FBC
$2—
3/19

BANISHED THREADS

Kaylin McFarren

Threads Series—Book #3

Distributed by:
Creative Edge Publishing LLC
8440 NE Alderwood Road, Suite A
Portland, OR 97220

ISBN 10: 1518806910
ISBN 13: 9781518806919
Printed in the United States of America
10 9 8 7 6 5 4 3 2 1

Cover Artist: Amanda Tomo Yoshida

PRAISE FOR KAYLIN MCFARREN'S THREADS SERIES

Severed Threads—Book #1

With plenty at stake, erotic chemistry, dastardly villains, a lost relic, an unusual setting, and a touch of the supernatural, this indie novel could stand on any romance publisher's shelf. The full package of thrills and romance. —Kirkus Reviews

Crisp writing and sparkling dialogue that will hold the interest of any reader who enjoys a good mystery story that's well told. —Mark Garber, president, *Portland Tribune*

I highly recommend this story for people who enjoy romance and suspense. Kaylin McFarren will not let you down! I look forward to future stories in this series. —Paige Lovitt, *Reader Views, Chicago Sun Times*

Buried Threads—Book #2

The many levels of this story will engross readers into the world of the Japanese syndicate, a Buddhist monk, and the American couple, while they quickly read to a satisfying conclusion, absorbing the culture the story is set in along the way. —San Francisco Book Review

Buried Threads, an erotic thriller, combines the action and adventure found in a Clive Cussler novel, the plotting and romance of Danielle Steel's books, and the erotic energy and supernatural elements of a work by Shayla Black. —Lee Gooden, *Foreword Review/Clarion Reviews*

More than a murder mystery, this mingles a treasure hunt, an international race against time, a dark prophecy, Japanese culture, erotic encounters, and a clever killer's modus operandi into a story that just won't quit. —Diane Donovan, *Midwest Book Review*

Banished Threads—Book #3
As with Severed Threads and Buried Threads, book three closes on a cliffhanger—one that indubitably will keep readers on edge. Well written and absolutely enthralling, Banished Threads is a wonderful addition to McFarren's award-winning series! —Anita Lock, *Pacific Book Review*

This intricate escapade is as carnal as it is cerebral. If you're into vivacious prose and bodice-heaving melodrama, this just may be your cup of tea. —Joe Kilgore, *The US Review of Books*

Family secrets, engaging characters, the heat of romance, and a standout suspense plot with a twisty, surprise ending make Banished Threads a must-read addition to McFarren's popular Threads series. —*Chanticleer Book Reviews*

AUTHOR'S NOTE

As many readers know, novels almost never belong solely to the authors who write them. They are in large part the property of editors, publishers, literary agents, advertisers, distributors, bookstore owners, and various retail outlets. Ultimately, the writers are rewarded with a single-digit percentage in appreciation for their originality, bloodletting, and painstaking commitment to completing a praiseworthy best seller.

By vast comparison, self-published authors have no pressing deadlines, no stagehands, no hand-waving directors, no commission-paid staff, and no designated committee to determine the design of their book covers or the acceptability of their nonformulaic genre-bending manuscripts. Although this might sound attractive to new aspiring writers, grandeur is a fleeting idea that is only realized when one takes the time to read the fine print on one's Willy Wonka ticket. You see, the negative often outweighs the positive when it comes to self-publishing. Although I'm delighted with the notion that I have no barriers or blinding signposts on my continuous journey to success, I also lack the advance and marketing team that accompany a lucrative, ego-boosting contract.

My editor is a hired, trained professional, followed close behind by loyal friends who simply enjoy reading and critiquing in their spare time. Distribution is limited to Internet sales, book fairs, and lovely independent bookstores that are willing to take a chance on an unknown author. Worldwide marketing is based solely on social networking, free giveaways, book clubs, advertising dollars, and word-of-mouth endorsements, which means sales are never as grand as one might hope. Yet despite the pitfalls and disappointments incurred on this rocky, misguided adventure, my dedication and ambition remain firmly intact, not as a result of the certificates and wonderful praise that come with writing award-winning books, but from the opportunity to introduce characters who are flawed and multidimensional—in many ways not unlike myself. These remarkable lost souls often possess the ability to overcome any obstacle or catastrophe blocking their paths to true happiness and success—something many of us can only hope to achieve.

With all of this in mind, I urge your tolerance and patience, as I often get lost while stretching the boundaries of reality and delving into strange, unfamiliar territory. As published authors are known to say, nothing is more rewarding than telling a story well or creating one that remains in the hearts of readers long after the last page is turned. It is the aspiration of every romantic, including this fun-loving, decrepit old soul.

So please sit back, relax, and enjoy the ride you're about to take as this *Threads* series comes to an end. New tales continue to form in the recesses of my mind and are only a night's dream away. Given time, they will materialize into typewritten pages and possibly self-published books. And if the fantastic should come to fruition, they will find their way to bookshelves belonging to wonderful readers like you. In the meantime, I would like to extend my appreciation to all the remarkable people in my life who have never failed to provide encouragement, constructive criticism, or unshakable support. Without each and every one of you, and the love you give freely, this Irish storyteller's voice would never be heard.

—Kaylin McFarren

DEATH AWAITS

"Whose child is this?" the coachman said.
"Will no one here speak for the dead?"
"She's mine," a mournful woman cried.
"The price for wedding vows defied."

The reaper smiled with thoughtful nods.
If coin should flip, what were the odds?
Sad truth be told, another lied,
An evil heart consumed with pride.

Her crimes would grow—increase with hate,
Allow him time to seal her fate.
The baby's soul was heaven-bound,
But hers would squirm deep underground.

"Dismiss your guilt," he told the source.
"Forgiveness comes with real remorse.
Torment will find a twisted mind
Whose love was built on cruel design."

The woman dried her tears of grief.
His heartfelt words brought forth relief.
Time would heal this banished thread,
Repair the loss where pain had fed.

The reaper climbed aboard his ride,
Without a villain by his side.
But one day soon he would return,
Collect a wicked soul to burn.

—Kaylin McFarren

"The truth is rarely pure and never simple."
—Oscar Wilde

CONTENTS

Prologue   xiii

1   A Storm Brewing   1
2   Unexpected Alliance   10
3   Rough Landing   33
4   Set Adrift   47
5   Tide Pool   63
6   Plundered   79
7   The Game Plan   87
8   Brief Interlude   91
9   Landlubbers   101
10 Revelations   114
11 Inquiring Minds   130
12 Boundaries   138
13 Flight to Freedom   154
14 Ultimatum   167
15 Visionaries   173
16 The Witness   186
17 The Scapegoat   193
18 The Advocate   202

19	The Treasure Trove	207
20	Absolution	214
21	Parley	222
22	Shared Vows	228
	Epilogue	235
	About the Author	239

PROLOGUE

A lone figure stood in the estuary lookout nestled in the trees above the North Sea on the Holderness Coast, waiting with restless anticipation as Gwen Gallagher approached the cliff's edge. A quick adjustment to the night-vision binoculars allowed the watcher a closer view of the twenty-eight-year-old secretary as she savored the last autumn sunset she would ever see. The crisp, cool air picked up speed, leaving her long black hair sailing like a ghostly pirate's flag behind her. It lifted the hem of her black skirt slightly, exposing her white, shapely legs and black suede booties to the wintry elements. Her blue eyes sparkled as they swept across the landscape, appraising the beauty surrounding them. She raised her chin toward the darkening sky and smiled, obviously believing the note she had received, inviting her here, had come from her married lover.

As Gwen moved even closer to the edge, the watcher took a deep breath. All that remained between this ludicrous woman and the vividly blue ocean was two meters of solid rock. From the lookout vantage point, there was barely enough light to confirm that she was staring down at the tossing sands and churning water, mesmerized by the early evening breeze. All it would take was one push, and she would feel the rush of wind through her hair and see the crystal-blue sea one last time as she slammed headlong into the jagged rocks.

The watcher's heart was fluttering erratically now as Gwen stood balancing on the brink of extinction. The sky darkened, and gray waves slammed into the rocks, blasting sea spray high into the air. By all appearances, she had become preoccupied with the black storm clouds collecting overhead and the hard-hitting raindrops striking her cheeks. The wind was whipping now, starting to voice its howling rage. Meanwhile, the watcher climbed down from the lookout and stepped hurriedly across the uneven ground, arriving only six yards away from the scene where Gwen now remained frozen in place. The soles of her shoes held her stoically on the uneven mafic rock, as the rising gale whipped and swayed her body like a frail willow. For a brief moment, the watcher was uncertain what to do next. Then Gwen turned around suddenly and stared back in a trancelike state. The watcher stepped forward, waking her.

"What are you doing here?" she called out. "What do you want?"

The watcher remained silent and took another step forward before pulling out an engraved, freshly sharpened steak knife. A look of fear crossed Gwen's rain-streaked face, making it impossible for the watcher not to smile.

"Go away! Leave me alone!" she screeched. She took a final step back, to distance herself, just as a massive wave hit. The spray washed over her and sent her plummeting fifteen meters down. The watcher dropped on all fours to maintain a protected position on the slippery, stony ground. Minutes later, the surge passed, and it was now safe to stand. A quick assessment confirmed the dangling binoculars were safe and in excellent working order, but the engraved knife had been washed away. After stepping down to a new viewpoint, it was easy to ascertain that Gwen had been injured from the fall and was now trapped in the jagged rocks below. She looked up at the watcher and called out for help, screaming at the top of her lungs.

Bloody idiot. If someone should hear her, they could interfere, and that would ruin everything.

Five minutes passed as poor Gwen continued to scream. Then, as good fortune would have it, the wind rose again. With the crush of another wave, she was pulled under and swept out to sea.

The watcher smiled and was about to leave when a tiny fraction of light picked up something on the ground. Careful inspection confirmed it was a gold hoop earring, plucked from its owner—a marvelous souvenir to add to the prized, growing collection. After the watcher slipped it into a pocket in the yellow-hooded slicker and removed the binoculars, a pleasant thought came to mind. Since it had become a moral right and obligation to dispose of the unworthy and undeserving in the Cumberforge Manor, it wouldn't be long before Gwen's lover would be joining her and the rest of the disloyal moneygrubbing fools who had been personally escorted to the bowels of hell.

1

A STORM BREWING

On a dreary night in late October, *Stargazer* sliced through the surface of the North Atlantic at fifteen knots, heading straight for the coast of England with Trident Ventures' five-member crew on board. Below deck, in the captain's quarters, Chase Cohen closed his leather-bound journal, set down his pen, and dimmed his reading light. With a filled brandy snifter in hand, he leaned back in his curved armchair and considered his poignant situation. His marriage proposal to Rachel Lyons had come on the heels of a wild adventure in Tokyo that had nearly cost them their lives. In hindsight, he might have withheld his offer had he fully grasped her inability to share his affections beyond their bedroom walls. Yet the thought of losing her in a fight or to another man was unimaginable. He was willing to play the fool for as long as necessary—accommodate her until his patience ran out. But there was nothing worse in his mind than wasting his time by making Rachel a priority in his life while he remained an option in hers.

Minutes slipped away, and Rachel's dreams seemed more troubled under his watchful eyes. She trembled, thrashed, moaned, and cried out as he gnawed on his bottom lip. Then, suddenly, her movements stilled. A loose strand of hair remained delicately resting on her face. Hardly aware of what he was doing, Chase stood and leaned over her to brush the copper strip away.

She remained motionless and reticent and appeared to be unaffected by his gesture. What was going on in that damn mind of hers? Would she ever trust him enough to share? Chase heaved a deep sigh and attempted to disengage his obsession. He looked out a nearby window and saw an orange glow emerging on the horizon.

The brilliant orb expanded, sending rays of white light toward their ship, shimmering like diamonds on the gentle rolling waves. It was a sight he would've enjoyed sharing with Rachel, cuddling under a blanket in a cozy lounge chair on the upper deck, sipping steaming cups of coffee and feeling the sun's warmth on their faces. But as usual, her morning ritual obliterated the fantasy.

With the precision of a fine-tuned clock, she awoke, pushed herself upright, threw off the sheets, and ran from the bed. He heard the sound of retching and choking in the adjacent bathroom. From a bystander's view, he watched her neck twist above the low-mounted stool and felt himself cringing inside. Sadly, he assumed full responsibility for her condition. His lack of judgment in not using precautions four months earlier had thrown a wrench in their plans...at least when it came to diving excursions and treasure-hunting expeditions. Personally, he didn't mind the idea of a new baby, especially if it meant keeping the woman he loved in his life. But Rachel hated the thought of giving birth. Not a day went by that she didn't object to his behavior or make her negative feelings known.

"I'm tired of being sick all the time," she had whined. "Between the constant motion on this ship and the smell of Ian's fried fish, I'm lucky to be standing. For crying out loud, Chase, why didn't you listen to me when I told you I wanted to fly to London?"

He shrugged and offered an awkward smile. While charting their course and stocking the galley with champagne, gourmet goodies, and enough provisions to last two months, he'd had a more romantic vacation in mind. One that entailed making passionate love to Rachel for days on end. Instead, reality had climbed on board, blurring his vision for the future. After traveling for five weeks, with stops in New York and Montreal, he now found himself haunted by how their eyes never met and how much her cold indifference had grown.

In an effort to comfort her, he wet a washcloth in the sink and held it against the back of her neck. More than anything, he wished he could ease her suffering and encourage her to appreciate the positive aspects of motherhood. But just as his Irish helmsman had predicted, irritability and morning sickness had become a commonplace occurrence. And according to the man's cynical outlook, the worst was yet to come. In less than five months, Chase would be forced to stand by in the delivery room while his sweet, darling wife screamed and cursed him for all eternity.

Ian Lowe would know better than anyone, Chase surmised. His helmsman had been through the same ordeal twice with the same petulant, ill-mannered hag, he had told him on more than one occasion.

"Left Dublin years ago for good reason," Ian had claimed. "That devil was always in me business, screaming and cursing. Tearing up the house and tossing me clothes whenever the mood struck her. If I didn't leave while the gettin' was good, we'd have killed each other by now."

Rachel took the cold compress from Chase's hand and wiped it across her mouth. Chase reached out to stroke her forehead, but she caught his wrist mid-movement in a deathlike grip. "That's it...I give up. I'll take the pills Dr. Evans prescribed. But then you have to promise not to blame me...if anything goes wrong."

Chase considered her words carefully before nodding. He remained in that position, crouched and confused, until Rachel's harried breathing slowed. She released her hold, and he in turn claimed her elbow to help guide her back to the bed. They sat across from each other, staring into each other's eyes. Slowly and cautiously, Chase brushed his hand across her warm cheek. Rachel gazed back at him with a peculiar mixture of emotions dancing across her features. Her eyes crinkled in catlike contentment, but her face was marked with indecision. She made no effort to deepen his gesture as he stroked her hair. Instead, she placed her hand over his—cold and clammy in spite of its soft appearance.

"I'm trying to be happy—honestly I am. But it's hard to get excited without worrying about the what-ifs. Like, what if this trip becomes more stressful than it's already been? What if something terrible happens, and we end up losing the baby? Even though I try not to think about it, what if we wake up one day and realize the passion we have for one another is gone?"

Although Chase wanted to squelch her fears and assure her that his feelings would never change, he realized his promises meant nothing without a shared commitment. He told himself that whatever love she felt for him had been diminished by this ocean voyage—by his inability to put aside his own interests and consent to her wishes. Once again, his lack of common sense had overruled his better judgment. Just like the day when he thoughtlessly swam off in search of sunken treasure and had returned to find Rachel's father drowning. The guilt he carried in his heart would always be there...as certain as the marble headstone marking Sam's grave.

Chase released a strangled breath. "That's not something we need to worry about, honey. We're going to be married next month like we planned, and everything's going to be great. You'll see."

"Really? But what if my uncle—"

He pressed his finger to her lips, silencing her. "No more what-ifs. We're arriving in England...a nation filled with shop-keepers just waiting to take our money. We're going to spend the next five days shopping, exploring castles, meeting new people, and making wonderful memories together. As soon as your feet hit the ground, that's all you need to think about."

His gaze dropped to her luscious lips. To the little dimple that played on the corner of her mouth whenever she smiled. *God, she's so beautiful. How could I ever let her go?*

She leaned forward and kissed him softly on the cheek. "OK, I'll try. Even though I can't seem to keep my eyes open for more than five minutes at a time. I don't think I've been this tired in my whole life."

Chase smiled. It was time to get out of his head and into his heart—to have faith in his emotions. He couldn't change the past no matter how much he wanted to, but if he was willing to put his fiancée's needs ahead of his own, he could create a good life for both of them. Provide a bright future for his daughter and her new baby brother or sister. Yet be that as it may, everything he could hope for—love, happiness, and security—all hinged on Rachel's ability to trust him.

Outside their cabin window, in the blue skies overhead, the sun's judging eye was all that was left to watch him as he curled up behind Rachel, laid his hand on her tiny bump, and drifted soundlessly off to sleep.

$$\mathcal{Q}$$

Two hours later, Chase sat up and glanced at his watch. Apparently sleep deprivation had caught up with him, as it was now 9:30 a.m. His stomach growled suddenly, reminding him of the meal he had skipped the night before. Mindful of Rachel's presence, he eased himself off the mattress and slipped on his deck shoes. Then he pulled his blue nylon jacket over the top of his white cable-knit sweater. After glimpsing her tranquil expression, he closed the door quietly, ascended the stairs, and made his way to the galley. The aroma of fresh-ground coffee, maple-flavored bacon, and scrambled eggs filled the air, stirring his appetite. As he stepped into the room, he spotted Devon Lyons sitting alone in the corner booth with a white steaming mug in hand and concentration darkening his brow. The last thing he needed after his short-lived night was a lecture on the care and feeding of pregnant women from a guy who didn't have a clue. However, despite the man's distaste for idle conversation and useless advice, Devon's presence was an instant reminder that this self-assured former stockbroker would soon be the closest thing to a relative he'd ever known. With the coastline rapidly approaching, more than anything he could use a strong ally to bolster his defense, and who better than a future brother-in-law?

"I see Ian's been busy," Chase said. "I suppose you've already eaten?" He scooped a generous portion of eggs onto his plate and then snatched a few pieces of bacon from the broiler.

Devon watched him from the rim of his cup. "Just finished off a second helping. So how's my sister doing?"

"Sleeping peacefully at the moment. But I know she's eager to get off this ship."

"Well, it won't be long now. By my best estimate and Ian's calculations, it's only four hours till we land."

"Dock," Chase corrected. He stuck a piece of bacon in his mouth and poured himself a cup of coffee.

"Yeah, right. Anyway, I talked it over with Ian, and we agreed that a vacation was long overdue. He's planning to see his kids, and there's this gal living in Kilkenny I used to know. So while Hawkins and the cleaning crew are taking care of things here, we'll be spending a few days in Ireland. For the record, I've never been particularly fond of watching my uncle destroy his enemies."

Chase released a humorless laugh. "And what makes you so sure that he's going to tear out my heart and carve me a new ass-hole? Since I'm the father of Rachel's baby, don't you think he'd want her to be happy and our child to be provided for?"

Devon sank back into his seat. "Oh, I wouldn't play that card if I were you. Like I said, my uncle never got over losing his brother...And knocking up his niece? Well, that's an entirely different matter. Far worse if you ask me." He gave a half shrug. "But hey, I could be wrong. With him having his own family for the last ten years, Paul Lyons might have grown a heart by now. You know, he could turn out to be a cool dude with no hard feelings at all."

"Which explains why you're not sticking around..."

Devon's hands were smoothing out the black sweater covering his taut stomach and adjusting it ever so slightly. "Things change, you know. Six months ago, I would've told you that you're wasting your time with Rachel, and just look...here you are trying to make an honest woman out of her."

"If she'll have me," Chase mumbled. He dropped into the seat across from Devon. Then he picked up his fork and rested an arm on the table. "So what do you think I should do? Disappear off the face of the planet after he tells me to go fuck myself?"

Devon chuckled. "Not exactly. You're going to have to be just as tough and determined as that old man is, but at the same time, you can't allow yourself to sink to his level. You're never going to win him over, no matter how hard you try. Believe me, I know. He shot me down years ago. But at least you've got one thing going for you: Rachel. If she's willing to convince him that she's totally in love with you, then you might stand a chance. It all depends on how well she makes her case. Or more importantly, how well you've sold yourself to her."

Chase swallowed a mouthful. "I know this is a dumb question, but do you think it's possible for her to be happy with me?"

Devon crossed his arms and angled his head. "Are you telling me that after everything you two have been through, you're still having doubts?"

"It's just that sometimes she seems so...confused. I don't know what to do. I love her and just want to make her happy."

"So, you're asking for my advice?"

Chase sat back in his seat and considered Devon's recent exploits, which had been openly shared by the police and discussed by half the population in San Palo, California. Prior to assuming the positions of navigator and mechanic on board the *Stargazer*, the self-proclaimed do-gooder had been kidnapped and held for ransom by drug dealers—the same shady characters he'd been trying to impress to win over his racy girlfriend. To everyone's amazement, she turned out to be a diabolical kingpin, who would have killed him without a second thought if she'd been given the chance.

Devon Lyons should have been the last person to ask for advice, but as it was, no one knew Rachel better than he did. At least that was what Chase had come to believe. "OK," he finally said, chewing a mouthful. "I'm listening."

Devon leaned forward on his elbows. "After Mom ran off, our father died, and you skipped town, my sister was diagnosed with clinical depression. She spent time with a therapist working through a shitload of stuff. Even though you're back now and both working together, trust will always be an issue for her. It'll be up to you to erase any doubts in her mind. Even though you have a seven-year-old daughter and a treasure-hunting career taking you around the world, you'll need to remind her that she'll always be the center of your universe. Now that might sound easy enough to follow through with, but I assure you it won't be. Rachel has always been a skeptic and as stubborn as they come. And what's more," he continued, with a look of intenseness gleaming in his eyes, "she needs to understand that accepting your protection doesn't mean she's surrendering her power, and having your baby doesn't mean she's giving up her independence, which she values above all else. If you can manage all that and still hang on to your sanity, then you might have a future together. Until then," he said, easing back in his seat, "I wouldn't hold my breath."

2

UNEXPECTED ALLIANCE

Paul Lyons awoke to a terrible morning, beginning with a blaring alarm that sent his arm slamming against an antique mahogany nightstand. He shrank back into his pillow, nursing the throbbing pain in his limb until it passed and waiting for his blurred vision to clear. Dream fragments floated around in his brain—disconnected nightmarish pieces riddled with shadowy faces, littered alleys, and haunting voices screaming his name. The most vivid recollection included the image of Gwen Gallagher perched on the edge of a dramatic cliff, fifteen meters above the ocean. In the harsh light of day, this vision morphed into horrific reality. His heart sank as he was doused with a fresh bucket of disbelief. The woman he was meant to love and spend the rest of his life with had fallen like a wingless angel, leaving him devastated and confused—filled with an endless reservoir of anger and frustration at never knowing the true reason for her death.

Surprisingly, his loud and violent rousing hadn't disturbed his semi comatose wife. Sara wore a green flannel gown arranged neatly around her slumbering form, her auburn-dyed hair fanned out over the pillow beneath her head. Her arms lay by her sides, and her chin was tilted up slightly with her lined lips parted, as if waiting to be kissed by a long-overdue prince. In lieu of her nightly regimen, a sleep mask had been pulled down over her dull-brown eyes and orange foam plugs had been inserted into her gossip-craving ears. A quick glance at the prescription bottle and empty water glass on her nightstand confirmed that sometime during the night she had found a cure for his constant tossing and turning. Yet despite the fact that she kept up appearances—portraying the loyal, dutiful spouse—there was no doubt in his mind that she knew about the guilt he had harbored for the past three months.

With lingering trepidation, he removed himself from the twisted bed sheets, sending the cat scurrying off the mattress and across the hardwood floor. Although Sara had discouraged it, the colorful creature persisted in sleeping on the foot of the bed and would often arrive there in the middle of the night without being heard or detected. But Paul had no issue with Abby's need to be close to them. In fact, he had secretly encouraged it, accrediting the glow from the Abyssinian cat's copper eyes as a remedy for keeping evil spirits away.

Reflecting on the last ten years of his life, he was reminded of the sequence of events that had led up to his incarceration in the Cumberforge Manor, which was about to end, if he so chose. By the age of thirty-two, the ink on his second divorce decree was barely dry when he became involved in a disastrous love affair with his brother's ex-wife. Following their breakup and his promise to stay clear of women, he found himself testing his sexual prowess on half a dozen young women while backpacking across Europe. Two years later, he settled into a leaky sublet in London's East End and managed to save up enough money from assistant teaching and part-time clerical jobs to purchase a reconditioned computer. He typed day and night with mindless abandon, determined to create the perfect suspense story. To his amazement, a literary agent by the name of Max Lancaster saw magic in his words and miraculously signed him. Seven award-winning books followed, and Paul soon found himself thrust into the limelight, sought after for television and radio interviews and jam-packed book-signing events. His story lines and casts of characters drew the interest of men and women alike. He became so enthralled with his own acclaim that the idea of failure never occurred to him. After scraping together funding and investing every dollar he could get his hands on, he presented his *Murderous Madeleine* play at the Steep Theatre. It ran for only two weeks before critics buried it, citing a lack of dramatic tension as the chief flaw in his overly ambitious project.

With his dreams of grandeur stripped away, he took refuge in a popular alehouse near Piccadilly Square and closed it down on a nightly basis for two weeks straight. Occasionally, his agent Max Lancaster would drop by and join him for a drink. But after hearing Paul ruminate over his blunder for more than an hour, Max would pull on his gray herringbone cap, make an excuse, and hightail it out of there. On one particular evening, when the place was filled to the rafters, an attractive middle-aged woman stepped through the front door, capturing Paul's attention in the middle of a complaint he was sharing with Max. Before taking the seat beside Paul, she smiled demurely and requested her reserved bottle of premium whiskey. She offered him a generous pour after introducing herself as Sara Rafferty. While he listened, she claimed to have seen his play a number of times. Despite what the papers printed, she absolutely adored it. She had read all of his novels and would always be his greatest fan.

As she continued to ply Paul with an endless supply of compliments, Max bade him farewell and left the two of them to their business. Time evaporated as the conversation and whiskey flowed. Although he'd been making a point of avoiding entanglements, Paul found himself fascinated by this remarkable woman.

There were only six people scattered about in the dark room when he became aware of the late hour. Sara handed a card to the bartender and asked him to phone her driver. Paul grabbed his cap and was anticipating the long walk home; however, to his surprise, Sara turned to him and laid her soft hand on his.

"I know this will sound strange with us having just met," she told him, "but I have a rather unique proposal I'd like to share that would benefit you tremendously."

"As long as it doesn't involve money," Paul quipped sarcastically. "I'm as broke as a crack head on the first of the month."

Sara's hand pulled away, leaving him feeling her absence even though she was right beside him.

Paul placed his hand on her arm. "That was an old joke, my dear."

After a thoughtful silence, she adjusted her posture and resumed her inquiry. "There's no way to present this without sounding completely insane, so I'm just going to say it straight out."

Paul leveled his shoulders, wrapping his defenses around himself like an invisible cloak.

"If you would be willing to marry me, no questions asked, fulfill your husbandly duties, and assume the role of a compatible roommate for a period of ten years, I'll provide you with a generous stipend, custom-made clothing, directorship at an art gallery, and full ownership of my late husband's Aston Martin One-77 with a price tag exceeding one point eight million."

At first, Paul laughed openly, believing his demented friends had hired a struggling actress and brought her there to torment him. But when Sara Rafferty's full lips curled into a disapproving frown, he sensed the wealthy widow really had come there of her own volition and was perfectly serious. Oddly, loneliness seemed to be her singular motive, yet it still didn't make sense. Why would someone so confident, classy, affluent, and well-spoken suggest such a thing?

"So what's the catch?" he asked. "Nothing comes that easy. Not without strings or a shitload of trouble attached."

"There's nothing of the sort," she assured him. "And I'm certainly not looking to cause problems, sir. I'm only interested in acquiring the companionship of an educated gentleman who appreciates the fine arts. I am fully aware of who you are, Mr. Lyons, and your present situation. Despite everything, I believe you're qualified for the position, provided you limit your drinking and smoking and abide by a few simple rules. When our contract expires, you'll be free to leave and keep the assets you've earned, or you can elect to extend your stay, if we're both in agreement. Either way, I'm sure you wouldn't mind the benefits you'd receive in exchange for your time and commitment. That is, if you're willing to accept my offer."

Paul leaned in closer. "This isn't some kind of joke? You're really serious?"

One swift, curt nod was the only reply he got.

He tilted his head as he looked at her. "What you're asking for is—"

"More than you're willing to give?"

His eyes failed to meet her direct gaze. "You might be surprised to know that I've heard that before," she said, "but I never let it stop me, especially when I've made up my mind. Just know that I've done my homework, Mr. Lyons. I'm very confident about you and the decision you'll make."

"Oh, really?" With his brain in a fog, Paul was tempted to lean forward and kiss her, but that would leave the wrong impression—make her believe the answer was yes, when it definitely wasn't. At that moment, he needed to get some fresh air, think clearly, and act accordingly. "I'll consider your offer, Sara. But I can't promise anything, especially if a job offer should come along..."

"Suit yourself," she said. Then she handed him a card with her name and number. "In case you change your mind."

He slipped it into his pocket, and as one might expect, they parted company the same way they had arrived. But when Paul's angry landlord met him at his front door and demanded overdue rent money, Paul realized he had no options at all. He stuffed his clothes into a black bag and spent the night shivering under his coat on a park bench. First thing in the morning, while still feeling his drink and the ache in his back, Paul called Sara on his cell phone and arranged for a meeting. Her lawyer witnessed the strange exchange as Paul signed his freedom away. According to the legal document, they were required to exchange their vows within forty-eight hours, and they did so in a very quiet, very private wedding. With all common sense thrown to the wayside, Paul slid into the limo beside Sara and departed for a honeymoon in North Wales with none of his friends or his literary agent being the wiser.

Surprisingly, Paul enjoyed their candlelit dinners, playful bedroom antics, and long morning walks. He even managed to overlook Sara's extreme mood swings, as no more than ten minutes would pass before her anger would subside and his sweet, adoring fan return.

After fourteen absorbing days and thirteen exhilarating nights, their honeymoon came to an abrupt end. With their bags loaded in the boot of Sara's limo, they traveled through the countryside and eventually rolled through the manor's automated gates. An antiquated housekeeper and a green-eyed, redheaded little girl met them at the front door. As Paul soon learned, Sloan Rafferty was Sara's orphaned granddaughter—a ten-year-old child who had been born to a dying mother and spent the last two years in a French boarding school. According to the housekeeper with frizzled gray hair, Sloan's expulsion was the result of mischievous pranks, and until other arrangements could be made, she would be staying with them in the manor.

Paul felt a little dizzy and mildly nauseous. He couldn't focus on anything, especially the crossed-armed waif standing before him. Despite what Sara might have hoped for, he had no interest in assuming the role of a grandfather or disciplinarian of any kind. In his mind, the string that Sara had cleverly kept hidden had the potential to become a knotted rope, strangling him with the consequences of his actions.

By the week's end, his fears had been fully realized. The little hellion had managed to rummage through most of his personal effects. She'd scribbled on his manuscript, buried his car keys, and drowned his cell phone. When confronted in the main entry about her invasion of privacy, she had the audacity to stand before him, with jaw set and arms akimbo in a damp, ink-stained dress, swearing her innocence to the high heavens.

As the years came and went, so did a bushel of frustrated tutors. The lead housekeeper attended to Sloan's needs as best she could, while Sara concentrated on tennis lessons, fund-raisers, and country-club galas. With absolutely no control over his life, Paul was physically and mentally drained—a store looted and left with bare walls. Then one day, when he thought things couldn't get any worse, Sara returned home from her monthly weight-loss hypnosis session acting strange and overly excited.

"Dr. Bradshaw is bloody amazing!" she raved. "After surpassing my goals, I called my buyer at Harrods and ordered a spanking-new wardrobe. You really should take him up on his offer, you know. Stop that filthy habit of yours. I don't know why you're so damn determined to keep smoking, anyway. It's ignorant and passé. My friends absolutely detest it. They're just too kind to say so, is all."

Paul pulled a lighter out of his shirt pocket and lit the cigarette dangling from the corner of his lips. He took a deep drag, blew smoke to the side, and then looked directly into her face. "Are you finished now?"

She heaved a disgruntled sigh. "There's no need to be rude, Paul. I simply wanted you to know that he has a talented young client who is desperately in need of a job. I told him you could use the help, and he—"

"Damn it, Sara, you didn't. What happened to promising to stay out of my business?"

Sara looked down and pursed her lips, feigning disappointment. "Up until this moment, I've never interfered, and I have no intent of starting. It's just that Peter has looked after me for years. He's been incredibly kind, you see, and he's always asking after you."

Paul snorted a laugh. "You don't say."

"Please, darling, do this one little thing for me. Why, we could even take that vacation we've been talking about for years. You still want to see the canals in Venice and the Palace of Versailles, don't you?" With the tilt of her chin and slow curl of her lips, his hard-edged defenses were crushed. Once again she had gotten her own way, and he had unwittingly allowed it to happen.

The very next day, a raven-haired beauty arrived at the art gallery at 2:00 p.m. sharp wearing a tight-fitting blue dress, tan strappy sandals, and the wisp of a smile. Her ocean-like eyes bore into his soul, and with a simple, soft-spoken hello, his heart was instantly taken. For nearly a month, he tried to distance himself by issuing outside assignments and painstaking clerical work. Yet in spite of how hard he tried, he couldn't stop thinking about her. Then one day, the soft brush of her hand during an innocent lunch meeting sparked an irresistible impulse. As soon as they stepped out of the hillside restaurant, he pulled her in close and kissed her lips hard, leaving her limp and breathless.

Paul's gut twisted in fervent misery at the recollection—memories of lewd, adulterous acts. Even though their trysts had been a weekly occurrence, and were reduced to obscure, cut-rate hotel rooms, they'd shared their most intimate thoughts and secrets while wrapped in each other's arms. There was no implication the relationship was merely a sexual one. It was emotional, endearing, and basically unforgettable. He had found his one and only, the true love of his life, and now she was gone...forever. Even though the team of investigators and medical examiner had attributed her death to suicide, he held himself accountable—the underlying cause of it all—leaving him questioning his reason for carrying on with his own pointless existence.

He glanced at Sara still sleeping soundly as he moved quietly through the master bedroom. After reaching the sink in their bathroom, he noticed his hands were shaking more than usual. Perhaps it was the aftereffects of the dream he'd just had. Whatever the problem, he dismissed it and climbed into the shower.

As soon as he finished, and the steam in the room cleared, he began shaving. But he nicked his chin as he always did when he was nervous or preoccupied with personal matters. A few beads of blood dripped into the basin, and he quickly wiped them away. He didn't have to look into the mirror to know his worries from the past few months were etched on his forehead and at the corners of his light-hazel eyes.

With a dot of tissue adhered to his chin, he stepped into the closet and picked out a gray Hermès turtleneck sweater and tweed jacket, matching the color of his thick, slicked-back hair. The black tailored slacks were a bit loose in the waist, reminding him that he had skipped a few meals and dropped a few pounds in the process. But despite Sara's urging, food had become lackluster, just like the identity he had regrettably assumed. Nothing, including the maid's apple strudel, would make up for that day... that horrible moment when he was told that a homeless beachcomber had discovered Gwen's broken body lying in a heap beneath a fifty-foot drop.

Somehow, in spite of the stories in the local press, Paul had managed to hide his sorrow and forge on in his usual buttoned-up fashion. He attended an opening at the art gallery two days after Gwen's funeral, deflecting the ugly rumors from community leaders and the gossipy women in their ranks. Why, oh why, did he allow their meaningless words to affect him?

Paul drew another deep breath and exhaled slowly while counting to ten. *Steady your nerves,* he told himself. *Today is another day, like any other.* After securing his black leather belt, he wandered downstairs to make himself a cup of strong coffee. To his surprise, the pot was already brewing, and the washer was whirling in the adjacent laundry room.

"Hello?" he called out.

No answer. Red roses had been placed in a tall cylinder vase, and bags of fresh vegetables were resting on the granite countertop.

"Hello?" he called again.

Several women from the house staff had arrived an hour earlier than usual, puzzling him, until he remembered that his niece and her crew of treasure hunters would be showing up later that evening. Normally, he wouldn't mind seeing a few friendly faces, but with his emotions in turmoil, he had no interest in entertaining a houseful of excited, chattering guests...especially when they included the likes of Chase Cohen. The idea of Rachel marrying the despicable scavenger was inconceivable—a foolish, irresponsible act on her part. And now she was intent on coming here, expecting a blessing he had absolutely no intention of giving.

Paul raked his fingers through his gray hair and stood before the kitchen window staring out at two fiery-red maple trees in the garden. "Bloody hell," he grumbled aloud. "If she has any sense at all, she'll do the right thing by leaving on the same ship I entrusted to her." As if hearing his thoughts, the wind suddenly picked up and tossed a dozen dead leaves in the air.

"Why do they have to come today of all days?" He opened the cupboard above the sink and was about to collect his cup when the sound of footsteps in the hallway jolted his senses. Turning toward the source, he spotted Margaret, the sixty-nine-year-old housekeeper who had become a fixture in the mansion. Her gray hair was pulled back in a messy pinned bun, and her arms were filled with the wet towels she had been gathering while visiting the bathrooms scattered throughout the house.

"Good morning," Paul said. "Please tell me you made the coffee."

"Oh yes, sir." Margaret said, smiling warmly.

"Thank goodness. For some unknown reason, my wife seems to lack the skill."

"Heidi and I have been trying to anticipate your wife's needs, but she's more determined than ever to take care of you herself. Anyway, I hope I didn't startle you, sir. There's a young man at the front door asking for you."

Paul retraced her steps to the entry, where the door stood slightly ajar. Opening it wider, he was surprised to find a uniformed messenger waiting on the doorstep with a clipboard and large envelope in his hands. The man was clean-cut, straight-backed, and broad-shouldered and had the youthful appearance of a third-year college student.

"So, what are you advertising?" Paul nonchalantly asked.

"Nothing, sir. Although I did sell subscriptions before becoming a soldier," he said diplomatically. "And now I'm a full-time messenger. One must find a way to make ends meet in this economy, you know." He stepped forward with his clipboard and silently watched as Paul signed his name on the delivery receipt. Then he surrendered his envelope, and with a quick two-finger salute, he climbed back inside his vehicle and drove away.

Paul closed the door with his eyes fixed on the packet. He turned it over and was trying to decipher the return address when Sara suddenly appeared in the entry. Her mink-trimmed mask had been pushed back on her head, and for a brief moment, she seemed dazed and confused—perhaps from the pills she had ingested the night before. However, when her dull-brown eyes landed on the object in his hands, they instantly brightened.

"Is that for me?" she asked.

"I'm not sure." He ripped open the package and dumped out a folder containing a business proposal. A yellow sticky note was attached to it, with a scribbled message from Max Lancaster thanking him for taking a look.

"So, what is it?" Sara asked. "A signed contract from a new artist?"

Paul flipped open the folder and quickly scanned the pages. "It's information about that development I mentioned to you. The one Max wanted you to invest in."

"Oh, you can toss that, darling. I make it a practice to never get in bed with strangers. Aside from my husband, of course."

"But you told me you would take a look. That it sounded promising. Are you saying you're not interested now?"

"I never was, Paul. I just told you that so you would drop the subject."

There was an awkward silence, and the space seemed to stretch between them. As if realizing the hurt she had caused, the corners of her mouth lifted in a slow, deliberate smile. "I set the timer for your coffee, darling. Go have a nice cup and relax. I'll be down in a few." Then she turned and hurried back upstairs, shutting the door quickly behind her.

Paul crossed his arms over his chest and huffed to further display his displeasure. He considered going back upstairs to argue the point when her face suddenly appeared above the railing.

"Don't forget about your lunch date, darling. Of course I would go with you if I didn't have my dress fitting and foundation meeting this evening. And then there's the hospital luncheon to attend. I've missed three in a row, and I'd hate to disappoint all the members. But putting all that aside, I'll be most interested in hearing what Sloan has to say. Especially when she discovers her funding has been cut off."

"Are you really sure you want to do this?"

"I've thought it over carefully and come to the conclusion that there's no other way." With that said, Sara closed the door again, ending any further discussion.

Damn it! Paul wandered into the living room and plopped down on the sofa. Why in hell did he agree to do this? It was Sara's idea, not his. But somehow she had made it seem like they'd shared in the decision-making process. For the next five minutes, he watched the second hand on the mantel clock above the stone fireplace. He laid his head back and cursed at the ceiling. It seemed more apparent than ever that the comfortable lifestyle he had traded his freedom for had come at the price of his pride and self-worth.

He glanced mindlessly at the cat contentedly licking her paw. "What's keeping me here, Abby? I should pack my bags and stow aboard the *Stargazer*. By tomorrow night, I could be long gone before anyone noticed." However, the more he thought about it, the more he became convinced that no purpose would be served by his leaving. And being locked away with Chase Cohen on Rachel's luxurious yacht could turn out to be more troublesome than attending to the needs of his imperious wife.

In his own contemptuous way, Paul had grown accustomed to being distant, unappreciated, and unaffected by public opinion. Loneliness had become his security—his way of tolerating the wealthy people he'd been forced to cater to on a daily basis. Settling the way he had would never advance his career, and for all intents and purposes, he was losing ground fast.

In less than eight days, though, the terms on his marriage contract would end. He would finally be free to walk away and resume his old life. Maybe be the person he always wanted to be. But reengaging in the world would mean getting up and moving on...opening his mind to new possibilities.

After all these years, with his wife controlling the purse strings and every aspect of his life, Paul knew he didn't have a leg to stand on or an identity to assume. Any future he might have hoped for had fallen off the edge of a cliff months earlier, and now he felt confined once again in a loveless, dead-end marriage with forgiveness being dealt out in small increments, especially when it came to Gwen Gallagher and the affair Sara had conveniently chosen to ignore.

Paul peered over the top of his *London Times* at his wife's nine-teen-year-old granddaughter, who was scowling and studying the basket of rolls on the table. After living with a collection of photos chronicling her mother's life, he could easily determine where this fair beauty had inherited her good looks. But sadly, these looks also came with a foul mouth and an explosive temper, which he'd had the unfortunate experience of witnessing on more than one occasion.

"I suppose you came here to lecture me," she said, watching him with her brilliant green eyes. "As usual, Gran must have had more important things to do." Sarcasm dripped from her words. She eyed the croissant in her hand before tearing it tremulously apart. After dragging a large piece across the marinara sauce on her plate, she popped it into her mouth. "So, I take it she still hasn't forgiven me for that shoplifting thing."

Paul cleared his throat before answering. "I guess she hasn't made up her mind yet." He almost added, "Can you blame her?" but skipped it, knowing the cruel gibe would only add fuel to the fire. "So how's that job search going?" He folded his newspaper neatly in half and set it aside. "I hope you found something more lucrative than—"

"Emptying store shelves?"

The girl's insolence had worsened with age. Whether she was attending a formal dinner party or gallery show or seated directly across from him in a popular upscale restaurant, Sloan turned the air sourer than curdled cream with her paranoia and tedious self-pity.

Paul shifted in his seat. "Given the chance, I was going to say the perfume counter at Fenwick's." His eyes fell on the green and black snake tattooed around her wrist—a symbol of teenage rebellion designed to impress her delinquent friends.

"Well, it was an easy mistake," she said. "Veronica called while I was trying on wraps. I just stepped outside for a moment. I didn't need to be strip-searched like a common criminal. If given the chance, I would have returned it..." She brushed her long bangs out of her face, but they fell back in place, burying her left eye.

Paul snorted. "That wrap, as you call it, was a dress that cost nine hundred dollars. You're just lucky the security guard was an old friend of mine."

She rolled her eyes and smirked. "Oh yeah...I almost forgot. Thanks for adding rubbish collecting to my glowing résumé."

You ungrateful brat. Paul bit back his anger and was instantly reminded of her most humiliating transgression. At the age of fifteen, she had an argument with a young neighborhood girl over a stupid boy and retaliated by smearing dog feces on her front door. If Paul hadn't sworn up and down that Sara's granddaughter was visiting a nonexistent relative, the police would have hauled her in years ago.

Ah, yes...dear, sweet Sloan. There would always be an excuse, someone else to take the blame. A dozen reasons to be given another chance. She was moody and morose and had snapped at the cabdriver who had brought her here, claiming she'd been deliberately overcharged. Today, of all days, she seemed in an especially bad mood. Anything he might say or do would rub her the wrong way, leaving him bitter for days. But there was still the matter of delivering Sara's wonderful birthday news—the solution to everyone's problems.

Or so she had claimed.

"Since you'll be turning twenty next week and plan to live off your grandmother's trust," he said, "I thought it most important to inform you that—"

"—it's none of your business," she finished. "If that's the reason you insisted I come here, then you might as well—"

"What? Go fuck myself? Or better yet, leave before you do something we'll both regret?" He shook his head and looked away to hide his frustration. A fresh group of customers was coming through the front door, laughing, closing their umbrellas, and removing their rain-drenched overcoats. The room had reached full capacity, with the bar and every table now filled. Paul turned back to face Sloan and found her nonchalantly spinning her fork.

"As I was saying," he continued, "last week your grandmother met with her attorney. I thought you'd like to know that she's arranging to have your trust revoked as soon as possible."

Sloan's first bite of spaghetti dangled from her gaping mouth. Not just a fetching strand, but a dripping gob-full. By all appearances, it seemed the insolent young woman was determined to eat in record time, as if feeding at a pig trough.

"I could be a drug addict...or a raving lunatic," she said indignantly. "Don't you both realize how lucky you are?"

Yeah, real lucky. Paul was about to shut her down when he noticed a bald, heavyset man seated across the room in the dimly lit corner. Out of all the people he hated most in this town, Neville Murdock topped his list.

The deplorable hack reporter was a notorious gossip who made his fortune selling trumped-up stories to scandalous rags. After reading the insidious articles he'd written about Gwen's death, Paul was convinced the weasel would enjoy nothing more than adding another nail to her coffin.

Unfortunately, he realized too late that he'd already been spotted. Murdock was on his feet, crossing the room in seconds flat. "What a coincidence to find you here, Mr. Lyons," he droned. "Did you get the messages I left? I called your house last week. Like I told your wife, our readers would be very interested in your response to hearing about the recent robberies in town. Especially with you being a gallery owner and all. But then, come to think of it, that's not entirely true, is it? The way I understand it, your wife still owns the place."

Paul half expected a wretched insult to follow, but then he quickly realized that was exactly what he'd been served. He took note of the elderly couple seated nearby before feigning complete ignorance. "Robberies, you say? I'm sorry, but I don't have a clue what you're talking about."

Rather than reveal possible suspects, missing artworks, and burglary locations, Murdock stole Paul's valuable time to expound on the government impact. "According to the British police, organized groups are targeting art in the United Kingdom. With the estimated loss at three hundred million pounds in the last three years, it's become the second-highest-grossing criminal trade in the country. I'm honestly surprised you weren't aware of the problem. But then you also didn't seem particularly interested when I brought up the subject of rising murder and suicide rates in our quiet community."

Paul glanced at Sloan, holding her knife and casually smearing butter on a fresh roll. "As you can see, Mr. Murdock," he said, "we're having a nice lunch here. I really don't believe this is the right time or place to discuss such matters. Perhaps you could stop by the gallery...after making an appointment, of course." He had hoped to silence him, but Murdock remained relentless in his pursuit of idle gossip.

"I just thought you should know the head of Scotland Yard's Arts and Antiques Unit has his hands full. It seems quite unlikely that they'll get this problem under control before your art exhibit opens tomorrow night." Murdock lowered his dark eyes and shook his head, simulating deep concern. "The fact that you're featuring Morris Graves's paintings is even more disturbing, Mr. Lyons. He may have earned a degree of notoriety in the United States, but here in England, the public will find him extremely controversial in light of his political views."

Paul leaned forward a little, palms flat against the table, and raised his chin in defiance. "So now you're an art critic? I thought you only wrote slander for a living."

Sloan choked on a half laugh.

"Joke if you like," Murdock fumed. "You're not above the law. No one in your family is, Mr. Lyons. Plagiarism, murdering husbands, destroying private property…and then there's always the curious matter of Gwen Gallagher and the reporter who vanished from the face of the earth."

"What? When? Are you talking about Ned Healey?"

Sloan shook her head. She wasn't having any part of it. "My, my, Mr. Murdock," she scoffed. "Narrow-minded, tiny-dick men like you never fail to amaze me. Why anyone would care what a creepy old man like you has to say is beyond me… especially when your shitty stories come from rubbish bins and self-serving creeps. One of these days, you're going to be bitten by the same snakes you keep company with, and no one's going to give a damn." She picked up her fork and speared her salad, but her eyes never left his. "Before it becomes necessary for my grandfather to jump up and beat the shit out of you, I suggest you move your fat ass back to wherever you came from. You're ruining everyone's appetite…including mine."

While three young women giggled at the next table, Murdock openly glared. Paul made a quick move, as if intending to charge him, and the portly man nearly fell over. He scampered back to his safe corner while the roomful of customers stared. Then he hid like a wounded child behind his oversize menu.

A half smile lifted the corner of Sloan's lips. "Nicely done, Gramps," she said. Then she raised her fork and returned to her meal.

For the next five minutes, Paul peered over the edge of his coffee, watching her with curious fascination. Not until that moment had it dawned on him that behind her tough-girl facade lay a wary heart. She was the scarred product of her cruel environment—damaged by rumors, falsehoods, and conjecture, not unlike him.

She finished off the last bite on her plate and returned her napkin to the table. Then she rose to her feet, preparing to leave. "Thanks for lunch. We really must do this again sometime."

In another place and time, he might have been hurt or disappointed by her catty tone. But after realizing the truth behind her actions, he could only smile.

"I want you to know that grandfather thing…It was purely for effect," she said. "Nothing for you to get worked up over, Paul."

He snorted a laugh. "Of course. As I'm sure you're more than aware, I never signed on for that role. But I have to admit it was nice to hear you say it, just the same."

"Yeah, whatever." She slipped her arms into her charcoal wool coat and wrapped her black knitted scarf around her neck.

"Oh, and by the way, I'd like you to have this." He held out a thick envelope containing the gallery's weekly receipts. After peering inside, her eyes grew wide with disbelief. For a few seconds, he was sure she would hand the money back, calling it an insult to her integrity. But apparently, forced emancipation had leveled her pride and resolution.

"It's not a lot, mind you," he said, "but maybe it will help… until you get back on your feet." He flashed another quick smile, but she didn't seem to notice. With her gloves gripped in one hand and the envelope in the other, she stared down at the ground, presumably plotting her next move. However, when she lifted her chin, a trace of hesitancy showed in her eyes.

"It's all right to take it," he assured her. "No one's going to care."

The perky blond waitress returned with a coffeepot in hand, eager to refill his cup. But Paul was quick to wave her off, preferring to hear what Sloan had to say.

For an endless stretch of time, she remained silent, as if stumped by the degree of his generosity. After glancing around the room at occupied diners, she slung her graffiti-covered backpack over one shoulder and jutted out her chin. In spite of their show of strength against a common enemy, all evidence of an alliance had vanished in a flash.

"I want you to know that I can take care of myself," she said, "just like I always have. It's never been about the money…my sticking around. Gran can keep every penny of my inheritance as far as I'm concerned. I was just hoping she'd see me—give us a chance to talk things through before I left town." Her facade remained firmly in place, safeguarding her emotional wounds. "Maybe you could pass that along. If you really care anything about her, that is…"

Sloan's brilliant eyes were locked on Paul as he adjusted his posture, flipping one leg over the other. He forced himself to remain calm and collected—untouched by her icy indifference. "Sure," he said. "I suppose I could do that." Then he picked up his newspaper and feigned interest in the latest European trading report.

As Sloan approached the door, he lifted his eyes to watch her leave. He found himself wondering why after all these years they couldn't manage to get along for a lousy twenty minutes. Perhaps it was the result of their inability to compromise—to give each other the benefit of the doubt. Or maybe they'd both simply lost the ability to trust another human being and believe anything good could come of this world.

As Paul picked up a whole-wheat muffin and smeared it generously with marmalade, he came to the conclusion that, much like him, Sloan was drifting mindlessly through this world, an empty soul searching for the right balance of sanity. If someone didn't come along soon to set her on the right track, she could turn out to be as lost and ineffectual as he'd become.

"Paul?" A man's small voice pulled his attention to the opposite side of the room. Max Lancaster was standing next to the bar wearing a thin blue sports jacket and wrinkled gray slacks. The white dress shirt he had on looked unlaundered and slightly frayed at the neck. His white beard was cropped close, and his white eyebrows overhung his soulful brown eyes. "Hi. I thought that was you," he said. "Mind if I join you?"

"Hello, Max," Paul said with forced joviality. His former literary agent was down on his luck and was sure to be even more so with the news he was about to share. "Help yourself." He gestured at the seat across from him and moved his newspaper out of the way. "Can I get you some coffee? Something to eat?"

"I don't want to take up your time," Max said, removing his herringbone cap from his shaved head. "I know you're a busy man." When the waitress came by with a fresh cup and pot of coffee, he declined the offer.

"What can I do for you?" Paul asked.

"I was wondering if you got the papers I sent. You know, about that place over on Brighton Avenue. I think it's going to be a real winner...bring in a killing for both of us."

Paul swallowed hard and looked down at his strong black coffee, knowing there was no easy way to destroy Max's dream, especially after shooting him down four months ago for a loan and 60 percent stake in a get-rich-quick scheme. "I'm sorry," he said, lifting his eyes. "Sara didn't bite on this one, old man. I tried, but she just…" Paul shook his head and curled his lips. "I don't know what to say. I wish I could help you. I honestly do. But you know the situation. I don't have access to the kind of money you need."

Max dropped back in his chair. His eyes lowered to the top of the table and stayed there for endless seconds. When he looked up, his lips were fixed in a tight, thin expression, and his brown eyes were darker than usual.

"I see," he murmured.

Paul pulled out his wallet and looked inside. He had given all the cash he had to Sloan with the exception of seventy-five euros. He had considered keeping something for his tab, but realized he could cover it with a credit card.

"I'm sorry…This is all I have with me," Paul said as he laid down every last bill. "I wish I had more that I could give you, but…"

Max glanced down, shaking his head. "Keep it. I don't need your charity." His voice was low and unfamiliar. He looked dejected and offended, but most of all, he had the look of a man who hated the world. "I don't want to owe you anything." He slipped on his cap and came to his feet. Then he turned and walked out the door.

Paul watched him through the window as he traveled up the street and climbed into a dirty white van. As it pulled away from the curb and continued on its way, he realized that if Sara hadn't come along when she had, he could have ended up as destitute, bitter, and miserable as his unfortunate former friend.

3

ROUGH LANDING

C hase Cohen closed his pale-blue eyes behind a pair of dark aviator glasses, tilted his head back, and blew out a deeply held breath. After surviving sword-wielding yakuza gang members, ghosts, goblin sharks, man-eating eels, and complete culture shock in Japan, he was grateful to be in London, where the streets were safe, and the conservative populace spoke old-fashioned Americanized English. Granted, a number of expressions and terms were different when it came to naming the subway and various parts of an automobile, among other less relevant things, but for the most part, he could navigate through any uncertain British terminology and unforeseen challenge with his beautiful partner at his side.

En route on the *Stargazer*, Chase had perused dozens of travel books and watched an equal number of videos, educating him on the highlights of England, and now that he and Rachel were finally here, moored on the banks of the Thames at Saint Katharine Docks, he could more fully appreciate the city's beauty and the ancient history surrounding them.

With his first step on British soil, he had the energy of a young boy—eager to see and experience everything in the eight days they had allotted themselves. But of course their visit with Rachel's uncle would have to come first. Paul Lyons's blessing on their forthcoming nuptials was the true purpose of this trip, not touristy sightseeing attractions. If he had any hope of surviving the man's wrath and walking away with his precious prize, he needed to appear strong, completely focused, and self-assured.

Remarkably, as he and Rachel walked by dozens of restaurants, bars, and shops in central London, his enthusiasm rose to a new level. He couldn't help but feel a vibrant pulse of humanity resonating within. "This place is incredible," he said. "If the right job came along, I'd have no problem living here."

Rachel wrinkled her nose and halfheartedly shook her head. "Really? After barely an hour in this place, you see yourself drinking tea, wearing a soggy raincoat, and scuba-diving in the countryside?"

"I know it sounds crazy, but now that you mention it, I did read an article a few days ago. Seems there's a multitude of flooded quarries in this country, and divers come here to explore them all the time. Who knows? There might even be treasure hidden in one."

"Yeah, right…if you don't mind diving in frigid waters." She glanced up at the dark, threatening clouds gathering above them. "Which is what we'll be standing in if we don't find our way to the train station soon."

Chase looked up at the dark clouds and felt a few sprinkles on his face. While Rachel waited, he opened a neatly folded map and searched for directions. "Looks like a twenty-minute walk, or we can grab a bus ride to the London Bridge station. It picks up in front of that gray building over there." He motioned with his head before stowing his map and claiming their luggage.

Then he watched her lift the handle on her rolling duffel bag. "You sure you don't want me to take that too?"

"No, I'm keeping it close to me. Got all my essentials inside." It didn't take much imagination to know she was referring to her impractical high-heel shoes, starched shirts, pressed slacks, and bangle bracelets—all necessary components for surviving the elements. As she wobbled across the cobblestones in her five-inch heels, towing her bouncing bag behind her, Chase followed closely, smiling all the way.

They reached Thomas Moore Square and stood inside the bus-stop shelter to watch for the next arrival. However, to their dismay, they soon discovered that all the buses were traveling full. Worst yet, the waiting taxis were demanding a ransom to make the winding two-mile drive. They'd both been warned by Devon to avoid the gypsy cabs lurking about—the cars painted black to look like taxis but lacking company-marked license plates.

As they waited, five minutes turned into ten and then dragged into fifteen. Eventually, a cab pulled up, dropping off a happy Asian couple. Rachel asked the smiling driver to use the meter. He agreed, and they set off for the train station lickety-split.

"You have an interesting accent," Rachel told him. "Can I ask where you originally came from?"

The driver paused for a lengthy moment before answering, "Pakistan." Then he picked up his cell phone and carried on a loud conversation in Urdu, a language Chase had overheard during his travels. It seemed the man's personal life had taken preference over his job. Any effort to communicate with him would be wasted.

Rachel rolled her eyes and shook her head. She sat back in her seat and watched Chase thumb through photos of tall ships they'd seen earlier that day in the harbor. After a while, her interest waned. "What's this all about?" she asked.

Chase looked up from his digital camera only long enough to notice the driver's practice of giving way to other cars at every possible opportunity. "I've heard of being polite on the road, but this is ridiculous," he said.

The short drive had grown to thirty minutes by the time they reached an intersection near the train station, and Chase was somewhat surprised to notice that the meter was rapidly approaching forty pounds. As Devon had informed him, cabs in London, much like those in China, had two costs: the distance meter, and the time meter. The distance ticked up while the car was moving, and the time meter counted in seconds whenever the cab was stopped in traffic. As they slowed for a rail crossing, Chase watched the time meter double and the total price increase accordingly. After he pointed this out, the driver frowned and sullenly stared straight ahead without saying a word.

"It's all right," Rachel whispered in Chase's ear. "I'll pay his ridiculous fee...as long as we arrive in one piece." But Chase wasn't interested in being swindled. He sat forward in his seat, grumbling.

"I think we've gone far enough," he told the driver. "Let us out here."

Instead of following his instructions, the Pakistani driver sped up dangerously, circled the station, and came close to side-swiping another car. They jerked to a quick stop, and the driver pointed at his meter, which had jumped to an astonishing eighty pounds.

"Give me a receipt," Rachel told him. "I'll pay what you're really owed." The paper slip came out of the machine, and the driver handed it off. While he waited, she fished inside her purse and extracted forty euros.

"That's only half," he said. "Where's the rest?"

Rachel's eyes narrowed. "There doesn't seem to be a driver's ID on the dashboard or back of your seat, which tells me you didn't earn a driver slot legitimately. If you don't want to take what I'm willing to pay, then so be it." She pocketed her money, opened the door, and dropped her duffel bag on the street. Then she jotted down the license-plate number and stole a quick snapshot of the driver while Chase called the number of the taxi company printed on the receipt.

"We have no record of that license plate," the dispatcher said on the phone. "Are you sure you've written it down correctly?"

"Yes. I'm sitting in the cab with that number."

By now, the trapped driver was extremely agitated. A small crowd had gathered behind the elderly taxi wrangler at the drop-off point at the station. Chase was still inside the car and calling the police when the driver panicked. He jammed on the accelerator, hitting the wrangler in the leg and sending him reeling across the ground. The cab sped away with Chase hanging out the open passenger door, and Chase could see Rachel staring after them in shock. From a side street, a truck pulled out in front of the cab, bringing it to a screeching halt. Behind them, adrenaline had kicked in: Rachel was now sprinting toward the car, with a group of bewildered witnesses close behind. Meanwhile, Chase debated whether he should go for the driver's throat or drag him from his seat and smash his head on the concrete curb.

"Chase!" Rachel screamed. "Get out of the car!" Suddenly, people were coming from everywhere, shouting at the driver and threatening him bodily harm. As Rachel reached the rear of the cab, Chase stepped out calmly. The driver took one quick look in the rearview mirror before stomping on the gas pedal and careening down the street with the back door wide open.

"Are you all right?" Rachel asked, still panting and obviously shaken. Chase threw a protective arm around her shoulder and drew her close.

"Not even a scratch," he said. "And do you know what's even more amazing?"

Rachel gazed up at him solemnly and slowly shook her head.

He half laughed at the absurdity of the situation. "The cab ride was free."

Rachel took a step back. "But the rest of our luggage wasn't."

As they disembarked from the train at Whitchurch and stepped through the station's main door, Rachel's excitement rose at the prospect of seeing her uncle. He was a younger version of her father, with the same chiseled good looks. He would have been easy to spot, even in this busy place. But from her vantage point, he was nowhere to be seen. Believing he had forgotten about her arrival, Rachel's heart sank. She turned to Chase and was about to voice her concern when she caught sight of a handsome man in the passenger-loading zone: white cable-knit sweater, tight jeans, in his mid-thirties, shaggy brown hair, rugged jaw, easy smile, dimples, and unforgettable emerald-green eyes. He was leaning against a silver Mercedes, flashing his perfect white teeth and holding up a sign reading, "Welcome to England, Rachel Lyons."

For a moment, she could hardly breathe, and she wondered if it was possible to fall over and die from shock. Or maybe from the idea of coming face-to-face with the last person on earth she ever expected to see. Although she had spoken to his Irish mother at a fund-raising event years earlier and was told that Killian was living with relatives in Northampton, she had convinced herself that the chance of meeting him was as unlikely as the sky turning green.

Killian Reed. His shimmering eyes were loving and warm and full of laughter. Rachel gasped and dropped her purse and overnight bag. She pulled off her high heels and ran to him. He swept her up and spun her around. When he set her back down, she buried her face in his chest and hugged him with all her might. She took a deep breath, inhaling the familiar scent of bay-rum aftershave. He kissed the top of her head, and she gazed up at him. She didn't realize she was crying until he reached out and wiped a tear from her cheek.

"I can't believe it's really you," she whispered, gratified to see unshed tears in his beautiful eyes.

"It's me, seaweed brain," he said. "I'm really here."

Rachel stood on her tiptoes and wrapped her arms around his neck. He put his arms around her waist and held her close. His hand smoothed her hair as he whispered, "I missed you, girl."

She looked up at him and smiled, and it suddenly dawned on her that you meet all kinds of people in your life. Some you never think about again. Some you wonder what happened to and if they ever think about you. And then there are some you wish you never had to think about again, yet somehow you do. Killian Reed just happened to be one of those disconcerting, unforgettable beings. He was part of her past: a distant, bittersweet memory that had lingered for years.

With their last parting, they had grasped each other's hands with a rush of melancholy, tender, and inexpressible feelings, and had gone their separate ways.

But time had moved on, and there was someone else in her life now—a silent observer patiently standing by, watching their every move with an annoyed pinch between his brows.

She took Killian by the hand and led him to Chase. More than anything, she hoped they would become fast friends, but as they shook hands, Rachel found it difficult to ignore the frowns tugging at the corners of their mouths. They both took a step back and just stood there, regarding each other silently, the air now seeming as cold as a razor blade.

"So...I guess we should head out," Rachel said, hoping to ease the tension between them. "I can't wait to get my feet up. It's been a long, trying day."

Chase's head turned. An unreadable expression filled his eyes. "I think you meant to say *trip*." She watched him collect her bag and purse and deposit them in the back of the car.

Killian tossed his head toward Chase. "Don't let that bother you," he said in a hushed tone. "A little rest will do everyone good. I'm sure things will look better in the morning."

Rachel offered a weak smile. "We can only hope."

"So where's your luggage?" Killian asked. "That bag can't be the only thing you brought."

Chase joined her before the open rear door. "Long story," he mumbled. "Nothing you need to worry about...unless you're a cop." He extended an arm toward the rear bucket seat. "After you, dear," he told Rachel, sarcasm laced in his tone.

She tried her best to ignore him by turning her attention toward Killian. "I'll be curious to hear how you ended up here. I didn't even know you were still in the country...let alone working for my uncle."

He waited for Rachel and Chase to be seated before shutting the car door behind them. As soon as the key was in the ignition and the engine was running, he glanced into the rearview mirror.

"I don't usually do this, Rachel. Your uncle's driver called in sick this morning, so I offered to pitch in. For the past two days,

I've been helping set up the new show at his gallery. Now that everything's done, I plan to head back to my studio and finish painting myself."

Chase snorted a laugh. "Working on a self-portrait, huh?"

Killian smiled in the mirror. "No, Mr. Cohen," he said lightheartedly. "I'm a plein-air painter. I'm not sure if you're familiar with Ferdinand Burgdorff, a renowned artist from California, but critics have likened my work to his coastal landscapes. My publisher and agent are always after me to paint more. With my work represented in more than twenty galleries and most of my shows selling out, I have a hard time keeping up."

Chase harrumphed. "Must be tough being so wonderful."

Rachel glared at him. "Really? Are you kidding me?" She shook her head in disgust and dropped back in her seat.

Killian stole another look in the mirror. "I understand you spend most of your time traveling around the world looking for buried treasure on Rachel's yacht. How's that working out for you?" Although his question sounded innocent enough, Killian had found Chase's greatest weakness by delivering a jab to his pride. Rachel glanced to her left and noticed that his lips had tightened and his nostrils were slightly flared. A growl rumbled low in the back of his throat. She clamped her hand on his forearm.

"Actually, it's *our* ship," she corrected. "Chase and I are business partners, and soon we'll be more than that."

"Heard about that. Been putting in some long hours. Didn't mean to sound rude. Congratulations, by the way."

Rachel turned to Chase. "We good now?"

Chase's eyes were fixed on Killian's reflection in the mirror. "Since you've spent a lot of time with Rachel's uncle, what's your take on how he feels? About us tying the knot, I mean."

Killian flashed Chase an uneasy look before returning his attention to the highway. "You sure you want to know?"

"Yeah, I do. Is there a problem?"

Rachel slid her hand up to his shoulder. "Honey, there's no reason to go into this. I'm sure it'll be fine...after we settle in and I've had a chance to talk to my uncle."

Killian cleared his throat. "For your sake, I sure wish it was that easy, Rachel."

"What's that supposed to mean?" she asked. "Did he say something to you about our engagement?"

"You know it really doesn't matter, does it? I mean if you're both in love and want to get married, whether your uncle approves or not shouldn't make a difference. Not unless you're planning to be single for the rest of your life."

Chase sank back in his seat. "You don't pull any punches, do you?

"Sorry, man, but it happens to be the truth."

"Which you would know because..."

"Because I asked permission to marry Rachel when I was eighteen. Her father blew me off as a stupid kid, and his brother told me to go screw myself. If by some miracle you receive Paul's blessing for marrying his niece, you're a far better man than me, Mr. Cohen."

Chase's gaze dropped then swung back to Rachel.

"That was a long time ago," she said. "We were just kids. My uncle was a guest in our home. His rudeness was inexcusable and completely uncalled for. But it doesn't really matter. As it turned out, I wasn't ready to settle down. Not with anyone." She reached for his hand and held onto it. "Not until now."

Killian rolled up to a stop and turned in his seat. "You know, Rachel, given how your uncle feels about you, I could have read him all wrong. He might surprise everyone and welcome both of you with open arms. If you told me three years ago I'd be working with him, hell, I would've said you were crazy." He flashed her a quick, easy smile.

Chase shifted in his seat. "Yeah, right. He's going to welcome me into his home with a big smile and knife behind his back."

Rachel glimpsed the rearview mirror and spotted Killian's eyes looking larger than normal. "I don't know why we're worrying about all this," she said. "I'm sure my uncle will give Chase the benefit of the doubt. After a few days, he will see we're meant to be together and will have no reason to object. In the meantime, let's just forget about the past and talk about more pleasant things, shall we?"

Chase whispered, "What happened to having no secrets between us?"

Rachel let out an exasperated sigh and rubbed her forehead. "What's that supposed to mean?"

"You never mentioned being engaged."

Six months ago, when she made a promise to share everything in her life, she never expected to see Killian again or to have Chase questioning her better judgment.

"What...no answer?"

"It doesn't deserve one." Rachel shifted her view to the side window and focused on the stately manors and rolling green hills in the distance.

Killian cleared his throat. "I'd love to hear about your trip. I imagine you had quite an adventure."

Rachel leaned forward and placed her hand on the top of the seat. She chose to answer for both of them, skipping over their month-long journey to describe their gypsy cab ride. When she finished her tale, Killian shook his head.

"I'm just glad you're both all right. The cops are sure to be on the lookout for that maniac driver. If things turn out as they should, you might even get your bags returned before the night's over."

"I sure hope so. Chase lost all his clothes, and I only have enough for a few days."

"If you don't get word back by tomorrow, I'll make arrangements to take you shopping. I've had a few bags disappear at airports myself, and I know exactly how you feel. There's nothing worse than losing everything you brought with you."

"We would appreciate that very much." Rachel eased back in her seat and squeezed her hands in her lap. She glanced at Chase's scowling face, confirming the matter between them was far from over.

"Our trip here has just started," she said quietly. "Can we please make peace?"

The corner of his mouth lifted in a quirked smile. "I'm just curious why you never told me about your former fiancé."

Rachel noticed the tension of Killian's hands on the wheel before returning her attention to Chase. "Why can't you wait until we get there? Until we're completely alone?"

"Ah, that sounds familiar. Always another time, another place. You know what? Better yet...just drop me off at the next town. When you're ready to talk, you'll know where to find me."

They were obviously suffering from cabin fever after being cooped up on the *Stargazer.* There was no other explanation for the pointless tension between them.

"Ah, come on," Killian told him. "Loosen up, mate. There's no need to get carried away."

Chase scowled. "Do I look like your mate?"

Rachel leaned into Chase. "I'm asking you to stop this. *Right now.*"

Chase looked down at his cowboy boots. He seemed to be mulling over her words and slowly coming back to his senses.

"Why can't you just tell me what's bothering you straight up? Then maybe all the fighting between us would end."

Rachel sealed her lips and clenched her teeth, caging her instinctive retort. As far back as she could remember, she had always kept her personal dilemmas a secret. Whether she stayed single or chose to marry *any* man, handing them over would never be an option. She pressed her palm against Chase's warm cheek and turned his face toward her. When their eyes met, she kept her voice level and tried to sound sincere. "Love comes from the depth of one's being. I don't take it lightly. I don't abuse it. And I don't think it's necessary to prove I love you on a daily basis. When I say I care about you, take me at my word, Chase, or don't take me at all."

Without warning, he grabbed her head and pressed his lips on hers in a hard, possessive kiss. Then he bit her lip and sucked on it, sweeping his tongue under it and into her mouth, touching every area as if trying to memorize the taste and texture of her. She kissed him back with newfound hunger that would have amazed her had she been in any state to consider it. But she wasn't. Her head swam. Her bones turned to water and her soul ignited. Deep inside, her body throbbed and ached.

Rachel suddenly became aware of Killian's gaze in the mirror and pushed Chase away. She felt the rush of heat to her cheeks as she lowered her lashes, her embarrassment preventing her from holding his look.

Chase grabbed her chin again and stared down at her lips. "The reason why relationships end is because one person tries to do everything in his or her power to save it while the other looks for any excuse to end it. I don't want to wake up one morning and discover I've been written off as another mistake." He raised his eyes to hers, released his hold and sat back.

What the hell? Rachel fell back in her seat, simmering in a stockpot of emotional turmoil. She couldn't help but notice Killian's arched brows in the mirror, plainly amazed by Chase's actions.

Damn it, Chase. As much as it pained her to remain calm and unaffected, there was no escaping the undeniable truth. She glanced down at the yellow diamond resting on her finger—the same engagement ring she had reluctantly accepted and now found herself nervously twisting. As each day had passed on board the *Stargazer*, Chase's disbelief in her ability to love had become more apparent, and his determination to somehow control her simmered as a constant threat. He had become the king of mixed signals, delivering romantic promises with fervent ultimatums, while she withdrew into her cocoon of apprehension, becoming the queen of second thoughts.

4

SET ADRIFT

Killian's eyes watched Rachel in the rearview mirror. "Can we stop by your uncle's gallery? It's not far from the house, and it will give you a chance to preview the Morris Graves show at a private gathering we're having right now, before the official opening tomorrow night. I could also use a little extra time to double-check the lighting. That is, if you don't mind..."

Rachel turned from her window and flashed him a lackluster smile. "Sure, no problem. Will my uncle be there?" At that moment, it really didn't matter. She couldn't wait to get out of the car and as far away from Chase Cohen as possible. Although he had tried his best to pull it together on the ship by being available to her and her needs, Rachel had remained unwavering in her determination to keep him at a physical and emotional arm's length. She couldn't escape the fact that he had left her at her weakest moment—when her guard was down and the pain from losing both parents had almost destroyed her. Now, with a child to worry about, how could she survive if he left her again? What if she wasn't the mother or wife he expected her to be?

Rachel rested her mouth against her turned fist and felt the tears in her eyes. She couldn't help but wonder if her love for Chase had prompted her rash suggestion for coming here. From the day they first met, she had made it clear that she wasn't the demonstrative type, and yet he refused to believe it. They were so far apart in how they dealt with their feelings, she couldn't help but wonder if they'd ever truly be happy together or if they were just lying to themselves.

When they arrived outside the gallery, Killian stepped from the car to speak with the parking attendant. He circled the vehicle to open the rear door and then froze in place, smiling. A tall, toned, short-haired blonde who looked like she did Pilates for a living was rapidly approaching from the side of the car. She was wearing tight leather pants and a tight pink sweater that drew attention to her large breasts. They hugged for an endless moment and then exchanged a quick kiss before engaging in an indecipherable conversation. Rachel watched with curious fascination. Was this female bodybuilder his lover? The woman who had healed his broken heart?

Without provocation, Chase suddenly reached for Rachel's hand and kissed it. He turned it over and brushed a warm, firm kiss over her palm. Fire roared in her blood, and her breath hitched. But she was determined not to give in—not to wipe away the memory of his bad behavior with a sexually charged act.

She clenched her fist, struggling for control.

"I'm so sorry, baby," he said. "I don't know what got into me. That's not who I am...You know that."

Rachel arched a brow. "I do?"

His lips spread into his all-too-familiar smile. "I guess it's that glow on your face...making me act like an idiot. Making you more beautiful than ever."

Rachel looked down. It seemed her pregnancy had become the focus of their lives—perhaps the only reason for staying together. But with the baby resting under her heart and no noticeable outward signs, she preferred to keep the matter strictly between them.

Chase lifted her chin with a curled index finger and forced her eyes to meet his. "Are you OK?"

"We'll get there. Just give it time. I'm still trying to figure out what my life's going to look like five months from now." He was even more handsome up close, which seemed impossible to her. His broad chest and muscular arms reminded her of the male models in fitness commercials. His tousled wavy blond hair hung to collar length and was neatly combed back. She couldn't help but stare into the beautiful blue depths of his eyes, and her throat literally closed in reaction. Was sexual desire all that she felt? There had to be more, but Chase seemed to think the answer to everything was kissing and touching. And to be honest, the distractions usually proved right.

"I love you, and…and I never want you to forget that," he said. "Regardless of how badly I behave."

She stared down at his hand holding hers. "I love you too, but we're here now…trying to make the best of it."

Chase shook his head, and a sigh slipped out. "I wish I could stay in a hotel with you…maybe order in and watch a few movies. I want to show you how much you mean to me. How you seriously are the only person who will ever have my heart." He leaned forward, and his lips lightly brushed over hers. "Please don't give up on us," he said softly against her mouth and kissed her again.

Rachel blushed and nodded slightly. She bit her lip but was unable to stop a giddy smile from erupting.

For an endless moment, they drank in the sight of one another and were devoid of the world outside. Then Killian returned, breaking the magic between them. "We should probably get going…"

Rachel stepped from the car. She pulled her black coat closer to her, suddenly cold; Chase immediately followed, reaching out and slinging his arm around her. At first glance, the gallery was not at all what she had been expecting. It was half a block long, glass-encased, trendy, and entirely too modern for her liking. But before she could deliver an unfavorable review, Killian was holding the door open, escorting her Prada-clad feet inside. Her eyes lit on the reception area, where her uncle was seated on a tan sofa directly across from two men wearing casual street clothes and brown paper bags over their heads. If not for her uncle's amiable expression, she would have thought they'd come there to rob the place.

Weird. Nothing about this place was normal, especially its other visitors. Although most of them were dressed in classy nightclub attire, a good portion resembled anime characters and band members from Kiss. She had been under the impression that Goth died years ago, but tonight it appeared to be experiencing a rebirth.

Rather than interrupt her uncle's conversation, Rachel decided to explore the room's eclectic wall art and gravity-defying sculptures. Killian touched her elbow and offered her a tall glass of sparkling cider. She slipped out of her coat and handed it to him before accepting the glass. Her eyes were taking in her surroundings, homing in on a bronze figure she quite liked near the back of the room. With the fluted glass pinched between her fingers, Rachel walked toward the object. The life-size sculpture was exquisite in every aspect. Great care had been taken to duplicate a stunning woman in a midcentury lace-trimmed gown. Her long hair curled around her face and trailed down the center of her back. The most intriguing feature was her soul-piercing eyes, looking over one smooth, polished shoulder. They were surprisingly intense—almost hypnotic—following her around the room from every possible angle.

To Rachel's amazement, the sculpture resembled an aged photograph of a woman perched on a rock that she had recently discovered in the attic of her father's coastal home.

Grandma Lily. It was too perfect to pass up, and it would fit seamlessly into the cottage's newly remodeled living room. Although her father would have venomously objected, knowing Lily had run off to Europe just like his unscrupulous wife, Rachel couldn't resist the idea of bringing her grandmother home. She knew acquiring the heavy bronze would involve costly shipping, but that didn't faze her. She had to have it, regardless of the price, the artist, or its current position in her uncle's ostentatious gallery. It would stand directly across from the entry, and she could see it every day, remembering the woman who had braided her hair, read her stories, and kept the scary monsters away.

"Chase, wouldn't she look incredible at the end of our sofa? It's almost as if we came here to find her."

He took a sip from his glass and grinned. "I think she'd be happier in the guest room, actually." When Rachel's brow dipped, he quickly added, "But then I know as much about art as you do about car engines, sweetheart. If that's what you want, then you should get it."

"*Really?* You don't mind?"

"Of course not. If it makes you happy, then why not?"

Rachel considered hugging him but was too captivated to move. She reached out a hand, running it along the edge of the bronze.

"I'm going to grab a real drink from the bar and look around for a while," he said. "Let me know if you need anything else."

As he walked away, a half-remembered voice registered in her mind. It sounded so familiar, so kind and inviting. A trill of laughter that couldn't be forgotten hung in the air, and suddenly Rachel felt uneasy. Her hand dropped to her side.

What am I doing? Perhaps the sculpture was too extravagant. Perhaps she should keep looking—find something smaller and more practical. There was probably a good reason why the price tag was missing. It might be that no one in his or her right mind could afford it.

Rachel backed away from the bronze rendering and collided with another body. She immediately turned, fully prepared to apologize, and was met with a brunette's backside. The woman groaned with anguish, clutching her midsection with both arms. Rachel stepped closer to study her face. The woman appeared to be of Indian descent. Her large brown eyes were watery, and her breathing came out in sharp, shallow rasps. Sweat covered her forehead in a thin sheen, indicating she was in terrible pain.

"H...Help," she croaked. "I need...help." Her desperate tone made her words almost inaudible, but they found their way to Rachel's ears.

Not knowing what else to do, Rachel clenched her hands and looked down at the woman's enormous belly.

"Don't you understand?" the pregnant woman gasped through clenched teeth. "I'm in pain."

Rachel scanned the half-filled room, willing the absorbed art critics to look in their direction and come rushing to her aid. She couldn't be responsible for this; she wouldn't have a clue where to begin. Then the woman groaned louder, and Rachel's instincts took over. She reached for the young woman's hand and led her to a nearby bench. Killian was talking to clients on the opposite side of the room, and Chase was nowhere in sight. She signaled for the bartender to come quickly, and then sent him running for a glass of water.

"What's your name?" Rachel asked, patting the woman's hand reassuringly.

"Melina," she said, wiping her moist eyes. "I'm so sick of this false labor. It keeps me from sleeping, and it screws with my head. I had a terrible bout a few days ago, and it's been on and off ever since. I'm only two weeks away, and now I've got back-aches and irregular contractions. I'm really pissed off that the midwife won't help. I've tried every remedy in the book. I just want this damn thing to be over so I can get on with my life."

Rachel swallowed the lump in her throat.

The dark-haired bartender returned, looking slightly flushed. Rachel accepted the glass from him, noticing the tattoos covering both his arms. He walked away, casting a quick look over his shoulder as Rachel sat down beside Melina and coaxed her into sipping the water. After a few minutes, their eyes reconnected, and the strain in Melina's face seemed to have lifted.

"Feeling better?" Rachel asked. She received a slow nod.

"I had a bit of a scare," Melina told her, "but I'm all right now." She rose to her feet, smoothed out her black dress, and pinned on a suitable smile. "I couldn't help overhearing part of your conversation. Was there a particular piece of art you were interested in purchasing?"

Rachel raised a brow. "What? You...work here? But what about..."

"My baby? Oh, you needn't worry, Miss. I plan to work as long as I can. Especially with my five-year-old son in private school and the carpenters hammering away."

Rachel spotted a sizeable diamond ring on the woman's left hand. Although she knew it was none of her business, curiosity drove her to ask the next question. "What about your husband? I hope he's helping you out…"

Killian had obviously overheard Rachel's words, as he crossed the room quickly and took Melina's hands in his. "My fiancée and I are managing just fine, thank you," he said. "Melina's never been the stay-at-home type, and fortunately, our nanny doubles as a housekeeper, allowing Melina the time to work here."

Rachel stretched her eyes in disbelief. "You two are…getting married?" Her line of vision traveled between their faces before involuntarily dropping to the woman's protruding belly. "That's…remarkable. After seeing you outside with that blonde, I just assumed—"

"Oh, that's Britt Easton…a former schoolmate," Killian said, addressing the concerned look on Melina's face. "We were just catching up. Anyway, when I saw you over here with your heads together, I just assumed you'd already made each other's acquaintance and knew all about the two of us." He kissed the top of Melina's head and smiled brightly.

Unbelievable. There was no denying Killian had changed, but never in a lifetime would Rachel have suspected to such a degree. She watched the interactions of this unlikely couple with renewed interest and kept a quiet lookout for Chase. They chatted about a new remodeling project, their honeymoon trip to Barcelona in the spring, and the commission Killian was currently working on. After ten long minutes of boring, idle chatter, Melina reached for Killian's forearm and smiled.

"Would you mind bringing me another glass of water, love?" she said. "I seem to have finished off this one." She handed him her empty cup and watched him walk away, glancing back once over his shoulder. "I understand you've known Killian since you were children and almost married him." Melina tilted her head slightly and smiled.

Unsure how to react, Rachel nodded.

"It's a shame things didn't work out the way you had hoped," Melina added. "Now, which pieces of art were you interested in buying?"

Rachel had become the client again. She pointed at the large bronze poised directly across from them. "That one."

Melina's face looked quite surprised at first but soon settled into a warm smile. "Wonderful! That particular piece was commissioned by Lily Lyons and created by Pete Medlow. Although it's worth considerably more, it is very reasonably priced at forty thousand dollars. It's actually from your uncle's private collection and only recently became available. If you look closely, I'm sure you'll see that—"

Her sales pitch fell short when Rachel handed her a black Visa card. "Can you please arrange to have the sculpture crated and shipped to my home address in San Palo, California? Our wheels will be touching down in nine days, so I'm hoping it will arrive soon after."

"You're flying home?" Melina appeared to be genuinely surprised. "But I thought you came here on your father's yacht. From what your uncle said, I just assumed you'd be returning the same way."

Her comment gave Rachel pause. "So he talked to you about me coming here. Did he happen to mention my fiancé?"

"No. Only you, Miss Lyons."

A thoughtful frown settled on her face. "Oh…I see." Although she preferred to avoid being the center of attention whenever possible, Rachel's uncle had barely acknowledged her existence. Even a nod of his head would have been nice.

"He didn't say anything about how beautiful you were, either, or about your uncanny resemblance to Miss Lily. She was a remarkable old soul…as kind and generous as they come."

"You knew Lily? My grandmother?"

"Oh yes, everyone did. She ran a house for young single mothers on the outskirts of town up until the day she died—three years ago. After hearing about her impressive list of suitors, I was surprised to discover she'd never married. There were politicians from America and Brazil, a well-known investment banker, a famous race-car driver...even a wealthy sheikh who flew in by private plane to see her. He wanted to put her up in a castle, but she turned him down flat. I suppose she never saw the advantage in settling down, not when she valued her freedom most." Melina's smile widened. "Silly me...going on and on. With you being her only granddaughter, I'm sure you know much more about Lily than I do."

No, I don't. Rachel gnawed on her lip. She wanted to go back in time, crawl into her grandmother's lap, and fall asleep in her arms. As she stared at the statue, disappointment, frustration, and uncertainty mixed painfully in her heart. If Lily hadn't had such a soft spot for wayward young women, she might have had room left over for her grandchildren. A way to reach out and let them know she still cared. Obviously, her uncle didn't. Why else would he sell off Lily's sculpture to any customer willing to pay the price?

Hmm...another mystery to add to my list. Whatever her uncle's reason might be, Rachel was glad to be taking the flawless version of Lily back to the States, where she could gaze at her in wonder. Despite the empty holidays, her unexplained absence, and the secrets they would never share, Rachel would always remember the joy and compassion Lily left behind.

She waited at the register and signed her receipt. "I believe you have my address and phone number. Is there anything else you need?"

"Looks like we're all set." Melina handed Rachel's card back and smiled again. "Can I get you a glass of champagne to celebrate? We keep it chilled in the gallery kitchen for our special customers."

Rachel shook her head. Under the circumstances, there was no reason to give her more information than necessary. "Actually, I'm trying to watch my weight right now."

"Sure wish I was," Melina muttered. "Oh, there's Killian. He's probably looking for me." She gathered the skirt of her dress around her before maneuvering through the crowd.

"Rachel? Rachel—over here!" a man's deep voice called out, soothing and musical at the same time. She turned toward a vociferous group and was stunned to see a familiar face in the crowd.

You've got to be kidding me. There was only one person in this world she hated with unbridled passion: Brandon Reed. She despised him for his cowardice, for leaving her to fend for herself. Rachel was never a violent person by nature, but she had actually swung a balled-up fist and hit him square in the jaw. As it turned out, her greatest weakness had been her blind, idiotic faith in people. This man had fooled her with his charm and kind concern. By the end of their fourth meeting, she was unfooled, and Rachel hated him with every ounce in her being. But after some time, she realized her hatred was self-defeating, and she had somehow managed to tuck her anger away.

A quick assessment assured her that Killian's jet-setting cousin hadn't changed one iota. To his remarkable credit, besides being eighteen years older than the last time they'd met, he was as ridiculously handsome as ever. Even at twenty-two, Brandon had resembled George Hamilton—a dashing, daring Hollywood celebrity who of course also happened to be a sporting, self-promoting, and very ambitious playboy. As Killian had informed her years earlier, and anyone who had met him might suspect, Brandon's spot-on impersonations and happy-go-lucky attitude made him a hit at parties and left a long-lasting impression. His deep-set brown eyes, gleaming smile, and perpetually bronzed complexion drew the attention of men and women alike. Surprisingly, it didn't hurt his reputation to be kept by rich divorcées and widows wherever he traveled. They were the ones who provided his lothario funds, allowing him to thrive in the manner in which he'd become accustomed while he pursued his fledgling acting career.

Rachel still blamed him for the uproar he'd caused, but seeing him now in his elegant attire, she couldn't help but smile. He was dressed in pressed tan slacks and a black turtleneck sweater. His brown tweed sports coat was draped casually over one arm, adding to his cavalier look. If she didn't know whom she was dealing with, she might have actually considered Brandon a pleasant distraction…just as she had the month after they'd met. Yet there was no mistaking the fact that this man was pure trouble. With one steamy shower and the drop of his towel, he had intentionally ruined her only chance at repairing the damage her father had caused in her long-term relationship with Killian.

"I can't believe it's really you," he said. Before she could stop him, Brandon's arms were around her, crushing her against his chest. She wanted to separate herself from him as quickly as possible, but her arms were pinned at her sides, making it impossible to move. When he finally let go, Rachel's eyes found Chase. Even from a distance, she could see the tension in his stance, could imagine the dark cloud gathering above his head.

"My cousin told me you'd be here, but I didn't believe it was true," Brandon said. "God, you look exactly the way I dreamed of you. Only now you're more beautiful than ever."

She rolled her eyes and wrinkled her nose the same way she had when Chase's dog dragged a smelly bone into the house. "Go back to sleep, Brandon," she told him. "You're still dreaming."

"I see you haven't lost your sense of humor," he said with his slow, methodical smile. "Still as clever as ever." His attention shifted to Melina standing across the room, apparently still searching for her missing husband. Brandon winked at her, and she turned away.

"It seems you're just as despicable as ever," Rachel said. Her eyes landed on a strange painting hanging on the wall behind him. It was the depiction of an eyeless crow...as blind as she'd been on that warm September afternoon, practically a lifetime ago, when he came to California for a month-long visit. After a rugby match, Brandon had returned to Killian's apartment alone. She'd been studying for a final exam in the kitchen when he walked into the room covered in a layer of sweat and dirt.

"Do you mind if I take a shower?" he had asked. "I hate to be a bother, but I just feel so..."

"Gross? Yeah, go ahead." Rachel heard the water kick on and tried not to imagine him standing under the spray as naked as a needle. Halfway through his shower, she moved to the living room and dropped onto the couch to watch the latest weather reports. An unseasonal heat wave was headed their way, and the local officials were discussing rationing water and how the drought had been threatening the valley. She flipped to another station, when suddenly the television and everything else shut off.

"Goddammit," she had sworn, standing up quickly. The lights were out; probably a downed power line. *Great.* That was all she needed. The bathroom door opened quickly, and Brandon emerged with a white towel around his waist. In the last hours of daylight, she could see droplets of water clinging to his smooth chest and deep, defined muscles. Against her better judgment, she had found herself visually tracing the small trail of hair leading from his belly button down to the edge of the towel.

Brandon touched her shoulder as she stared at the crow painting, drawing her back to the present. His voice was a near whisper. "You know I always wondered what would have happened if Killian hadn't walked into that room when he did."

Her eyes narrowed. "Put it away, Brandon. I'm still not interested."

"Rachel?" Chase was at her side, reaching for her hand. "Are you all right, sweetheart?" He was speaking to her, but his eyes were fixed on Brandon, scrutinizing him from head to toe.

She nodded quickly. "Yes, of course."

Brandon took a step closer. "Don't believe we've met. The name's Brandon Reed. I'm Killian's cousin. You probably don't know this, but Rachel and I go way back."

Chase released his hold on Rachel and surprised her by grasping Brandon's hand. He glanced around the room and graciously nodded, acknowledging the roomful of eyes that were now conspicuously watching. "I'm Chase Cohen," he told Brandon. "But then I suppose everyone here already knows that."

"It wouldn't surprise me at all. The people in this close-knit community tend to be skeptical of outsiders. As for myself, I ran into Killian yesterday, and he brought me up to speed. So I understand you search for buried treasure. Sounds like a great life."

Chase glanced at Rachel and somehow managed not to roll his eyes. She understood that he had no interest in validating his profession, especially to someone who really didn't give a damn. But he managed to patiently summarize his history before turning back to Rachel.

"Didn't you say you were hungry?"

"Starving…now that you mention it."

"Yep, that's what I thought. If you don't mind, Brandon, I need to get this lady fed and tucked into a warm bed. As you can imagine, we've had a long day."

"That might prove difficult with her uncle having a dinner party at the house tonight. According to Killian, your evening's just beginning."

Chase blew out a breath, and then asked her, "Are you going to be all right until then? I can grab some crackers and cheese from the table over by that creepy bird art."

"That's Morris Graves's work," Brandon informed him. "The whole reason for this show. He died fourteen years ago and still has a following, including a society of mystics who worship his art. You'd be shocked to know how much it's worth."

"Well, no one needs to worry about me buying his stuff. It looks like crappy children's art. My daughter is more talented."

Brandon's eyes shifted from Chase to Rachel. "You have a daughter?"

If Chase hadn't been there, she might have looked for an excuse to leave. She didn't want to feel guilty for implying that she would never accept the role of a mother to Chase's illegitimate child; neither did she want to place herself under any undue strain in having to correct his assumption.

"Actually, I do," Chase volunteered. "A beautiful, brilliant seven-year-old, and I actually think she'd agree with me."

"Yeah, well, like they say...taste is a matter of opinion. For some people, it has to be acquired."

Rachel treated Brandon to a wry smile. "So I take it you own one?"

"Of course I do. Whether you're fond of Morris Graves's work or not, it's a great investment."

"Oh really?" Chase said. "Personally, I never waste my money or time on people or stuff I don't like."

Brandon shot him a faintly annoyed look. "Funny, I thought we were discussing fine art."

"I guess..."

Brandon issued a half bow and walked away. After he was out of sight, Rachel hoped with all her heart that nothing more would be said—that the whole matter would be left to die a natural death. But in true Cohen fashion, that was not to be the case.

"Seems you've got an infestation problem," Chase said. "Got any more annoying bugs I need to squash?"

Rachel shook her head. "Brandon is in my past."

Chase touched her chin. "I guess we all have experiences we're not proud of. Just wish I were better informed. Then I could've brought my rope and strung him up from the rafters." He grinned at her with his customary crooked smile.

Rachel reached up for an embrace. "Thank you for being so amazing." She felt his hands against her back, pressing her closer.

"I'm *always* amazing," he said with a waggle of his brows. He released her, and she dropped back onto her heels.

"I guess we'll be putting on a great front at the dinner table tonight," Rachel told him. "What do you think they'll be serving?"

"We can only hope it's not liver, fava beans, and a nice chianti."

Rachel laughed and looked to her left in time to see Brandon standing next to her uncle. Seconds later, her uncle turned toward the crowd with an angry, contentious frown. Scanning the room, his eyes fell on her, fixing her with a strangling gaze. Although she couldn't believe it, she knew Brandon had come there for a specific reason. If he had his way, every man she'd ever cared about would be ripped from her life, including Chase, simply because she had refused to sleep with him.

5

TIDE POOL

Inside the dimly lit bus shelter, Damien Hewes rested his arm on Sloan Rafferty's shoulder and leaned in close to brush a kiss against her cheek. It was the kind of casual peck they'd exchanged on various occasions, but always in the company of others. Tonight, as they huddled together, trying to keep warm, the gesture felt curiously intimate. She automatically stiffened against him as if anticipating something more, but then she realized she was being silly and overly sensitive. For the last five years, Damien had been like a brother to her—listening to her complaints, sharing her concerns, always ready with a helpful opinion. There would never be a reason to feel threatened by him or coerced into doing something against her will. At least that was what she'd come to believe.

He leaned in close. "You know I really admire the way you stood up to Paul Lyons. That guy's an arrogant bastard, just like my old man. Both of them walk around like they own it all, but we know they don't own shit."

Possibly the strangest young man in Sloan's circle of friends, Damien took pride in his computer skills, individuality, and dedication to problem solving. He had a medium build and snow-white hair, pale complexion, and calm blue eyes that turned dark whenever he felt threatened. As a child, he loved the idea of creating inventions, and on one summer evening, a botched science experiment destroyed an abandoned warehouse and left him in the hospital with a concussion and stark-white hair. But rather than color it back to its former natural brown, he chose to wear it as a badge of courage.

"Actually, he surprised me today," Sloan said. "Gave me enough cash to cover expenses in Pitlochry. I was planning to earn wages in London, but now I won't have to wait. I can take that job I was offered at the Festival Theatre."

"Painting sets?"

"No, silly. Performing with a repertory group. It's what I've always wanted."

Damien smirked. "So, you're running off to Scotland…leaving all your friends behind. I'm sure they'll be happy to hear that."

Sloan half shrugged. "Sorry, Damien, but for the first time in my life, this is about me. I finally have a chance to make it on my own."

"You *do* know Sky made plans for us to live in his London flat. If you're not there, everyone's going to be incredibly disappointed."

His reference to "everyone" not only included him, but also his sister Veronica. She was a strange, enigmatic girl who loved mysteries and judging people by the color of their auras. Despite fashion trends, she insisted on maintaining the persona of a gypsy with her long black hair, green highlights, lavender contacts, body piercings, and butterfly tattoos.

As the rain continued its onslaught, a car passed, splashing water in its wake. Sloan looked up at Damien just in time to catch the reflection of headlights in his eyes. "I thought everyone was meeting us here," she said, nervously glancing away.

"Right now, Veronica is tying ribbons in her hair, and Sky's kissing one of his girlfriends good-bye. But don't worry, Sloan; they'll be here soon enough." Damien tilted his head to one side. "What's wrong, sourpuss? You afraid to be alone with me?"

"Of course not," she said, more confident than she actually felt.

"You sure? Then why are you shaking?"

Sloan turned to reply, but before she could, Damien's mouth smothered her words, swamping her with his directness. Yet, despite everything, she found herself responding passively. His soft lips parted and moved in a slow, circular fashion before pressing down more forcefully.

Her head was confused, yet her body continued to respond as though she were oddly powerless to stop. Pushing him away would seem almost...rude. She closed her eyes, still slightly heady from the intoxicating effects of the alcohol they'd consumed, and relaxed momentarily in his embrace. Her senses were curiously roused as his teeth gently nibbled on her lips. As if by their own volition, her arms slipped around his neck. Then a roll of thunder clapped loudly, making the fabric of the shelter tremble, and she shrank back in alarm.

"Looks like it's setting in," she said to the air.

"Mmm...good. All the more reason to stay here." Damien swiftly pulled her back toward him so that their eyes were forced to meet.

"Damien...please..." A wave of panic overtook her, but it was too late. The signals of encouragement had already been sent. His gaze dropped to her breasts, and his hands held her waist, pulling her closer. She stiffened against him, but he was upon her before she knew it, pressing his lips hard against hers.

His kisses became more demanding, his tongue plundered her mouth greedily, and his fingers dug into her hips. He was rough, aggressive, and strong, and she never thought she'd like it—this feeling of losing control. A blood rush and wave of arousal surged through her like liquid fire. She heard his breathing quicken as his kisses grew more intense. A hand cupped one of her breasts and began rubbing faster and faster. She pulled away, but his hands had already moved to open her blouse, skillfully unfastening the front of her bra. Cursing the fullness of her nipples, she flopped back helplessly against the glass wall as his mouth covered one and he began sucking away like a hungry baby.

Sloan knew she should stop him, end his assault while she still could. But instead her arms hung at her sides like useless rags. She squeezed her eyes shut, desperate to block out what was happening. In the stillness, she could feel his tongue circling the areola of her nipple, and she shuddered at the involuntary tingling inside that it evoked. Then her juices began flowing, and she willed them to stop, knowing it was no more than a reflex. Yet her response repelled her. She took a long, deep breath and concentrated hard. But the movement of a hand across her abdomen, feeling its way over her contours, made her stiffen again.

Her heart skipped a beat and then slammed to a halt as he reached the crossroads of her limbs. A pair of straightened fingers began to rub up and down. Instantly, her mind splintered with confusion. She tried to push him away, but his reactions were quicker, and he grabbed her hand to pull it down onto his arousal instead. She heard the sound of air being sucked through his teeth and then felt his hot, steamy breath as he locked onto a nipple again.

Her stomach tightened, and then an odious stench of stale urine wafted up from the sewer on a gust of wind, overpowering all other sensations. Sloan's heart was racing. Her insides were churning. Swallowing against an acidic taste in her throat, she was unsure what was worse—the foul reek in the air or the equally vile sensation of touching him.

Revulsion rapidly turned to panic, and she tore her hand away. She stared down at white hair splayed across her breast, and it suddenly struck her how Damien's physical attributes had never been particularly relevant before, but now, on this cold, wet, and windy night, they seemed overwhelmingly significant.

The sound of a slamming car door turned his head. With his attention diverted, Sloan clutched the top edges of her wool coat, sealing the collar tightly against her throat and any further assault. She focused on the silver SUV parked below the corner lamppost, praying that a rescue was imminent. Her hero came in the form of a broad-shouldered young man in a shiny black rain-coat. He was crossing the street, running straight toward them with an upturned hand raised over his head. It was Sky Nolan, the strongest and most beloved member in their group.

"Sloan...I thought that was you," he called out. After enter-ing the shelter, he laid a gentle hand on her shoulder, causing her body to jump. "What's wrong?" he asked.

In the semidarkness, she struggled to make out his chiseled features, blondish-brown hair, and dark-blue eyes, and yet his deep, soothing voice was unmistakable.

"Nothing. I'm—I'm fine," she managed. "The storm...it, it startled me." She feigned a smile. Embarrassment was warming her cheeks, making it impossible to look at him directly.

Sky shot a curious look at her silent companion, who had already managed to distance himself. "Glad to hear that, Sloan. We wouldn't want anything bad to happen to you. Would we, Damien?"

Sloan had no intention of ratting out her troubled friend. Especially after sharing the half-empty bottle of Scotch he'd stolen from his father's bar. But more importantly, everyone knew Sky could be hostile and quick-tempered at times. He would get into a fistfight or draw his switchblade to protect the friends he cared about most, and Sloan Rafferty just happened to be one of them.

"Of course not," Damien mumbled.

"Good, good. Let's get going then. Your sister left early to grab seats at the club. I'm parked just across the street."

Sloan followed his lead in the torrential downpour. They were only a short distance from the car when Damien grabbed hold of her hand, turning her halfway around. "Sorry about that," he said. "I don't know what possessed me."

"Glenlivet," she said.

"Huh?"

Sloan looked at him long and hard. "Never mind," she finally said. "Just don't try anything like that again, or you'll be losing a hand instead of a friend."

As she approached the vehicle, Sky held the door wide open. She slid into the passenger seat while Damien stood outside in the rain with his eyes down and his hair dripping. From now on, Sloan knew, she'd have to make a point of keeping her distance from him, which could prove challenging with his sister pushing them together all the time.

"The door's unlocked!" Sky called. "You coming or not?"

Damien glanced at Sloan. "On second thought, I think I'll head home. My throat's a little sore. Might be a cold coming on."

"Suit yourself!" Sky shouted. He slammed the door shut behind him and turned the key in the ignition. As they drove away, he cast a sidelong glance at Sloan. "I might be a bit slow on the uptake, but I'm not stupid. I know something went down. Either that guy came on to you, or you've got worse problems at home. No matter what, you're staying at my place tonight. When you feel like talking, I'll be ready to listen."

Yes on both counts, Sloan wanted to say. Like all of her close friends, Sky had been deemed unacceptable. According to her grandmother, he was a misfit, a rebel, and a low-minded degenerate. The very underbelly of society determined to pull her down with him. However, after the way Sara behaved when Sloan asked about her own mother's death, Sloan thought Sara could have easily been diagnosed as bipolar...and her husband right along with her.

What right do they have to judge anyone when they're so screwed up themselves? Sloan stared through the window at the passing cars, hoping for a mindless distraction. But she couldn't ignore her frustrations. Since the day she was born, the only person she could count on was Margaret. The sweet, elderly housekeeper was her nanny and the closest thing she had to a mother. She had tolerated Sloan's adolescent tantrums and rebellion when no one else would, and she was always ready to offer a kind word of advice. Although Margaret urged her to make peace, Sloan wasn't interested in appeasing anyone, especially her grandmother. As far as that woman was concerned, forgiveness was a lost concept, along with love, tolerance, and understanding.

"Did you hear me?" Sky asked, breaking into her thoughts.

"Yeah, sure. Thank you." She sat back in her seat and flashed a smile. For the time being, she was determined to appear marginally happy, confident, and unaffected. At least until the details surrounding her mother's untimely death were revealed—the secret that everyone in the Cumberforge Manor seemed determined to keep from her. And just why was the greatest mystery of all.

Sloan glanced at her watch and saw it was half past ten, much later than she'd thought. A quick look around made it clear that no other place in London could change so radically at night. During the day, Soho held its breath in denial of what was to come: aromatic alleys, cheaply dressed, over-perfumed country girls, fresh-ground espresso, and as if by magic, a whiff of Peking duck that had the guts to find its way across Shaftesbury Avenue.

This was Sloan's playground—the place where her survival instincts were tested nightly. At this late hour, pubs and clubs were coughing up punters like dirty phlegm, and everyone was high, guided by pheromones that made sure they ended up in the sack, whether they liked it or not. That was how Sloan viewed this upside-down world—the one she'd been born into, ejected from, educated in, and now called home. At sunset, she would prowl the streets with her friends, or venture out on her own, assessing the damage. Despite warnings and crime reports, she always felt safe and protected, as long as she kept a pocketknife handy and her wits about her.

An incoming, seemingly endless tide of people filled the walks on their way to unknown destinations—bars and restaurants, or dark hole-in-the-wall theaters. There were tourists, fraternity brothers, divas, blue-collar workers, transvestites, queen bees, musicians, and beauticians. They came for chef specials and entertainment and to blow off steam. But mainly it was about experiencing the whole screwy scene.

Sloan climbed out of Sky's van and imagined that the congregation exiting the local church was an unstoppable wave, washing the city clean of its sins, while they had come to add a fresh new layer. As it turned out, the Red Room—where Veronica and other friends were waiting—was a backdoor velvet-lined nightclub in a restricted section of the city. However, nothing about the dilapidated building was deficient. The entry was covered from floor to ceiling with enormous gold-framed mirrors.

Dimly lit sconces dotted the walls, leading the way into the booming, high-energy joint. Sloan and Sky stood and watched liquor flow from every spigot in the place. The Red Room was filled to capacity with folks from all walks of life. The strange melting pot was built so far underground that it seemed like heat from the center of the earth could be warming the floor. The mist rising from the concrete softened the edges of the club, while strobe lights threw it into sharp relief. All races, all cultures—outlandish and swank—seemed to have found a temporary escape here. Drugs, sex, and alcohol mingled in the back rooms, and even the moans sounded in time with the constant pounding rhythm. LED strobe lights pulsed, and the damned souls of the Red Room pulsed right along with them. The music was not really music—at least not like any Sloan had heard—but a constant throbbing bass wove its way into your core and refused to leave.

Veronica had positioned herself among the crush of dancers, bouncing up and down with the romping and stomping beat. Brice Stanton, one of Sky's former classmates, was sandwiched between her and an unfamiliar redhead, grinding away. As the energy continued to build, the crowd thinned a bit, making it possible to see Veronica in action. Her body flowed and curved with liquid motion in a sheer purple top and hip-hugging black skirt.

Sky kept his arm protectively resting against Sloan's back and waved his free hand in the air. Veronica spotted them and smiled. She rushed over and escorted them to a corner table littered with empty beer bottles, wineglasses, and two overfilled ashtrays. "It's about time!" she yelled at them.

"We got here as soon as we could!" Sky called back. "Some of us work for a living."

"Yeah, right. It's a good thing I don't, or you wouldn't have a place to sit." Veronica leaned in toward Sloan and sniffed. "Shit, girl, what kind of poison have you been drinking?"

"Something in a gold bottle that your father's probably missing by now."

"Damien, huh? I told him stay out of the high-end stuff, but he never listens." Veronica ran a hand across her forehead, smearing her foundation with dripping sweat. Then she slid her fingers beneath the edge of her purple chemise and yanked it about to suck air down her filmy layered top. "It's a good thing my dad's not a boozer, 'cause half his stash is pure water." She let out a soft chuckle. "So where's my goofy bro, anyway? Lost as usual?"

Sky was quick to answer. "Damien was feeling off. He's probably at home by now."

Veronica knitted her brows. "Really? That's odd. He was totally stoked an hour ago. One of his favorite bands is about to go on. Oh, well, his loss is our gain." She slipped a white packet into Sloan's breast pocket and smiled. "For later." Then she pulled out a plastic Tic Tac dispenser and held it before Sloan. "Breath mint?"

Sloan smiled, recognizing the code word for speed. She took the container and popped a pill into her mouth before offering it to Sky.

"No, thanks."

Veronica motioned her head toward the crowded bar. "They got a new guy working tonight. He's been secretly pouring me free drinks and telling me he'll recoup his losses after hours. I'll be back soon. Time to check in."

She crossed the room to the bar, where a handsome Latino was serving fruity concoctions and draft beers to anyone willing to pay. Sloan looked around for familiar faces and was about to stand up to continue her search when a shirtless male server arrived.

"What'll it be, folks?"

"Pint of Wadworth!" Sky yelled.

"What about you, gorgeous?"

"Shot of Black."

Sky stared at her in disbelief. "Johnnie Walker? Are you nuts?"

"Make it a double," she told the server. She waited for him to leave before turning to Sky. "Back off, angel. I'm capable of making my own decisions."

"Try *mistakes*," he blasted back.

"Yeah, whatever." The sound around her suddenly dulled, as if she were experiencing a rapid change in air pressure. She tried yawning to open her eardrums, but the strange sensation continued, turning voices into muted echoes.

"Sloan? Sloan! Are you all right?" Sky yelled, but she could barely hear him.

Damn it, Veronica. What the hell did you give me?

Sky reached across the table and covered her hand with his. "Is something wrong?"

"My head feels like it's full of cotton. It's probably the music. It's so loud!"

"Do you want to go outside?"

She unfastened the top three buttons on her blouse, exposing her cleavage. "Is it hot in here?"

Sky got up and grabbed Sloan by the arm. "Let's get the hell out of here."

She looked up at him, angry and confused. "What are you doing?"

"I'm trying to keep you from passing out in this dump!" he yelled. When she pulled her arm back, he glared at her for a moment and then dropped into his seat.

The server approached with a tray full of drinks. "Did you say *dump*? You can leave anytime, you know…right after you cover your bill."

Sloan reached up and snatched a large shot glass from his tray.

"Not cool, bitch," the guy said, frowning. "Next time you do that, you're going to end up with a dozen drinks in your lap." He dropped a filled beer glass on their table and moved on to his other customers.

Sky glared at Sloan. "Are you tripping? Is that what's going on?"

She tossed back the whiskey and then slammed the glass on the table. *Shit!* Her throat was on fire, and the flames were shooting through her chest, leaving her coughing and gasping for air.

"I warned you. Are you ready to go now?"

"Stop staring me like that," she choked out. "I thought you were leaving."

He crossed his arms over his chest and glared at her from the tops of his eyes.

"What's your problem?" she snapped. "Why aren't you drinking like everyone else?"

"Changed my mind after I realized you'd lost yours. I thought you didn't belong in this place. But, man, was I wrong. You fit right in."

Sloan snorted. "Belong? You're kidding, right? Since when do I belong anywhere?"

"Sounds like a pity party coming on," he grumbled.

"Really? Guess you'd know better than anyone." Her lips twisted into a wry smile. "Everyone's under the assumption that I grew up with a silver spoon in my mouth…like all of you." Sloan glanced at her friend, standing at the far end of the bar, smiling and waving. "But you know what? I wouldn't know silver from tin."

Sky scoffed at her remark. "What makes you think any of us had it better than you? Get over yourself, Sloan. Just because there was money floating around doesn't mean any of us had access to it. It's time you wised up and figured out who you really are."

"Who I am?" Sloan stared at him, imagining he had the power to read her thoughts. "What the hell is that supposed to mean?"

"I honestly had no idea what we were walking into," he claimed. "If I had, we wouldn't be here. This was Veronica's bright idea. From the dust under her nose, I would put money on her finding what she was after. So why don't we just leave while we can? I'm sure she'll find a ride home with Brice or one of her other friends, just like she always does."

Sloan sat upright in her seat. She was too numb for this gar-bage—for whatever he had in mind. "Hmm, let me guess. You want to go home and shag me like Damien. Is that what you have in mind?"

He leaned into her, sweeping his eyes up and down like he was mentally measuring her. "Ah, that's what went on. Now it all makes sense. The way he was acting and his lame-ass excuse. I knew it had to be something. So tell me, how far did he get?"

Sloan blinked repeatedly, struggling to keep her eyes open and her mouth shut. She had no intention of dropping her guard and exposing herself to ridicule. But the combination of booze and pills had loosened her lips, and mindless words kept pouring out. "Are you waiting for a blow by blow? 'Cause if you are, it ain't coming, and neither are you. Not inside this girl."

He snorted a laugh. "You're kind of sexy when you're inco-herent. You know that?"

Sloan drew back and tried to focus. "You're the one who shouldn't be here, Sky. You're too good for this place. For any of us..."

"Someone should have told me that before we walked in," he quipped. "Veronica and Brice are totally in their element. They love playing stupid games. Dropping acid, tagging walls, hiding from cops. Disappearing for days just to get noticed by their pinhead parents. That's their thing, honey, not yours."

Ignoring the impeccable logic of that statement, Sloan tried to form a counterattack only to have her thoughts interrupted by Brice physically throwing himself at them.

"Bloody hell, Stanton!" Sky exploded, shoving him away. "I was hoping to go through the rest of my life without seeing you fucking mindless."

Brice turned around so fast in his torn-up jeans that it was dizzy to watch. "Sloan! There you are! Are you here to have fun?" He waggled his eyebrows, making her laugh.

Sky answered for her. "She's here to watch an idiot get his head dropped in the loo, and by the way you're acting, I wouldn't be surprised if it was you."

Brice snorted a laugh. "Stop being such a stick in the mud, Nolan. Look around. Everyone in this place is frigging nuts." He went back to throwing himself at the bouncing redhead and Veronica with total disregard for anyone else.

Sky turned to Sloan. "So, are you ready to leave for my place—sleep it off and tell me who you really are?"

"You think I'm joking, but I'm not. I'm invisible. I'm a figment of everyone's imagination."

"OK, so now you're a blooming fairy. How 'bout buttoning up and giving me your hand?"

"Why? We just got here," Sloan slurred. "I haven't even danced yet." She stood up and realized her mistake too late. The room tilted to the right and began spinning. She squeezed her eyes shut, fearing that if she moved too quickly or moved her mouth, her stomach would protest and add a new layer to her humiliation.

Sky was on his feet. "Sloan, look at me. It's going to be all right. I'm going to get you out of here."

She reached for him to keep from falling over. He tossed a few bills on the table and guided her through the crowd with her arm slung over his shoulder. After claiming her coat, they emerged through the exit and into the cold night with their arms around each other's backs. In both directions, music lovers, minors in micro-minis, and bohemian misfits waited in line for their chance to witness the alternative rock band's performance. In a matter of minutes, the club would explode, with Brice and Veronica in the center of all the action.

"Ah, bullock," Sloan slurred. "Left my clothes at the gallery. Did you see them?"

Sky halted next to a lamppost. "I need you to stay right here. I'm going to grab my car and be right back. OK?"

Sloan nodded and wrapped her arm around the lamppost. As he walked away, she closed her eyes and leaned her head back. *Breathe, breathe. Just breathe...* She needed to gain control over her mind and body. Take her finger off the self-destruct button and conquer her fears before they conquered her. But where to begin? Even the shrink she had visited weekly offered no answers, solutions, or worthwhile advice, leaving her more perplexed than ever.

"Let go of your past, Sloan," he had said. "Concentrate on the future and the positive aspects of your life, and before you know it, you'll find yourself reengaging in the world, in the lives of the people around you."

Dumb-ass advice. At the end of each session, he rewarded her with a new prescription—a quick fix designed to dull her anxieties and sweep her frustrations under the rug.

Ah, shit. Where were those pills when you needed them?

The air suddenly grew cold, stinging her ears. Sloan tugged at her coat with one hand and held onto the post with the other. She began wondering why Sky was taking so long when a car suddenly pulled up. The passenger window was rolled down, but the driver was obscured in darkness.

"Get in!" a man's voice yelled.

Without a second thought, she opened the door and climbed in.

6

PLUNDERED

When Sloan came to her senses, she realized she had been blindfolded and was completely tied up. She had an agonizing cramp in her neck, and her wrists and legs were fast asleep from the duct tape cutting into her skin. Her fingers were going numb by the second, and with no way to see, she had to trust her other senses to figure things out.

First, she determined that she'd been left on a hardwood floor. Next, she inhaled a light pine fragrance in the air. There was also an unpleasant odor she couldn't identify. Perhaps it was sweat or the smell of mold in the room. The area around her didn't seem to be that big; however, her instincts told her it was larger than a closet.

It appeared that someone had kidnapped her, but why? Did they want money? If they did, the cash Paul had given freely was still in the gallery apartment, where he had allowed her to crash and store her clothes for the last two weeks. With all the trouble Sloan caused her grandmother over the years, it was unlikely that she would pay any kind of ransom. Sloan sighed and scrunched her brow at the thought. Her grandfather had a good amount of money, but he wouldn't spend a dime after forking over the weekly receipts from the gallery. And besides, he was her step-grandfather. He was under no obligation to help her.

If the men who had taken her didn't want money, then what did they want? A shudder traveled down her spine as a frightening idea came to mind. She fervently hoped it wasn't true. She knew she couldn't survive if they wanted her as a sex slave. She'd find something sharp and kill herself first.

Sloan wondered how long she'd been there and how long they planned to keep her. If she could just get her blindfold off, she could figure out what to do next. She rolled onto her stomach to relieve the pain in her neck, only adding pressure to her aching back. She fell onto her left side and decided to stay put, since gravity was determined to keep her there anyway.

A noise came from the next room. A man was yelling. She could only pick out a few muffled words—insults like *jackass*, *bloody cheap shit*, and other curse words. Whoever this guy was, he was definitely pissed off about something—things were even being thrown against the wall. The sound of crashing left her cringing and dreading that more pain would be coming soon.

Please don't hurt me, please don't hurt me. The words became a chant in her brain. Tears pooled in the corners of her eyes, brought on by growing fears. The next thing she heard was slamming doors, and she realized that one of the men who had taken her was rapidly approaching.

Oh, shit! Sky, where the hell are you?

Someone grabbed her upper arm so tightly that a bruise was sure to form. Then a fist slammed into her cheek. Her assailant hit her repeatedly in the face, and kicked her sides until her ribs were on fire. The rest of her body hurt, and she knew she would feel the full effect of the beating in a short matter of time.

Why is this happening? What did I ever do to deserve this? Sobs escaped her throat. Tears rolled down her cheeks as the beast continued his attack.

"What the fuck are you doing?" A second voice demanded from the other side of the room. Quick footsteps followed, and the man who was brutalizing her was jerked away and pitched against the wall. Although she assumed he'd been injured, his voice sounded unfazed.

"It makes me feel better." The tone in his words was higher, throaty, and coarse, not husky like the second guy. "I've wanted to beat the crap out of this one for months."

Sloan continued to cry. Every inch of her body hurt, and the taste of blood filled her mouth. She wanted to crawl into a ball and hide. But she couldn't while she was still hog-tied.

Her attacker was talking again, and she couldn't believe what she was hearing. "The way I figure it, if she's covered in bruises, that cheap bitch will have no choice but to pay us what we want."

The second man let out a heavy sigh. "I made the call, just like we planned. You know what that bitch said? 'I washed my hands of her months ago. I don't care what you do to her. She's your problem, not mine.' Now what kind of bullshit is that? Why would she say such a thing?"

Sloan couldn't help but flinch after hearing her grandmother's words. She knew the woman had plenty of reasons not to like her, but she never expected to be disowned. At least, not entirely.

"Because she's the Queen of Sheba," the beast growled. "What the fuck do I know? Just move! I'll get my money out of her my own way."

Sloan's body froze with the realization that she was about to be raped. With her hands and feet tied, there was nothing she could do to stop it.

Oh God, don't let him do this.

The next noise sounded like someone being punched and dropped to the floor. Sloan exhaled a deep breath. As long as they were fighting among themselves, they wouldn't be bothering her. It was the only hope she had to hang on to.

Suddenly, the rope binding her legs was cut, and she felt herself being dragged out of the room. She hissed involuntarily when he grabbed her sore arm. Her inability to move was a reminder that her wrists and ankles were still taped together. Tears leaked from her eyes as she tried to fight against the person who was dragging her across the cold floor.

"Please...I beg you," she whimpered. "Don't hurt me."

"What are you doing? Get your hands off of her!" the first guy yelled. "I'm not done yet!"

"Neither am I," the second man said. He picked her up and dropped her on what she could only guess to be a bed. The next sounds she heard were the door slamming and a lock sliding into place. She gulped hard and closed her eyes tight, waiting for what would come next.

Sloan remained motionless, wondering if the guy who had dragged her there was still in the room. Everything around her was silent. The only thing she could hear was her heavy breathing. She moved her head to the side and was able to figure out that she was lying on her stomach with her nose pressed against the bed's scratchy comforter. A gasp escaped her lips when a weight fell on the bed, causing her to roll into a man's solid body. Her back was pressed against his back, and she quickly surmised that he was facing away from her on the bed.

"Why are you doing this?" she asked in a quiet, weak voice.

A grunt was his only response. He suddenly stood up and moved closer. She could feel his presence above her, staring down, studying every inch of her.

"Are you going to rape me?"

"Do you want me to? Is that what you're saying?"

A scream froze in her throat as he leaned over her body. His hot breath was on her skin. He wiped the blood off her face with a cold, damp towel and gave her a quick, soft peck on her bruised lips, causing her to wince.

"Don't hold your breath, sweetheart. It's not happening."

He surprised her by removing her blindfold. After having her eyes covered for so long, the room seemed extremely bright. Stars danced in front of her eyes, and she squeezed them shut again, waiting for her irises to adjust to her unfamiliar surroundings.

"Sorry," she heard him say, more sincerely than she thought possible. She opened her eyes more slowly this time. The beige ceiling in the bedroom was the first thing she saw, followed by the four gray walls surrounding her. She looked for an exit, a window, a door...any means by which to escape.

Her eyes landed on the man at her side, and she was oddly calmed by his appearance. He was surprisingly handsome and close to a foot taller than she was. His caramel eyes were striking, and his long brown hair was slicked back, giving him a dashing *GQ* look—so unlike the terrifying criminal she had imagined. He had an average build, and his snug black T-shirt revealed muscle definition in his biceps, chest, and abdomen, indicating he worked out. His five-o'clock shadow and golden tan further suggested an unconventional lifestyle. But what good would clues do her if she was already dead? After removing her blindfold and allowing her to see his face, he would have no other choice but to kill her.

Right?

She watched him move toward a wood dresser, where he appeared to look for something. When he turned around, she spotted a switchblade in his hand. He flipped the blade open and used his thumb to examine the sharpness of its edge.

Oh, shit! Sloan tried to roll off the bed. He grabbed her arm and pushed her face into the mattress. "Please don't," she sobbed into the sheet. The words were muffled, yet she knew he could hear her. She tried to move again, to distance herself, but before she could, he dropped a knee into the middle of her back, eliminating any possibility of escape.

"I'm begging you not to do this," she pleaded, all the while kicking out at him.

"Stop it," he hissed. He increased the pressure of his knee on her back, restricting her movements, mercilessly trapping her.

"No!" she cried out, frantically swinging her feet. "I won't let you hurt me!"

"Oh, for the love of hell," he muttered.

Sloan ignored him and kept screaming. "Please let me go! You can't do this!"

The guy actually had the nerve to laugh. "I can't? And who's going to stop me?"

"Please...I'm not a bad person. Honest, I'm not."

"Really? Well, you definitely had me fooled." He used the knife to cut the tape on her wrists and tore it off. Then he freed her feet.

"Save that sweet ass for me!" Sloan froze in place after hearing the man's voice in the next room. She watched her captor's brown eyes and noticed the annoyance resonating there. He looked down at Sloan for a prolonged moment before grabbing her hand and pulling her up after him. He stopped before an inside doorway and shoved her through. She landed on her hands and knees on the cold linoleum floor. Was this a bathroom?

"Stay in there," he directed. "And forget about climbing out of that old boarded-up window. Even if you were covered in grease, you wouldn't fit through." He slammed the door shut and instructed her to lock it.

She did as she was told and called out to him. "I'll live in here forever if it means I'm safe." She stood up and stared at her reflection in the mirror. Tears ran down her cheek. She gingerly touched the large bruise on the side of her face. There were scrapes on her forehead, and her bottom lip was cut and swollen. She hugged herself as fear and confusion rose.

Minutes later, she heard a repeated rap on the door. "Let me in," the same man told her. "You have nothing to fear from me. I promise."

"No! Go away and leave me alone!"

"I want you to think back carefully," he said. "Tell me…have I done anything to hurt you?"

Besides pinning her down with his knee, he honestly hadn't. He'd been protecting her from his psycho partner in the next room—a man who apparently would beat her to death if given the chance.

She slowly opened the door. Then she slid down to the floor and stared straight ahead, waiting like a mouse in a trap.

"Do you think you can trust me a little more?"

She lifted her eyes and met his. "I won't tell anyone. I promise. Just let me go. OK?" Tears were streaming down her cheeks, an endless supply she couldn't stop.

He laid his head back against the tile wall and closed his eyes. "I can't."

Sloan huffed. "After everything that's happened, how do you expect me to believe anything you say?"

He righted himself and took her hands, pulling her back onto her feet. "Trust me, kid. You have nothing to fear from me." He paused for a moment before adding, "I mean it."

"You kidnapped me! How am I supposed to trust you?" She looked around the room for something to protect herself with—a makeshift weapon of some kind. Anything she could use against him and the monster waiting outside.

"Oh, I think I can tell you something that will change your mind." He closed the distance between them and placed his hands on the wall above her head. Then he leaned in close, increasing the tension in her aching body. He lowered his face, bringing his lips to her right ear, and whispered softly, "I'm an undercover cop."

7

THE GAME PLAN

"That is the most cliché line ever," Sloan said with an unladylike snort. "You don't honestly expect me to believe that. Why would I, especially when you—"

The would-be cop put his large hand over her mouth. "Shut up," he whispered. With his free hand, he pushed the bathroom door open. He walked her back to the bed, staring down at her the whole time. Then he bent over the nightstand to turn on the radio and cranked up the sound. He wiped his hand on his jeans and motioned for her to sit down and be quiet, but she refused to follow orders. She covered her ears with her hands, attempting to block the horrible noise. Was it rap? Screaming hip-hop? Whatever the crap it was left her teeth clenched until he turned the dial and managed to find an oldies station—something that was tolerable while he attempted to explain himself.

"Why do you find it so hard to believe I'm a cop?" He leaned toward her. "Don't I look like one?"

Sloan crossed her arms and leaned back against the wall. "If you want me to believe you, then show me your badge."

He was staring at her, kind of tilting his head to the side. "Not like I'd carry it here with me." He sounded displeased, but she didn't care. "I'm working undercover, remember?"

Sloan stared at him, her insides winding into a tight ball. "If you're a real cop, then you must be dirty."

He groaned and leaned his cool forehead against hers. "I'm not a dirty cop, and I'm not a bad cop. I'm just doing my job."

"Fine, whatever. Just leave me alone."

"Not until you believe me," he said through tight lips.

Sloan sighed through her nose. "How are you going to make me believe you then?"

The guy opened his mouth and then closed it.

"Can't think of anything?"

"Just give me a second. I'll come up with something."

"Like another lie?" Sloan ducked out from between his arms and waited. "Who are you, anyway?"

His lips flirted with a smile. "You can call me Tor, like everyone else. And don't bother. I know who you are, Sloan. Shoplifting, right?"

"What did you say? Do you know my grandfather? Have we met before?"

"No, we've never met, but I know all about you. I really am a cop, and a good guy too. But that jerk in the next room isn't. We're talking drugs, smuggling, robbery, and extortion. When Julien was twenty, he served seven years for assault and battery after almost killing a guy in a bar fight. As long as he's helping me on this case, I can't haul him in on kidnapping charges. And I can't let you go. Not until his friends are rounded up."

"Bullshit."

"I mean it."

"Guess I'll be screaming bloody murder then."

"OK!" Tor scratched his neck. "You were just in the wrong place at the wrong time."

"Yeah, sure. Try again."

"All right, all right. I'll tell you the truth, but you have to listen and do exactly as I say."

A wry smile twisted her lips.

"I'm not joking. I mean it."

She dropped onto the mattress and scooted back against the headboard. "Fine," came her tight-lipped reply. "But my friends will be worrying about me. I don't want to stay in this crummy place any longer than I have to."

Tor half shrugged. "I'll see what I can do."

"So what gives?"

He sat down next to her. "Your grandmother's art gallery has been targeted. The same place where you've been living for the last two weeks. Julien is under the impression that you were snatched as a bonus, but the truth is I needed you to be out of there. I'm after the ringleaders who have been stealing and smuggling art all across Europe. Right now, I've got the unfortunate job of looking after Julien, a complete asshole who loves to beat up women and threaten kids. But he also has connections to the right people. If it's not too much trouble, I need you to sit tight for a few days so I can concentrate on my job and make sure your family stays safe."

Sloan watched him thoughtfully before asking the question that had been plaguing her for almost an hour. "Tell me the truth, Detective. Did you really talk to my grandmother? Did she say all that stuff about me, or did you make it up?"

Tor sighed before answering. "Have you given her any reason lately not to believe you?"

Her brows dipped. "Yeah...a few times, I guess." *Actually, too many to count.*

"I could easily say, 'Well, there you go.' But I'm not that big of a jerk," he quipped. "No one called her, and she didn't disown you, at least not that I know of. Parents boot their kids from the nest all the time, and I just figured with your current living situation, something must have gone down."

Sloan stared at the cracks in the ceiling, mulling over his words, trying to decide if there was any truth to them. If this guy was a real cop, why was his department allowing him to orchestrate such a ridiculous scheme? Why would they entrust him with a psychotic hoodlum who was hell-bent on killing her? And why did she still doubt his story?

He shot her a crooked smile. "I was thinking I might let you beat the shit out of Julien before we put him away for good. How's that sound?"

It sounded nuts; that was how it sounded. And sitting there twiddling her thumbs while her friends beat the bushes looking for her was even crazier. She'd give this character twenty-four hours max. Then she'd find a way to pry the board off the bathroom window—the wood framed escape route someone had deliberately hidden. After hightailing it out of there, she would find a way home before Tor discovered she was missing. Yep, that was her plan, and nothing he could say or do would change it. Because if the cop's story was as crocked up as it sounded, he was after more than art thieves, and her part in all of this could turn out really badly.

8

BRIEF INTERLUDE

After traveling for months to get to the remote Cumberforge Manor and spending the last two hours at the Lyons' gallery—hours Chase would never get back—he was relieved to finally arrive and be rewarded with forty-five minutes of solitude. Rachel plopped herself down on the white brocade couch in the lavish guest bedroom, looking almost as worn out as he felt. She hadn't said much of anything while they were buying clothes, and she spoke even less while passing through the bronze gates and doorposts leading to the mansion's stately threshold. During their short guided tour, she had only issued a few quick nods and polite replies prior to being shown to their room by the curly haired, bow-tied butler, who had insisted on carrying her bag. When the door finally closed behind him, Rachel's long, weary sigh said it all. The idea of attending a formal dinner party that same evening with a roomful of strangers would be excruciating after the miles and misadventure they'd endured to get there.

For a moment he thought he saw wariness in her eyes. But then she blinked, and her face looked merely tired. His gaze drifted down her body, covered in a black wool skirt and white cotton blouse. His muscles tightened. The soft material couldn't hide the lush curves beneath it. "So, what gives?"

"What do you mean?"

"I don't know. You seemed to have unhooked after leaving the gallery. Is something bothering you?"

"I guess my expectations were higher."

Chase glanced around the elaborately decorated room. "Than this?" His gaze fell to her lap where her fingers were fiddling with her engagement ring, rocking it back and forth.

"I'm talking about my uncle. For some reason, I thought he'd be more welcoming, and now I feel like he doesn't want me here."

Yeah. Chase got the same impression the moment he walked into the gallery. Her uncle glanced up once and hadn't even offered him a quick handshake. Just nodded in his direction and instructed his driver to take them wherever they needed to go. Whatever Brandon had said didn't improve the atmosphere, either, but only added more tension between everyone, making Chase wonder what was actually said.

"Chase, I'm thinking we should stay in a hotel room after all. Maybe check in first thing tomorrow. We could stick around a few days, make an appearance, and fly back on Friday." When Rachel looked up at him, it was easy for Chase to imagine that his fears were pointless.

"Is there something I should know about Brandon?" he asked, saying the words he'd been thinking for hours.

Her chin came down. "I'd rather not talk about it."

"Baby, it can't be that bad."

"It doesn't involve anyone. It was just…stupid kid stuff." Her voice trailed off. "Let it go, Chase."

Somehow it was worse not knowing. His imagination was going crazy, leaving him envisioning all kinds of twisted sexual stuff. He shifted in his seat and checked out the time on the mantel clock resting on the stone fireplace. It was ten minutes to eight. He fully expected her to jump up and insist he take a shower any second, but when he laid his right arm along the back of the couch, the entire left side of her body ended up against his.

He froze and waited for her to squirm away, keeping the mandatory two feet of personal space between them. But she didn't. Holy shit, she didn't. He glanced down at the top of her head, forcing his breathing to remain steady. Over the next half hour, every cell in his body became aware of her weight, her warmth, and her deep, even breaths.

Chase's heart skipped a beat when her head came down on the spot just below his shoulder. Was she asleep?

"Rachel?"

When there was no answer, he determined that she had, in fact, fallen asleep on him. There was a swelling in his chest, bigger and tighter than the knot that seemed to form whenever he was around her. And then the strangest damn thing happened as he stared down at her. Parts of his body hardened at her closeness, but his insides softened like butter left out in the sun.

You're so fucked when it comes to this woman. Those words kept coming back to him, time and time again. Maybe he was fucked, but he wouldn't trade this moment for anything. Carefully, so he didn't wake her, he brought his arm off the back of the couch and gently guided her down so that her head rested comfortably on his thigh. And something not too far north enlarged. Perhaps that wasn't the smartest idea, because it was too tempting to have her this close, but this…well, it felt right in a way that it had never felt with any other woman—the way he'd always wanted it to be with Rachel.

His chest lurched as she snuggled in, folding her hands together under her chin. He watched her for a long moment, soaking up the smooth line of her jaw, the curve of her cheek, and those irresistible rosy lips.

Damn, he was fucked in all the right ways. He tried to focus on the vintage artwork, antique writing desk, carved chair, gold duvet bedspread, and matching velvet curtains. For a while, he even stared at the freshly lit fire, flickering between uneven split logs. But his eyes were on Rachel once more. He wasn't even sure if his attention ever left her.

He thought it was still cool in the room, so he pulled the brown patchwork quilt from the back of the couch and draped it over her body. The bare expanse of her shoulder caught his attention. Her white shirt had slipped down her right arm, exposing the white strap of her bra.

The soft glow of her skin lured him in, and, once again, he was absolutely powerless to resist it. Lowering his hand, his breath caught as he touched the elegant curve of her shoulder. Rachel murmured in her sleep and wiggled a bit, but she didn't wake up. It probably wasn't fair to keep touching her, but he couldn't resist dragging his fingertips down her arm, relishing the feel of her.

Stopping at the hem of her shirt, his fingers grazed her silky skin all the way up to her cheek. He was glad she was asleep, because the thought of her knowing how badly his hands shook would probably have been embarrassing as hell. Boy, they were trembling too, like he'd never touched her before. Rachel...hell, she completely undid him.

Tipping his head back against the couch, he closed his eyes and swallowed hard as he rested his hand on the flare of her hip. He could probably count on one hand how many times he'd spent the evening with a beautiful woman curled up against him fast asleep, content just to be there with her. Part of his brain was telling him to kiss her hard, allow his hands to move over her body, while his cowardice convinced him to hold back. This was the woman he intended to marry—the amazing creature who was carrying his child. So why the hell was he feeling intrusive? Like he was invading unfamiliar territory?

"No," Rachel murmured, and his eyes flew open. Her brow wrinkled, but she seemed to be asleep. "That's not why we're here..."

Chase cocked his head to the side, straining to hear what else she was saying, but the only other word he could pick up was *sorry* before she settled back down. His heart pounded as he turned those words over. They didn't make any sense and probably didn't mean anything, but a ball of unease formed in his gut. Why did she feel the need to apologize? Whom was she talking to? What was going on in that secretive mind of hers?

Time passed, and he didn't sleep—not really. He was stuck in the weird in-between phase, half awake and half dozing. But he knew the moment she woke up. Her body stiffened, and she dragged in a deep breath. Several moments slipped by, and she didn't move or speak. God, he would've cut off his right hand to know what she was thinking.

Rachel slowly rolled onto her back, surprising him and leaving no time to react. His hand slipped from her hip and landed on her lower belly, fingers reaching the top of her pants. God knows he should've pulled his hand away, but he didn't. His hand had a mind of its own and did something entirely unexpected. His thumb moved in slow, idle circles just below her navel. He watched her under his lashes, nearly groaning when she sucked in her lower lip. Then his gaze flicked up, and he could see the hardened tips of her breasts pushing through the thin, filmy material. He was hard again—no surprise there.

This woman was making him crazy. He wanted her so badly he was physically aching. No matter what, he could always count on her response to hold her to him. But now, he could feel her slipping away. It terrified him to know his claim on her was so fragile.

Chase turned his head to the side, his lips tipping up at the corners as he drew in a deep breath. He clenched his jaw as she tipped her head back against his thigh, coming close to his erection.

"Chase," she breathed.

He opened an eye. "Rachel?"

"You're not asleep," she said, voice husky and unbelievably sexy.

"You were…and I was too." Total lie, but he doubted she'd be all right with knowing he had sat there almost the entire time watching her like a sex-starved pervert.

Rachel wet her lips, and damn it if Chase didn't want to swoop down and catch the tip of that tongue. "I'm sorry I fell asleep on you," she said.

"I'm not."

Her cheeks flushed. "What time is it?"

"Almost eight," he said, staring at her moist lips.

"You didn't even look at the clock."

"I just know that kind of stuff."

"Really?" she whispered.

"Yeah."

"That's a remarkable talent." Her hand curled into a loose fist on her leg. "Are you going to take a shower?"

"I suppose I should. You wanna join me?"

She made a face, but her eyes glimmered up at him. "That's not why I was asking. I was just curious, silly. We're supposed to be downstairs at eight thirty."

Using his other hand, Chase smoothed a few strands of auburn hair off her face, and then he rested his hand on the top of her head.

"I guess we should get ready," she said, making no effort to move.

"You think so?"

"Yes," she half whispered.

When her eyes drifted shut, he wanted to kiss her but found himself resisting the urge.

"I'll let you go first this time," she said.

"But you always take longer than me."

"Correct, and it's probably because you don't have makeup and nylons to put on. Normally, I would race you to the bathroom, but I'm hoping to take a long, hot bath later. If I step under a shower right now, I'm going to wilt, and you'll have to scrape me off the floor."

He took a deep breath. "Sure you're not going to miss me while I'm gone?"

She smiled coyly. "It'll be like a vacation for me."

Chase laughed. "That was entirely mean."

"Was it?"

"I know you're lying."

"You do?"

"Yep." He moved his hand, gently touching her cheek. Her eyes snapped open, and he smiled down at her. "You're going to miss me, but you'll never admit it."

Rachel was silent as he trailed his fingers from her jaw to her chin, coming close to her bottom lip. "I'll miss you."

"Really?"

"Yeah. Fifteen whole minutes."

Her eyes drifted closed as she relaxed against him once more. He continued to trace a path from her cheek to her lip, haunted by what she had said in her dreams. "You talk in your sleep," he said.

Her eyes opened, and her face paled. "I do?"

Chase nodded.

"Are you messing with me? Because I swear to God if you are, I'm going to hit you so hard."

That unease was back, and he wasn't sure why. "I'm not messing with you, sweetheart."

Rachel sat up, twisting on the couch, facing him. "What did I say?"

"Nothing really."

"For real?" Her expression was so earnest and so serious he wished he hadn't said anything.

He leaned forward, scrubbing his hands down his face. "You were just murmuring stuff. I couldn't really make out what you were saying." He looked at her. "It was kind of cute."

She held his gaze, seeming to take what he said as the gospel truth, and then glanced at the clock. "Holy crap, you suck at knowing the time without looking."

Chase shrugged. He knew it was well past eight thirty and the party downstairs was in full swing. "I guess I'd better get ready."

She opened her mouth, closed it, and then tried again. "He's not going to be there, you know."

"He?"

"Brandon Reed. He wasn't invited. I asked Melina…just to be sure."

Chase nodded. "That's good."

"So you have no excuse for not being on your best behavior tonight. Promise me right now that you won't say or do anything to upset my uncle."

Standing, he stretched his back. "I won't. Don't worry," he said, and before she could freak on him, he bent down and kissed her on the forehead. "Get ready, Rachel. You're the one everyone's waiting to see."

Her eyes were closed, and her hands were balled together in front of her chest. When she spoke, it sounded like she was whispering a prayer. "Everything's going to work out fine. I know it."

He made it to the bathroom door before she sprung up like a tight coil, hands gripping the back of the couch. "Chase?"

"Yeah?"

She took a deep breath, and that heartfelt expression was back on her face, back where it belonged. "I'm glad we're doing this together."

He couldn't help but smile. "So am I, sweetheart," he said. "Now move that beautiful ass of yours before I have to come over there and help you." Rachel jumped up and grabbed a throw pillow from the bed. She pitched it in his direction, hitting the edge of the bathroom door. "Gutter mouth," she said, giggling softly while turning away.

His heart beat wildly as he continued to watch her from the partially open doorway. She bent forward slightly, pulled down her tights, and stepped out of them, exposing her smooth, shapely legs. Her skirt dropped next, and so did his willpower. He raced back into the room, wrapped his arms around her waist, and planted a kiss on her neck. He whispered in her ear, "How 'bout I just keep you here all to myself? Then you can tell me what you really think of me."

She turned in his arms and hooked her hands around his neck. Then she looked up into his eyes. "I think you should do what makes you happy."

What? Surprise undoubtedly showed in his face. He licked his lips and nodded, his eyes on hers. "OK, gorgeous. You asked for it." He pulled her hard against him and sealed his mouth over hers. The moment she stroked her tongue along his, he put both hands under her butt and lifted her, turned, kicked a chair out of the way, and set her on the edge of the writing desk. His fingers found the buttons on the front of her shirt and quickly freed them all, spreading the blouse open. He unhooked the front of her sheer bra, releasing her full breasts, and stepped back to admire their beauty.

Bang! Bang! Bang! There were persistent knocks on the bedroom door.

"Are you kidding?" Chase growled. It had taken him weeks to get this far. He was hard as a rock and wasn't about to stop now. He leaned in to kiss Rachel again when a woman's intrusive voice rang out.

"Mr. Cohen! Miss Lyons! I'm sorry to disturb you, but you're wanted downstairs right away. Mr. Lyons has asked if you're planning to attend his party or if you prefer to hide out in your room for the duration of your stay."

9

LANDLUBBERS

Chase walked through the open French doors and out onto the long terrace, where cocktails were being served, trying his best to look interested. Three small groups had already gathered there, laughing and glowing in their finery. With hundreds of candles flickering, and outside roof heaters cranked on high, Chase was immediately reminded of a magazine ad he'd seen weeks earlier promoting a Montana ski resort that only the rich and famous could afford. However, like the red roses filling the cut-glass vases throughout the house, the glittering designer jewelry adorning necks of various sizes lent an air of gaiety that anyone could appreciate.

As it turned out, the dinner party was much larger than Chase had imagined. He followed some guests into the house to find a wall of backs in every doorway and people spilling out of the drawing room and into the conservatory. As he was searching the room for Rachel's uncle, a woman in a black lace dress loomed up and tapped him on the shoulder. Her sleek ebony hair was pulled back severely and held at her neck in a thick silver clip.

"Why, hello, Mr. Cohen," she said. "I've heard all about you. The great American treasure hunter. What a treat to have you here. I must have read a dozen stories about you and Miss Lyons. All that gold, and a sunken ship too. I sure hope you don't mind my saying so, but after hearing about you from Paul, I never expected you to be so handsome...so fit and so tall."

Chase couldn't begin to respond to that and didn't try. But that didn't discourage her one tiny bit.

"The Lyonses always put on super parties," she said. "The flowers and decorations are absolutely perfect. It's just a shame Sara didn't take my advice on the caterer. Didn't you notice the appetizers? It's all doughy stuff and spicy skewered chicken bites. They didn't even include stuffed mushrooms, smoked salmon, or roulades. But I'm sure dinner will be lovely, all the same."

"I sure hope so," he said with terrible joviality. A waiter offered gold shots from a large silver tray—some type of bourbon, if he heard correctly. Chase took a glass and threw it back, almost certain it was the last thing he needed.

"Well...I'd best be moving along," the woman said. "My husband Albert accuses me of monopolizing conversations. Rude, boring bastard. He's always on his cell, reading reports, ranting about one thing or another. If anyone's a jabber puss, it's him, Mr. Cohen. Not me." She lifted a winged eyebrow and smirked. "Oh, damn, there he is. Do have a pleasant visit, won't you?"

Albert's wife scurried away in the opposite direction, leaving Chase to debate the best way to approach Paul. With all the preparations for the party, the opportunity to meet him privately and correct any misunderstandings had been missed. He needed to remedy that, but finding the opportunity to vindicate himself was going to pose a challenge. Especially with 120 of Paul's closest friends and business acquaintances present.

A female staff member called out to him from an open doorway. "Excuse me, Mr. Cohen. I'm sorry to disturb you, sir," she said in a hushed tone. "I was just wondering if you and your missus would like your bed turned down this evening." The middle-aged woman had medium-brown hair, soft brown eyes, and age-appropriate bags under her eyes. She was carrying beige pressed and folded sheets over one arm, and she seemed to be emanating a tremendous amount of nervous energy.

He noticed a black embroidered name on the upper right side of her gray dress and addressed her accordingly. "Why, yes, Heidi. I think my fiancée would like that very much."

Her cheeks flushed, and she softly smiled. Then she nodded and shyly looked down. She continued on her mission down the hallway, vanishing discreetly into the inner workings of the house.

Wearing his best smile, Chase moved through the oversize living room and resumed his search for Paul Lyons. He finally spotted him next to a massive stone fireplace talking to a well-dressed man and his blond-helmeted wife. It occurred to him that they were customers he'd met earlier in the day at the gallery—a couple who had spent more money on art than his shipmates could scrape together in six months. From the look of the well-heeled man's smile and the sound of his reoccurring guffaws, he was being politely agreeable while in Paul's illustrious company.

Killian and his wife-to-be hadn't arrived yet, and Rachel was still upstairs styling her hair. There was no one else at the party that Chase was particularly interested in talking to. At least not at the moment. He took a flute of champagne from a dark-eyed young waiter and strolled off through the open French doors into the knee-high maze of manicured shrubs. The curlicue path brought him round to a view of the house again, but the waiter who had served him had moved off, and instead Sara Lyons was ambling toward him.

"Good evening, Mr. Cohen," she said. "You clean up quite nicely." She was, of course, referring to the navy Westbourne suit, white pinstriped shirt, and burgundy noose he had purchased from an exclusive downtown merchant. With his luggage still missing and only having Levi's jeans and the white Merino sweater he'd arrived in, acquiring suitable attire for the evening, T-shirts, socks, and a few comfortable changes had been a requirement and not an experience he hoped to repeat any time soon. The snooty salesman in the overpriced men's store tried to insist he buy the hand-stitched Italian dress shoes he had tried on to complement his high-end wardrobe, but Chase forcefully declined. In defiance of Rachel's well-meaning advice, he had opted to wear his broken-in Laredo cowboy boots, and that was exactly where Mrs. Lyons's eyes landed.

Chase cleared his throat. "Great place you have here. When we drove up, I thought Killian made a mistake by taking us to some fancy hotel."

Sara smiled as she fiddled with her diamond bracelet.

"So how many bedrooms you got in this place?" he asked.

"Eight in the east wing, four in the guesthouse, and six in the south wing, which are used mainly by our maids and housekeeping staff." Sara glanced up at a slender young woman with long red hair crossing the terrace and then returned her attention to Chase. "Is your room suitable, Mr. Cohen?"

"Extremely. It's like staying in a palace, Mrs. Lyons. I can't thank you enough for having us."

She smiled sweetly. "It's my understanding you'll be with us for a week. If you need anything at all, please don't hesitate to let Margaret know. She's in charge of our staff here, and she will be happy to assist you."

"Thank you," Chase said. "And by the way, I really appreciate you allowing my fiancée and me to share quarters. She was a little nervous about asking, and we didn't want anyone to feel—"

Sara raised a hand, silencing him. "There's no need to say more, Mr. Cohen. I wouldn't have it any other way. You and my husband's niece are engaged, after all." She laid her manicured hand on his forearm. "Oh, and I thought it best to inform you that even though we have arranged for our guests to be here this evening, the dinner party is being given in your honor. My husband has specifically asked me to make an official announcement regarding your engagement to Rachel at the end of our meal. Perhaps that will put your fiancée's mind at ease, and you can relax and enjoy the rest of your visit. How does that sound, Mr. Cohen?"

Sara cast a satisfied look at his expression of utter amazement. "Wow, that's unbelievable. Rachel's been a wreck all day. I'll let her know the good news. Right after she finishes primping."

"I hope she doesn't feel rushed. The cocktail hour always runs much longer than it should. But then Paul has always preferred it that way."

"I guess he must enjoy celebrating…"

"Oh, no, thank God," Sara laughed good-humoredly. "I was referring to our last-minute arrivals. There are always a few stragglers competing with traffic. You can imagine how busy it gets at this hour. Anyway, Paul likes to have everyone present for special occasions. We'll give them just a few more minutes before we begin."

Chase glanced at his watch and mentally noted the time. At this rate, they wouldn't be eating until 9:30 p.m., but that came as no surprise. Europeans were famous for dining late.

"And now you'll have to excuse me," she said. "I still have some last-minute details to address." She disappeared back inside with her white gown trailing behind. Chase stared after her, astonished by her welcoming words and gentle demeanor. It seemed Rachel's first impression of Sara was entirely wrong, which was so unlike her. Her instincts were always spot on, but she had obviously missed the mark this time. Sara was thoughtful and very supportive. She would make a wonderful ally when the time came to officially ask her husband for Rachel's hand in marriage, or more precisely, his blessing.

Chase blew out a tense breath. Thanks to Rachel's brother, Devon, he'd been worrying all this time about nothing. *Sara's a blue blood. Don't get sucked into believing she cares about you or anyone else.* Obviously, the guy didn't know his aunt as well as he thought.

"Thanks for nothing," Chase mumbled. He couldn't wait to share the good news with Rachel. If Paul Lyons turned out to be half as kind and understanding as his wife, he and Rachel could be married within days and spend the rest of their vacation traveling around England, enjoying the sights and sounds. The revelation left him smiling and throwing back his glass of brut champagne. Even though he detested the highfalutin stuff, somehow it never tasted so good.

❧

When the guests were seated for dinner, Chase engaged himself in a conversation with the two guests seated closest to him. As it turned out, the kind gentleman to his right was Peter Bradshaw—an ascetic-looking elderly Oxford graduate with narrow shoulders and bespectacled eyes, reminiscent of a scholar or scientist. He was also a hypnotherapist who had been assisting Sara with her allergies, memory loss, and weight management. His silver-haired assistant, Ida Ainsworth, was seated beside him. Although eager to occasionally add her two cents, she appeared to be preoccupied with her cell phone and Facebook friends most of the night.

"So tell me something about Paul Lyons, Dr. Bradshaw," Chase said. "Do you have any idea of what he's into?" They were dining in the manor's great hall with a dozen round tables scattered about, and had finally reached the end of their five-course meal. As Chase waited for an answer from the doctor, he became aware of the mood of noisy expectancy permeating the room. He glanced at Rachel, who had been seated at an adjacent table throughout the evening. Her uncle's auburn-haired wife was positioned on her immediate right, staring mindlessly into a glass of burgundy wine. To Chase's delight, her eyes had the fine glaze of preoccupation—like someone who was about to make a very important speech.

"Art," Peter Bradshaw said. He twirled his glass on the rucked tablecloth. "Very expensive fine art. His wife, on the other hand, is more focused on—"

"Power," Ida said, dabbing a white linen napkin on the corner of her heavily lined mouth.

Peter nodded his agreement. "Ah, yes…power. With tourists, electronic firms, and international billionaires moving into our community on a daily basis, it's essential to our survival."

Ida looked up from her phone. "He's also very keen on Stilton cheese, professional theater, and competitive fencing."

"Oh, and Richard Wagner's music," Peter added. "*Tristan und Isolde*, in particular. He often plays it in the library while he's writing his novel. I understand he's determined to put another one on the best-seller list."

Chase panned the room again, glimpsing the collection of international guests at nearby tables. A stocky German man was drumming his fingers on the back of a gold Chiavari chair while talking to the dowdy silver-haired woman seated in it. The two Chinese travel agents he'd met while searching for the loo were staring at the cleavage of the well-endowed French vocalist seated across the table from them. Chase shifted his eyes to another table and tried to be discreet by not listening to the snippets of gossip going on around him. It seemed there were mixed reviews pertaining to the dining arrangements and the gallery's new art exhibit. He glanced back at Rachel when the group of guests next to Paul erupted in laughter and caught a peek at the servants watching from the gallery above. He pushed his chair back to get a better view of his fiancée in her low-cut lavender dress, blushing and looking away pensively with a strained grin. He smiled back at her, hoping to catch her eye. He wanted to alleviate her obvious discomfort, but remained powerless to do so, of course.

Paul stood and turned toward the two masked men entering the room. With a wave of his hand, they stopped in their tracks. "I'm sure everyone's been wondering about the gentlemen on my right whom you might have had the privilege to speak with this evening. For those who haven't, let me officially introduce two fraternal brothers from the order of the Morris Graves Mystic Society. Although they're here at my request, I'm sure you'll understand their need to leave and fulfill other obligations before returning to the States."

"Thank you for your support," one of them said.

The second one croaked, "Enjoy the show tomorrow."

Chase turned to Peter Bradshaw. "I wish someone would tell me why they insist on wearing paper bags on their heads. It's some kind of gimmick, right?"

"Gimmick?"

"You know, a way to protest what people have been saying about Graves and his…unusual art." He wanted to say *crazy, weird shit* but then thought better of it. Modern art and the people who raved about it like it was miraculous conception left his mind itching and wondering if they'd all lost theirs. He would take a nice painting of a ship on the rolling sea any day over psychedelic faces, bird-filled orbs, and a flock of eyeless black crows.

The doctor chuckled. "Of course not," he chastised. "Those men are here as a show of support. They prefer their anonymity and belong to a pseudo secret society that believes in supporting struggling artists and promoting the ideals of their deceased leader." Peter leaned in closer. "I'm not sure if you're aware of this or not, Mr. Cohen, but Morris Graves was the only American artist to be honored with the prestigious Windsor Award. Unfortunately, the recent controversy over the grand polemarch's beliefs and his Nazi ceramics has tarnished Mr. Graves's reputation. You see, according to the polemarch's podcast, he'd like the public to believe that the Holocaust was an exaggerated myth. An elaborate way for persecuted Jews to promote multiculturalism and globalization. Coming from America as you have, you can imagine how that was received."

"Grand polemarch?"

"Charles Krafft. A white nationalist, and leader of their organization."

OK, the doctor was educated and well-spoken. There was no doubt about that. However, the creepy art exhibit Paul Lyons was promoting and the "hidden" people behind the scenes were thoroughly messed up, which further explained why he was excited at the prospect of hosting it. The press he would receive alone had the potential to draw thousands of curiosity seekers. Good or bad, relevant or ridiculous, he was making a name for the Lyons gallery. But at whose expense?

Sara shifted in her seat several times, as if nervous with anticipation over her unspoken announcement. Through the clapping and roar of laughter in the room, Chase caught

Rachel's eye again and held it for five long seconds, giving her perhaps a transfusion of reassurance. She was looking around nervously and, it seemed, imitating the laughter of others rather than laughing at the remarks or jokes themselves. He surveyed the room, which reminded him of a courtroom where Paul Lyons and his influential friends might hold sway. Up in the arcade of the gallery, two servers from the kitchen staff listened impassively, as if waiting for the next act to begin in a carefully scripted play.

A massive ten-foot pendant fixture, with upward-curling gilt branches holding frosted lily lights, hung from the ceiling in the center of the room. Killian's fiancée had refused to sit under it, which was why their whole table had apparently been demoted to the far corner of the room. If it did fall, Chase realized, it would crush a thickly bearded man and his giggling wife. Even from where he sat, he couldn't help but feel a little nervous about the pretentious, abstract fixture dangling from the prehistoric-looking hook.

Chase took another sip from his bottomless wineglass, refilled every time it reached the halfway mark. He spotted the dark-haired bartender from the art gallery standing in the door-way directly behind him. The stern-faced man was following the proceedings at the head table with a disconnected, vacant stare. Chase turned back around and noticed that Ida was now empty-ing the ornate fruit-and-nut bowl into her oversize purse. She was flashing irritable looks at Peter Bradshaw, while he silently mouthed, "What the hell are you doing?"

Sara stood up with her champagne glass in hand. "We're here for a very special occasion," she said, raising her voice and still-ing the room. "A celebration we can all appreciate and greatly admire. Tonight we drink to love, life, happiness, and everything they bring. I offer my best wishes and heartfelt gratitude to my darling husband on the success of his phenomenal art show. Everyone, please raise your glasses and join me in congratulating Paul."

"To Paul!" The overlapping burble went up, followed by a sudden release of tension in cheers, whistles, and applause… applause for Paul Lyons, not for Rachel, who was now staring at Sara in utter disbelief.

What? Chase was caught up in the heightened, unreal acclaim for this trumped-up occasion and found himself sipping champagne from his flute to mask his obvious disappointment. Rachel jumped her chair back from the table and hurried out past a waiter, who followed her for a second to see if he could help.

Meanwhile, Sara Lyons displayed a self-satisfied smile, while Paul prepared to rise to his feet. Despite Rachel's absence from the room, Chase was damned if he was going to let some psycho woman ruin everything. He loved Rachel more than anything in the world, and everyone in this goddamn room was going to know it. Especially Paul Lyons and his manipulating wife.

Chase abruptly stood, nearly knocking his chair over. "Rachel and I came here with no expectations—only to profess our love for each other," he declared. "I know you have your reasons for disapproving of me, Mr. Lyons, and you'll probably never fully understand our commitment to one another. But I can assure you that the time we've spent apart has only strengthened our love. Despite what you believe or what others might have told you, there's no safer place for Rachel than with me. I will love her, respect her, honor her, and protect her for all eternity. We're just asking for your blessing, sir. That's all we want. All we really…need."

The room was silent. Paul's face was ashen; even the high color from his jovial exchanges had drained from it. Contempt, disdain, scorn—it was hard to define the exact look on Sara's face, but her censoring stare wasn't missed by any of her guests, particularly those sitting at the closest tables.

Then Ida began clapping, loud and resounding. "Splendid job, Mr. Cohen, just splendid," she said. Soon the whole crowd was riotously applauding and cheering him on.

Ah, shit. What have I done? Chase looked around for Rachel and found her standing at the far end of the room near the butler's pantry, staring back in utter shock—paralyzed by dismay.

"Big mistake, huh?" Chase said aloud.

Peter Bradshaw's mouth quirked slightly. "You might say that. But then again, how can Mr. Lyons say no in front of his friends, customers, and VIP guests? You've made it virtually impossible for him...without coming across as a dick."

Oh, great. Chase would be lucky to have a bed to sleep in for the night when the room was emptied and Mr. Lyons's simmering anger was free to erupt.

"Excuse me! Excuse me, everyone!" Paul Lyons's booming voice reverberated throughout the room. "The hour is late. I'd like to thank all of you for coming and for your kind words of support. I'm sure many of you have plans tomorrow, just like me, and hopefully they'll include a visit to the gallery for our opening of the Morris Graves exhibit."

Jesus. The knot in Chase's stomach tightened, and his head throbbed. He looked down, riddled with shame. He could barely imagine the apologies he needed to voice. But where would he begin? Mr. Lyons's humiliation would leave them barely speaking, if at all. And Rachel...oh, God, Rachel. How could he explain? He had to get to her and clear this mess up before it was too late.

Chase started toward her at once, weaving his way through the surging crowd. He could feel her eyes on him, watching his every movement. She had to give him the opportunity to vindicate himself—the chance to admit she was right. "Rachel, stay there!"

He was only ten feet away from her when the housekeeper's voice rang out. "Wait! Stop! Listen to me! You can't go inside!"

A tall young man with shaggy brown hair burst into the room from a side door with a look of panic covering his face. His long black coat hung wide open, exposing his rain-soaked clothes. From the sound of his heavy breathing, he'd obviously been running through the waterlogged gardens to get there. "Mr. Lyons, I'm Sky Nolan," he announced. "It's Sloan, your granddaughter. She's disappeared!" A collective gasp filled the room. "I looked everywhere. I called all our friends, everyone she knows, and she hasn't turned up. Please, I beg you, sir. I need your help to find her…before something terrible happens."

Peter Bradshaw maneuvered his way into the scene to deliver his thoughts. "Consider the source," he told Paul. "You know as well as I do that Sloan is determined to cause havoc in this house. She enjoys nothing more than upsetting Sara. I'm sure this is merely a ploy to get your attention."

Paul glared at him. "Really? Well, let me tell you something, Peter. I couldn't care less what you think. The only reason you're here is because of my wife. Now if you don't mind, I'd like to hear what this young man has to say without any further interruptions."

The doctor frowned and surveyed the shocked eyes of the remaining spectators before storming out of the room.

10

REVELATIONS

Paul Lyons had become the man in charge, and from that moment on, he intended to keep it that way. In the kindest way possible, he asked everyone to leave. Everyone, that is, except Sky, Chase, and Rachel. Although his niece and her troublesome boyfriend were new on the scene and unfamiliar with Bellwood and the surrounding cities, they had a reputation for finding what couldn't be found. And, at that moment, all he cared about was finding Sloan and bringing her back home safely.

"Before we get started," Chase said, "I wanted to apologize, Mr. Lyons. I wouldn't have interrupted your evening or said anything if your wife hadn't—"

"Please, let's not get into that," Paul said. "My wife has a severe migraine and is being tended to by her physician. I somehow doubt that your love life is more important than her missing granddaughter."

"Yes, of course," Chase conceded. "I wholeheartedly agree."

Rachel touched her uncle's shoulder. "Uncle Paul, it's after midnight. Maybe we should call the police. Chase and I aren't equipped for this sort of thing. We wouldn't begin to know where to look. I can only imagine that time is crucial in this matter and—"

Paul held up his hand, silencing her. After being interrogated by detectives on two separate occasions regarding his whereabouts, state of mind, and relationship with Gwen Gallagher, the last thing he wanted was to involve the cops and have them crawling all over the place. With his luck, the strained relationship he shared with Sloan could turn him into a prime suspect. Especially if, God forbid, her body should wash up someplace.

Paul seated himself beside Sky Nolan and looked into his worried face. "Tell us everything you know. Did you see the man who took her? The car, license plate...anything we could go on?"

One of the maids from the housekeeping staff was passing through the dining room, where tables would soon be cleared. She refilled Paul's water glass and asked Chase and Rachel if there was anything else she could do for them.

"Heidi, I thought I told you to go back to the kitchen," Paul said harshly, answering for them. "Return to your duties and close the door on your way out." His eyes and attention returned to Sky. "OK, let's hear it."

After exhaling a deep breath, the young man told them everything that had happened at the Soho nightclub earlier that evening. At last, he said, "It's all my fault. If we hadn't gone there, none of this would have happened."

Paul raked his fingers through his thick hair, making his frustrations more apparent. "So you're telling me that you don't know if she was really kidnapped?"

"No, sir," Sky said. "But I know she didn't walk out of there on her own. A guy in the parking lot remembered seeing a black

SUV circling the street outside the club right after we got there, and it disappeared the same time she did."

Paul wiped at his brow. The room was getting hotter by the second. "Could she be staying at a stranger's house tonight...a person you've never met before? Sleeping off all the booze she drank?"

Sky's face remained solemn. "I suppose it's possible. But I can't imagine her leaving without saying anything. It's just not like her, Mr. Lyons. She would never go out of her way to cause trouble or make anyone worry. And with the condition she was in..."

Paul looked at Chase and Rachel. They were standing apart from them, exchanging concerned glances. He ran his hand over his clean-shaven cheeks and reminded himself of Sloan's encounter with the reporter. She was as tough as they came—a street fighter in every sense of the phrase. But she was still an innocent in many ways.

"Under the circumstances," Paul said, "why don't we wait to see if she turns up in the morning? There's really nothing more we can do tonight." He sat back in his chair, drinking his water and loosening the tie around his neck.

For a moment, Sky seemed staggered, unable to comprehend the meaning of his words. Then he nodded silently, his eyes fixed with a troubled expression.

"Please don't think that I don't appreciate your concern," Paul said. "I just wish you had used better judgment where Sloan was concerned. Leaving her alone was probably not the wisest move on your part."

"I know. You have every right to be angry with me." Sky paused for a moment, his dark-blue eyes gazing earnestly into Paul's. "I wasn't thinking straight. That's the only explanation I can offer."

Paul exhaled an audible sigh. "I'm not angry at you, son. My wife's granddaughter is stubborn and hardheaded. She's always had a mind of her own. I don't envy anyone trying to control her."

"You're right. She can definitely be a handful." Sky's helpless laugh broke unpleasantly on Paul's ears. He continued talking, touching briefly on the chain of events that brought them together and the remarkable bond they shared. "She really means the world to me, sir. I would never forgive myself if anything bad happened to her."

Both men rose simultaneously to their feet. Paul placed his hands on the young man's shoulders, and standing face-to-face, they looked into each other's eyes as though each were reading the other's thoughts. "Sloan will be fine…I assure you," Paul said. "Just relax tonight. I'm sure she'll turn up." He forced a smile. "Somehow she always does."

"If you say so," Sky mumbled. He walked slowly toward the adjoining door, and Paul beckoned for Chase and Rachel to follow. They passed into the main foyer, where Killian and Melina awaited, expectantly.

"Thank you for staying and offering your assistance," Paul said. "After hearing everything, I don't believe Sloan is in any danger. In fact, I'm sure this young man will hear from her tomorrow."

Paul turned to Sky. "You'll let me know if there's anything new."

"Of course." He looked at the faces around him. "I'm sorry for interrupting. Good night, everyone."

As soon as the door closed, Paul turned to Killian. "I want you to get on the phone right away and call everyone we know. I need to hear if anyone has seen or heard from Sloan this evening, if there's any reason at all to believe she's in danger. But everything needs to stay in this house. I don't want any word getting out. Is that clear?"

Killian nodded.

"Sloan's been through enough," Paul told him. "The last thing we need is for the media to get word of this."

"What about the local police department or the MI5 security agency?" Killian asked. "Should I contact one of them?"

"I don't want to do anything until we hear something. At this point, we don't know if she's been taken against her will or if a ransom is involved. If it is, I'll get in touch with our bank and make the necessary arrangements. Nothing is worth risking her life over. Is that understood?"

"Yes, sir."

Chase stepped up. "Rachel and I would like to help. We can make calls and drive around the area where she disappeared. Just give us an assignment, and we'll do it."

Paul nodded. "Thank you, Chase. Right now I think the best thing to do is—" His cell phone rang. He looked down at the number and didn't recognize it. Was this the call he'd been waiting for? The kidnappers giving delivery instructions? His heart thumped wildly. He could feel sweat gathering at the back of his neck and covering his spine.

God, please tell me she's all right. Everyone's eyes were on him, nervously waiting. He brought the phone close to his ear and took a deep breath. "Hello. What can I do for you?" He closed his eyes for a moment and concentrated on the voice. It was a switchboard operator from the security company reporting a break-in at the gallery. Two responding officers had discovered a broken window, a bloodied towel, and two empty walls where eight Morris Graves originals had previously hung. Oddly, every security device in the place had been knocked out, with the exception of a rearview camera, which had captured a black van and Sloan's red Audi speeding away.

"Oh my God! You've got to be kidding me! Those paintings were on loan! They're worth millions! Have the police been called? Do they have any leads?"

The operator informed him that the police had in fact been notified and were actively involved in the case. But, unfortunately, there was very little to go on until the lab reports came back. Paul would need to meet with the investigating officers first thing in the morning to give a full report on what was missing.

You mean besides Sloan? He felt sick to his stomach and light-headed. His right arm was going numb. He had to snap out of it. Get his head straight. This was no time to be sick.

Killian was saying something, looking as stunned as the rest of them. "I couldn't help overhearing, sir. Did someone break into the gallery tonight?

Paul shook his head. "Fucking unbelievable," he growled. "I contacted a new insurance company three days ago and took out a new policy. It's going to look like I had something to do with this. Like it was some kind of bleeding insurance scam."

"What about the police? Do they have any idea who might have done it?"

Paul wiped the sweat from his forehead and took a long, deep breath. "I don't know. They're looking into something, but it's going to take time."

Melina placed a shaky hand on his sleeve. Her voice was small—so soft he could barely hear it. "What about the Mystic Sons and the show tomorrow? What do you want me to tell everyone?"

The dull pain in his chest was spreading across his right side. He couldn't focus and was becoming increasingly agitated.

"Crap...what do you want me to say? Tell them to go fuck themselves, for all I care!"

Melina took a step back, and Killian filled the void. "Sir, I know you're upset, and it's not my intention to make matters worse," he said, "but don't you find the timing of all this a bit strange? I mean with Sloan missing and art vanishing from the gallery on the same night? No one's heard from her, and none of her friends seem to know where she is, right? I mean, it does make you wonder, doesn't it?"

Paul shook his head. "No, she would never do anything like that. I'm sure of it."

Killian had a bone and wasn't about to let go of it. "Really? I mean, think about it. Would she have any reason to get back at her grandmother? Any reason to need money?"

Oh God. Something is wrong...terribly wrong. The room was closing in, and he was struggling to breathe.

Rachel rushed to Paul's side, as if sensing his distress. She stared into his eyes, concern and panic written all over her face. "Are you sick? Do you need me to call someone?"

He fell back hard against the wall and slid down into a sitting position on the floor. Rachel crouched down and laid the back of her cool hand against his forehead. Then she held his wrist and studied her watch closely. "Killian, call nine-one-one or whatever the hell the emergency number is. Melina, go into the kitchen and get some cold water, right now!" She blew out a heated breath and turned to Chase. "Where did he say that doctor was?"

☙

Chase was on his way—determined to rescue Paul and earn back the trust he'd lost with Rachel after his drunken outburst. He hurried up the winding wood staircase and reached the top landing within seconds. The long, dimly lit hallway was covered with photographs in matching gilded frames, and finding the exact location of Sara's bedroom was going to prove a challenge. After their late arrival and quick change, he hadn't seen her walk in or out of any of the rooms on the upper floor, but according to Rachel's instructions, she had to be here somewhere—and so did the doctor.

Rachel called out from the foyer. "Chase!"

He hurried to the top of the stairs. "What is it?"

"My uncle says he's feeling much better. He doesn't want to go to the hospital, but I think a doctor should still look at him."

"OK." Chase returned to his search. As he ventured farther down the hallway, a man's muffled voice drew him toward the fourth room on the left. He peered through the space in the slightly open doorway and spotted Sara stretched out in a recliner and Dr. Bradshaw sitting in a leather chair directly across from her, administering his medicine.

"...Two...One." As if by an unseen force, Sara's eyes closed, and her head drooped slightly. Peter Bradshaw quietly gazed at her sleeping, defenseless form. Her breathing was so calm and her expression so tranquil, but strangely, the doctor seemed to be savoring her response as if he was enjoying a bite of dark chocolate. That Sara trusted him enough to lower all of her defenses in his presence was mind-boggling.

"Sara," Peter cooed in a questing tone. There was a small pause before she issued a "Hmm" sort of sound. "Can you hear me?" the doctor continued.

"Yes," came Sara's immediate reply. Her voice was devoid of inflection or any kind of emotion.

"I'm going to ask you some questions, Sara. I would like you to answer me as honestly as you are able. Can you do that?"

"Yes."

"When was the last time you engaged in sexual intercourse?" came Peter's first question.

Chase covered his mouth to keep from coughing. *What the hell?*

"Three months ago…July," she answered.

"Who was he?"

"Paul, my husband. After Gwen's death, we couldn't anymore."

"Couldn't what?"

"Couldn't be together," Sara said emotionlessly. The doctor perked a brow.

"He doesn't want you?" he surmised out loud.

"Doesn't like my attitude, my activities…my friends."

"Do you plan to stay married to him?"

Her brow wrinkled. "I love him…more than all the others."

"Would you consider a lover?"

"No. I only want Paul."

"Do you relieve your sexual tension in other ways?" the doctor asked, lacing his fingers and resting his hands in his lap.

OK, this was the strangest treatment for a headache that Chase had ever witnessed. He wanted to interrupt, but he didn't know how and wasn't sure if it would be dangerous to snap someone out of a hypnotic state.

Sara remained silent, as if she weren't sure how to answer the doctor's last question.

"Do you masturbate, Sara?" Bradshaw rephrased.

"I can't," she responded.

Chase tilted his head slightly. What did that mean?

"You can't bring yourself to because of your dreams and imagination?"

Sara paused before answering yes.

"Whenever you close your eyes, begin to focus, touch your-self…you see the bodies, the ashes, and all the death."

Whose body? What ashes? Chase dragged his hand over the top of his head. What was Peter Bradshaw talking about?

"Yes." Sara's voice was lower now.

The doctor's eyes moved to the ceiling. "Stress manifests itself in many different ways. But there are as many relievers as stressors, and the release that comes from carnal pleasures is among the most ancient and prescribed stress relievers known to humanity. Your particular stressor happens to be the very thing preventing you from relieving it." Peter's gaze trailed back to Sara's reclining body. "I would like to help you relieve your stress. Would you like that, Sara? Would you like your headaches to go away?"

Chase glanced back down the hallway. Rachel had to be won-dering what was taking him so long. *Come on…come on. Get this over with, Doctor.*

"Yes," Sara answered, sounding almost desperate.

Another smile formed on Bradshaw's lips. "I want you to focus on the sound of my voice—only my voice and nothing else. Do you understand?"

"Yes."

"I will be the only one who can bring you the pleasure you need. Do you understand?"

"Yes."

Peter Bradshaw leaned back comfortably in his chair. "You are unable to masturbate because of the horrible images that fill your mind. We need to change this association. Blood has its own beauty to it, Sara. Death and murder are as natural as birth and living. You have convinced yourself that these things are ugly." The doctor crossed his legs. "You can never take back control of your mind until you start to enjoy and accept all aspects of your life. Fill your mind with ugly images. Keep them at a safe distance. They cannot hurt you in any way."

Sara's brow furrowed, but she remained obedient. It was obvious that Bradshaw's instructions were being followed to the letter when Sara uttered a soft, pitiful sound that was something between a moan and a whimper.

"Allow them to wash over you. Listen to my voice. Focus on me, Sara. I'm here with you."

Sara's expression softened.

The doctor's gaze was locked on her face. "Your breathing is quickening. Your heart rate is steadily rising. It feels good. You're excited…and it's good to feel excited."

Chase's heart was racing as well.

Sara began panting, her head tilting back, her throat exposed. Her hands were quivering, her muscles all working together to create a reaction of excitement.

"That's it, Sara," he said.

She moaned again.

"Your skin feels cool under the surface. The sensation is chilling your skin and warming the pit of your stomach. You are becoming aroused."

Chase swallowed hard. Was this guy a sex therapist?

Sara's lips parted, and her breathing became ragged. Peter watched her with the cool composure of his profession, observing the effects of his therapy with detached amusement.

"Don't cheapen the feeling by wanting immediate release. Let it flow inside of you, all over you. Your vagina is tingling. You're getting wet inside. Does it feel good, Sara?"

"Yes," Sara breathed, her body squirming slightly in the chair.

"Continue to breathe. Each breath is filling you with new life. Even though the images are there, in the dark corners of your mind, the pleasure is stronger. It draws energy from your most basic desires. Give in to those desires, Sara."

Sara's head rolled to one side, and a string of erotic moans escaped her lips. Bradshaw watched her face carefully as her eyebrows knitted and her mouth partially opened. He leaned forward in his chair.

"Sara. Would you like to be touched?"

Shit! Chase almost said the word out loud. Did anybody in this house know this was going on?

Sara bit her lower lip and nodded.

"I am touching your leg now. Can you feel it?" Bradshaw said huskily. At the suggestion, Sara's leg twitched. She let out a low groan. She clenched her jaw, nostrils flaring with her ragged breathing, and nodded softly again.

"My hand is stationary on your leg, but you can feel its heat through your dress…through your stockings. You can feel the muscles of my hand applying light pressure to your thigh. The contact feels good. It is not the touch of a friend; it is sexual. This hand is now moving. Gliding to the top of your inner thigh. Very close to your arousal."

Sara arched her back slightly, continuing to breathe heavily, her hands now gripping the arms of the chair for dear life.

Bradshaw tilted his head. "Tell me what you are feeling," he said.

"I…I want more," Sara choked out in a low voice, a tone one would use for a lover. "It feels nice…so amazing."

"That is good. You are doing very well."

Bradshaw coached his hypnotized patient further, slowly building her up and teasing her. His metaphorical hand glided up her stomach and over her breasts, coming to rest on her neck and jaw before sliding back down to her abdomen. He lingered there for several moments, watching Sara writhe and squirm in her seat, desperate for the contact but unable to do anything more than wait for the next suggestion.

"I'm inserting my manhood...long, thick, hard...begging for release. Can you feel it, Sara? Can you feel me inside of you?"

"Yes...yes. Ahhhh..."

What the fuck? Chase looked down the hallway to see if anyone was coming and would catch these two in the act.

"I'm sliding it around slowly inside of you. Around and around...increasing your wetness, increasing your need. I'm moving forward now...gently in and out...in and out. Faster and faster. Faster and faster. Over and over. Harder and harder... driving you to the brink. Leaving you panting. Wanting it, needing it, feeling it. Here it comes, Sara. Here it comes. Allow the bliss to fill your mind. Let it blot out the darkest bits of your consciousness until there is nothing left but pure pleasure."

Sara tossed her head back again, groaning without restraint.

Bradshaw licked his lips, watching her in the throes of ecstasy. Then his tone changed.

"You will not come. You can't...not now," he instructed firmly. Sara uttered a pitiful moan of desperation. "Feel me deep inside you. No matter how close you are, you will not find release yet. The pleasure must come first, Sara."

"P-Please..." she pleaded softly.

Bradshaw smiled. "Too much pleasure without release can bring pain. Pain and death are very similar. One often accompanies the other. So one might say that sexual satisfaction and death have much in common as well. The release. The beauty in death, and the pain in pleasure. They are all interconnected."

Chase couldn't move—couldn't comprehend what was happening. Was this sick fuck gratifying himself by mentally torturing his patients?

Sara groaned again, and Bradshaw seemed to regard her quietly for a moment as she squirmed and jerked, her body so close to release. But the doctor wouldn't let her climax. Not today. Carefully, he coached her back down from the brink with his reassuring words. "The air in the room is cool against your skin. Your breathing is calm and steady. All your desires and tensions are melting away...controlled entirely by my voice. When you hear your name again, you'll awaken feeling very relaxed, refreshed, and clear-headed." After a brief moment, he leaned forward and whispered, "Sara."

She smiled and opened her eyes. Whatever this therapy was seemed to have done the trick, although her body was no doubt sexually frustrated.

Chase wrinkled his nose, thoroughly confused. *Wouldn't that increase your headaches?*

Bradshaw sat back in his seat, readjusted his position, and started asking Sara questions about the country club's upcoming gala, as if nothing had happened. "By the way," he told her, "I made a recording of our session today. I'll mail you a copy when it's ready, just like I always do."

"Thank you for taking such good care of me, Peter."

"It's no problem at all, my dear. When you have another headache or are unable to sleep, listening to the recording of our session will put you into a state of meditation. However, the therapy can only be truly effective with consistency."

Sara nodded and smiled again. "I honestly don't know what I would do without you. I'll make sure a check gets mailed first thing in the morning."

Surreal. Chase shook his head in disbelief. Sara's doctor was a sadistic bastard, and she was paying for his abuse. No one would ever believe what Chase had just witnessed. No one.

"Chase! Where the hell are you?" Rachel's voice rose from the foyer at the bottom of the stairs.

He stepped back quickly from the doorway, hoping he would not be detected by the room's occupants. He waited only a few seconds before knocking. While he stood in the hallway, waiting for Sara's response, he debated how to tell Rachel about the weird relationship these two shared.

"Yes, what is it?" Sara asked sweetly.

Chase cracked the door open wider and averted his eyes from Sara. He would never be able to look at her in the same way; that was for sure. "It's your husband, Mrs. Lyons. He seems to be feeling poorly. Would it be possible for the doctor to come downstairs right away?"

"Of course," Bradshaw said, rising. He matched Chase's gaze as he approached the door and gave him a quick, awkward pat on the shoulder. "I know a great plastic surgeon," he said. "Let me know if you want him to look at that big nose of yours before you stick it somewhere it doesn't belong." He continued on his way, descending the stairs, leaving Chase gut-punched by the quiet ugliness of his tone.

The third door on the left suddenly opened, and a familiar housekeeper walked out, carrying a basket of towels. "I wouldn't take anything that man does or says seriously," she said, looking down at her load. "He's obviously jealous, sir. You have a fine nose, and lovely eyes too."

Chase smiled slightly and stepped back, providing Heidi room to pass. He stared after her as she boarded the service elevator at the end of the hall and was still marveling over her dedication and ability to multitask when Sara's voice called out from her bedroom. "Mr. Cohen, are you still there? Was there something else you needed?"

"An alibi and a poison-tipped knife," he mumbled.

"What was that?" she asked.

"I'll be downstairs with my future wife."

11

INQUIRING MINDS

As fate would have it, Paul Lyons was checked into the local hospital for three days to undergo a barrage of tests, leaving Chase in a quandary over the best way to rescue Sloan—not only from her captors but also from the police. In Paul's absence, Killian had become an eager informant, describing the missing art pieces and telling the investigating officers that Sloan had been camping out in the gallery's upstairs apartment for the last two weeks following an argument with her grandmother and banishment from the manor. It was only natural that she would know all the locations of the security cameras and alarms with the exception of a camouflaged unit mounted at the rear of the building, where her red Audi had been parked. After the police made a thorough search of Sloan's temporary living quarters and discovered an envelope containing a missing gallery deposit, the bloodstained towel became a crucial piece of evidence in the case against her.

An arrest warrant was issued for Sloan Rafferty, and a search for her whereabouts was soon under way, making Chase's job all the more difficult. After checking his watch and confirming it was 9 a.m., he picked up the house phone to call the hospital and asked Rachel to put her uncle on the line. When she did, he came straight to the point. "It turns out Sloan had receipts belonging to the gallery. The envelope was clearly marked and—"

"That's rubbish," Paul said. "I gave her that money."

"Does anyone else know that?"

Paul paused on the phone. "No...but I'm telling you the truth. Her grandmother was planning to cut her off financially. I was only trying to help her out."

"Do you think your wife would be willing to substantiate that?"

"I don't know. Sara isn't particularly fond of her at the moment. It's been that way for some time now. She could actually turn out to be a detriment if Sloan is arrested and her case goes to trial."

"I see. Do you know anyone else who would be willing to help me?"

"Talk to Sky Nolan again," Paul insisted. "He left his number with Margaret. It should be somewhere in the kitchen. And Chase...find her. I still believe Sloan is being held against her will. She didn't have a hand in any of this. There's no possible way."

"All right, Mr. Lyons. I'll do whatever I can. Please tell Rachel I might be gone when she gets back."

Chase returned the receiver and noticed a business card sitting on the kitchen table. He picked it up and flipped it over. Then he leaned back against the kitchen wall, debating what to do next. According to Sky's job title and the scribbled note on the back, he was working as an assistant manager at a local hardware store and wouldn't be available for two more hours.

Damn it. Chase left a message and blew out an exasperated breath. After hearing what Paul had said about Sara, involving her was completely out of the question. She was still seeing Peter

Bradshaw on a regular basis and coming home high-strung and increasingly irritable. For most of the day, she'd been locked away in her bedroom, doing who-knew-what. The fact that she wasn't spending any time at the hospital should have set off warning signals that something was amiss to anyone who bothered to notice.

While waiting for Sky to return his call, Chase poured himself a cup of coffee and then sat down at the kitchen table. To his surprise, Margaret walked in, set her broom aside, and politely asked to join him. It didn't take long for him to realize she was nervous and extremely eager to share information with anyone willing to listen.

"I'm telling you, no matter what Killian or anyone says, I'll never believe Sloan had anything to do with that robbery. She's a good girl. She really is. Just terribly misunderstood is all."

Chase sipped his coffee, fully engaged. "Do you have any idea where she might be? Does she have friends no one knows about? A boyfriend who worries you?"

"You're better at asking questions than the police, Mr. Cohen. I think you missed your calling."

The corner of his lips curled. "Really? Well, I've always been fond of mysteries, particularly anything surrounding deaths and disappearances. In fact, a few days ago, I accidentally overheard a therapy session between Dr. Bradshaw and Mrs. Lyons and…" Margaret gave him a knowing smile.

"Now that's an odd pair if ever there was one," she volunteered. "Always have their heads together, whispering about one thing or another. For the longest time, I was certain she was going to marry him." She refilled his coffee cup before resuming her train of thought. "After Zane Zimmerman died from congestive heart failure, I never expected her to come home with a third husband. And then when Andrew Langford died from the same thing and she returned from her fourth honeymoon with Mr. Lyons, I nearly fell over from heart failure myself. Poor romantic soul. She's had more bad luck with men than anyone I know. In fact, if memory serves me, none of them lasted more than ten years except Peter Bradshaw. He's been keeping company with Mrs. Lyons for the past thirty years and is completely obsessed with her. You would think she would have grown tired of him by now, with all his weird antics. Anyway, after treating Mrs. Lyons for one thing or another, he's completely ingratiated himself in her good graces and will probably never go away."

Chase shook his head, trying to make sense of it all. "How many husbands did Sara have?"

"Four, if you count Mr. Lyons. It's a good thing you and Dr. Bradshaw were here, or we would have lost him too."

Unbelievable. Chase huffed. "So, how did her first husband die?"

"Now that was one of those mysteries you were talking about, Mr. Cohen. You see, Gordon Cumberforge had a severe allergy when it came to nuts. So we never kept them in the house or anywhere near him on account of them closing up his throat and making it impossible for him to breathe. Anyway, one day when Mrs. Lyons was at her session with Dr. Bradshaw, her husband came home quite unexpectedly, complaining of chest pains and shortness of breath. He collapsed on the kitchen floor, and an ambulance was called. But as fate would have it, he died before it arrived. When Heidi checked his coat pockets a few days later, she found a packet of peanuts inside. You know, the kind you get on an airplane. Only Mr. Cumberforge hadn't been flying in months, and I took that coat to the dry cleaner's myself."

Chase's interest was piqued. "Don't you find it odd that Mrs. Lyons lost three husbands the same way?"

"Oh, I know a lot of folks thought that. But I believe it's purely bad luck. Besides, Mrs. Lyons was distraught for days after each death occurred. In fact, Dr. Bradshaw had to keep her sedated for a full week after Mr. Langford's cremation just to prevent her from hurting herself. Someone who makes a practice of killing her husbands wouldn't do that now, would she, Mr. Cohen?"

Chase offered a weak smile. "No, I guess not."

"That's what I thought too, but Lily's death was a whole different matter."

"Lily?" Chase asked.

"She was Paul's mother. A kinder woman there never was. Always free with cooking advice and remarkably dedicated to helping young girls." Margaret glanced at the closed door next to them before lowering her voice. "What's troubling me, Mr. Cohen, is I saw Mrs. Lyons and Lily sitting on Lily's porch drinking cups of tea on my way to church one morning. I waved a hand, but they were so deep in conversation they didn't notice. Later that day, Lily suffered a heart attack, and investigating officers came to the house asking all kinds of questions. I heard Mrs. Lyons tell them she never spoke to Lily, but that's not true at all, and everyone in this house knows it. Only I can't say anything on account of Sloan."

Chase quirked a brow. "What about Sloan?"

Margaret took a sip from her floral cup. Her hand shook slightly, and the cup rattled when she set it back on its matching saucer. "Miss Lily told me something I haven't shared with anyone before, and it's killing me inside, Mr. Cohen. Especially after her sudden death." Her voice was almost a whisper. "You see, it's about Mrs. Lyons's dead daughter and another young lady who was living in Lily's house at that time."

Chase leaned closer, completely captivated. "She didn't die of a heart attack too?"

"No, it wasn't anything like that. But on the other hand, I would consider it much worse."

The floor creaked in the hallway. Someone had been listening. Someone who didn't want to be seen. Chase slipped out of his chair without making a sound. He stepped next to the door and waited. After mentally counting to three, he reached for the handle and pulled the door open.

"Heidi!" Margaret yelped. "Good God, girl. I swear you're going to be the death of me."

The young woman stared back at her, grimacing. She jerked a dusting rag from her shoulder and jammed it into the front pocket on her apron. While Chase silently watched, she wasted no time in berating Margaret. "Mother, I've told you a dozen times it's not appropriate to share private information. Mr. Cohen is a guest in this house and doesn't need to know everything that's gone on over the years. Mrs. Lyons has told you herself that in order for us to reside in this household and maintain our positions, we need to respect her privacy and keep our personal opinions to ourselves. Do you understand?"

The elderly housekeeper lowered her eyes and nodded slowly like a reprimanded child. "Yes, dear," she murmured.

Heidi's frown lifted. Her dark eyes softened, and she released a soft sigh. "All right, Mother. There's no need to go on. You should get back to work and allow Mr. Cohen to do the same. We don't want Mrs. Lyons to get word of this." She met Chase's eyes. A soft smile formed on her lips. "Now do we, Mr. Cohen?" she asked, beseeching his silence.

Chase forced a smile. "Of course not. You don't need to worry about me." But Sara did. He needed to call the hospital right away and speak to Rachel about his suspicions. "I'll be upstairs resting for a while. Please ask someone to let me know when Sky Nolan calls back."

Chase closed the bedroom door and used his cell to leave a second message for Sky. Then he called Rachel's number. She picked up her phone as soon as it rang.

"Hi, honey," she said softly, sounding a bit rough. "Any news about Sloan?"

He'd been so consumed with Sara's granddaughter that the importance of Rachel's well-being had been nearly forgotten. His heart squeezed at the thought of her quietly suffering and his distracted insensitivity. "No, not yet," he said, "but there's something very important I need you to do." It sounded like her phone had slipped out of her hand, but then he heard a soft breath and realized she was still listening. "Tell your uncle's doctor there's a real possibility Paul ingested something toxic last night that might have led to his heart attack, and he needs to have his blood screened as soon as possible. I can't go into details on the phone right now, but I have good reason to believe Sara Lyons might have attempted to kill her husband."

There was a long pause and then a chilling voice on the phone. "Hello, Mr. Cohen," Sara said. "Your fiancée dropped her phone before running into the bathroom. It seems she's feeling poorly today. I sure hope there isn't something going around."

Chase swallowed hard. What could he possibly say now that the murderess knew he was onto her?

"My goodness. What a vivid imagination you have, dear. It seems a member of my kitchen staff has been filling your head with all kinds of ridiculous gossip, which is unfortunate, since you seem to have taken it all so seriously. I'm sure my husband and I will have a good laugh about it later."

Chase's gut tightened. "I'm sorry, Mrs. Lyons," he said. "I was obviously misinformed."

"Well, just to clear up any silly notions, you might be interested in knowing that Paul's tests came back today. He was diagnosed with angina and is receiving the proper medication to address it. Dr. Levy just informed me that he'll be home the day after tomorrow. Just in time to celebrate our tenth anniversary. Isn't that lovely?"

"Yeah. Real nice."

"In the meantime, I would greatly appreciate it if you would disregard anything you might have heard. It seems that it might be time to make changes in my household staff. Oh, and Mr. Cohen, even though my husband has asked you to find my granddaughter, I'd rather you didn't waste your time. She's obviously been up to no good again. I believe it would be best if the police handled the matter as discreetly as possible."

"But if she was kidnapped, don't you think—"

"If you recall, Mr. Cohen, you were standing right next to me when she ran by on the terrace. Don't you remember that red hair of hers? It couldn't be missed. And neither is she at the moment."

"That's a bit harsh, isn't it?"

"Not if you knew her like we do. I suggest you and Rachel enjoy what's left of your vacation and return to the States, where your talents will be much more appreciated."

The phone went dead, and so did any chance of helping Paul. Chase was annoyed, perplexed, and mentally spent. Sitting back and doing nothing would be a sore reminder of the irreparable damage he'd caused in his life. If Chase hadn't abandoned Sam Lyons during their treasure-hunting expedition years ago, Paul's brother would still be alive, instead of resting six feet under in a hillside grave.

Despite his best intentions, there was no escaping the truth, no mistaking his stupidity in having voiced unproven accusations. But what more could he do? Like the guilt he carried with him daily, worry had become a complete cycle of inefficient thought revolving around a pivot of fear.

12

BOUNDARIES

S loan closed her eyes and drifted off to sleep sometime during the night. When she opened them again, she assumed it was morning, but with no windows in the bedroom, she couldn't be sure. Tor had resumed his bodyguard position on the floor, leaning his back against the foot of the bed. In his hands, he held a manila folder opened on his bent knee, and he flipped through it, reading intently. Another folder sat behind him, next to an open backpack, and something else was on the floor, making her heart pound. It was a gun! Sitting there in plain sight, all shiny and powerful...just begging for attention. But could she use it? Could she fire it and actually kill someone? The silver solution to her problems held her captive, completely motionless. What was she going to do? She missed her friends, she wanted her things, and she needed to get out of town and away from all the crazies living in it.

Sloan couldn't help but notice that Tor was deeply engrossed in studying some kind of inventory sheet. She looked back at the gun and nibbled the corner of her sore bottom lip, considering what to do next. Without making a sound, she slid off the side of the bed and inched her way toward the black backpack. She had almost reached it when she noticed his open wallet lying beside it. If she could take a few bills, she'd have enough money to grab a ride, making her trip home even faster. He wouldn't even notice, not if they were tucked inside her pants pocket.

Her eyes widened when she picked up the wallet and brought it close to her face. *Shit!* Tor really was a cop, if the badge was as real as it looked. She touched it to make sure it wasn't a toy—it wasn't made out of tin or cheap metal like the one Sky had used at a Halloween party. She held it in her palm, weighing it before flipping it over. It was heavy. It was the real deal, all right. Tor was an honest-to-goodness cop. But was he really? She looked down at the printed name on his identification and realized he had been lying all along. Tor wasn't his real name at all.

"Pierce Torren?" The name had an interesting ring to it.

"What?" he said. It seemed they were both unaware that Sloan had spoken out loud. He glimpsed the wall in front of him and then snapped his head around. His eyes dusted the gun before landing on the wallet, but oddly, he didn't attempt to move either one of them. "So you've been snooping, huh?"

Sloan cocked a smile. "OK, I get it. You're real. Makes the story you told me the same, I suppose."

"Looks like you know who I am too." He sniffed and looked away.

"Tor must be your undercover name, right?"

He looked back over his shoulder. A smug, satisfied smile bloomed on his face. "Yeah, right."

"Does the creep next door know who you are?"

"No, and for your sake and mine, you need to keep quiet about that. I'm not looking to have my cover blown by some bright-eyed kid."

"I might not look like it, but I'm hardly a kid, Detective Torren. I'm twenty years old, or at least I will be in two days."

"You don't say? Guess I'll have to bring you back something special. In the meantime, breakfast is on the table. Eat something, and don't forget our deal. You stay put until I get back." He slipped on his black shoes and stood up. Then he belted his slacks and buttoned up his white long-sleeved shirt, leaving a thin patch of hair exposed on his chest. "Time to go to work." He eyed her up and down, as if determining if he could trust her. "As far as anyone's concerned, you're still missing, and we need to keep it that way. OK?"

Sloan paused before nodding.

"I also want you to know we're not in the best part of town. Julien's got a fan club and baseheads hanging out. I'm locking this door behind me. I expect to find it the same way when I get back."

He took his wallet and gun and tucked them into his backpack along with the folders he'd been reading. Then he slung it over his shoulder and smiled. "Sorry, no television, sweetheart, but the radio's all yours. Try not to miss me too much. I shouldn't be long."

There was nothing left to say as he left the room and secured her inside. She glanced at the croissant sandwich waiting on the nightstand and decided it was best to eat something. It wouldn't do her any good to starve, and besides, other than listening to static on the radio, what else was she going to do? Go to sleep and roll around dreaming about the cop with gorgeous brown eyes? *Sick!* She needed to focus on something more important. Like the best escape route.

Sloan dropped to the edge of the bed next to the nightstand. After picking up the egg and cheese sandwich and examining it carefully, she took a nibble and then another and soon found herself relishing each swallow. She was still in the midst of taking the last bite when she heard a sound coming from the bathroom. After edging closer to the doorway, she peered inside but saw nothing. Then she heard it again—a weird scratching noise coming from outside the bathroom wall.

She had talked herself into waiting until the time was right, but now she was having doubts. She had a feeling Detective Torren had lied to her about the boarded-up window being too small to crawl through, and she decided to investigate the possibility herself. If he was right, and she couldn't get through, then she could simply nail the board back on, and no one would be the wiser.

After pressing her ear against the wall and hearing no sounds, she grabbed the edge of the board and pulled hard. She tried again and again, but it was no use. Then she used a foot for leverage and jerked with all her might. She fell back when a large section broke off, exposing the small window beneath. Now all she needed was something to boost her higher—a way to see outside and discover what she was up against.

The bedside table! She moved the radio onto the bed. Then she carried the small table into the bathroom and set it under the window. It was higher than she needed, but she was convinced it would work, all the same. She felt bad about breaking her promise to Detective Torren, especially when he was being so kind. But if for some reason he didn't return, this might be her only chance to get away.

"All right, let's do it," she said as she climbed up the makeshift ladder. Although it was wobbly, it worked exactly as she'd hoped. With knees propped on the tabletop, Sloan put her hands over her head in a dive position and began her escape. She got as far as putting her arms and head through the opening before getting stuck on her boobs.

Stupid C cups! If she were a boy, she could have gotten out easily. After wiggling around and squashing her chest, she was able to free her upper body. She balanced her ribs on the windowsill and tried to determine her whereabouts. The chipped brown siding, dense woods, and overgrown vegetation confirmed that she was being kept in an abandoned house in an isolated area—a place where no one would look or ever find her.

She was just about to start climbing through the window again when she heard the sound of a twig breaking. Cranking her head to the right, she saw where the sound came from. It was a tall, skinny guy with a cigarette between his fingers. He was standing about ten feet away with his back to her, leaning against a rotting tree. With his slightly spiked dark hair, leather jacket, and torn jeans, he looked like a club kid—like someone she might have hung out with at one time or another.

Fortunately, he hadn't noticed her, and she needed to keep it that way. But she was in a bind, and her current options were extremely limited. If she tried to pull herself out, the noise would be heard, and this character could easily catch her. She had to get back inside and stay there until he was gone—until there was no one around to keep her from getting away.

Sloan shoved against the windowsill and tried blindly to find her foothold. To her dismay, one of her flailing limbs hit the table and knocked it over. The crash drew the attention of the creep stationed outside. He turned around and raised a brow, staring back at her with his dull-brown red-rimmed eyes as she hung helplessly from the window. It was Brice Stanton! Sky's schoolmate from the Red Room! He came closer with a lit cigarette dangling from his curled lips. After leaning down, he blew smoke in her face and laughed when she coughed.

"What do we have here?" he said, grinning.

He motioned for someone to join him—an unseen accomplice standing just out of eyeshot. "Hey, Ron. Come check this out."

When she finally saw whom he was speaking to, Sloan's jaw slacked in disbelief. It was too good to be true, and yet there she stood in her rumpled gypsy finery. Veronica Rose Hewes. Long black-and-green matted hair, twisted yellow ribbons, and pursed pink lips, looking pensive and completely strung out.

"Ronny!" Sloan yelled. There was no mistake about it. She had come there to rescue her, but how did she know where to look?

Brice blew another stream in Sloan's face, leaving her coughing and gagging. Then he looked at Veronica and shook his head in disgust. "Can you believe this bitch? Can't follow simple instructions."

"Why should you be surprised?" Veronica scoffed. "She never listens to anyone."

An evil smirk formed on Brice's face. "You know, some women should learn that the only reason they have big mouths is to suck dick."

Sloan glared at Veronica. "What's wrong with you? Why are you just standing there?" When Veronica said nothing, tears began to form in Sloan's eyes, betraying her bubbling emotions. "What have I ever done to hurt you?"

Brice jabbed his elbow teasingly into Veronica's side. "Looks like we got us a crybaby." He leaned closer to Sloan and stuck his lit cigarette against her neck.

"Fuck!" she yelled, jerking her head away.

"Like I said, some women shouldn't talk."

Veronica rubbed her crossed arms, demonstrating her obvious impatience. "Come on, Brice. That's enough. She ain't going anywhere."

His grin transformed into a nasty pout. "Hey, I'm just getting started."

Sloan was about to tell him to eat shit and die when her peripheral vision captured movement to her left. She turned her head and spotted a figure in a hooded yellow slicker standing about twenty feet away, watching from behind the seclusion of trees. With branches casting shadows, it was impossible to determine whether it was a man or woman. All she could do was hope the person would see her distress and call the cops on this demented creep.

"Help!" she screamed. She saw the white flash of a smile through the dark and felt her mind jolt. Were they enjoying this? Pleasuring themselves at her expense?

The watcher slipped away just as Brice turned. His menacing eyes slid back to Sloan. "I'll help you." His lips were on hers, demanding and cruel. She twisted her head to get away from him.

"Leave me alone!" she yelled.

Veronica glanced around, visibly uncomfortable.

"Got us a slow learner here," Brice said. He grabbed a fistful of hair from Sloan's scalp with one hand and jerked hard.

"Stop it!" she screamed. The pain was excruciating, and her pulse hammered in her ears. She could hear the sound of her shirt ripping as he tried to free her from her trapped space in the window.

"Come on," Veronica told him. "That's enough. I want to leave. It's getting cold out here."

"What about Damien? Didn't your brother tell you she's nothing but a tease? It's time she had a taste of some of her own medicine." He rubbed his thumb into her neck, hard.

Ahh! Sloan's mind screamed. A heavy sob escaped her lips. She clenched her teeth, determined not to let him know he was getting to her.

"Such a pretty little thing," he said. "I knew you could listen. Just required a little reminder is all."

Sloan squeezed her eyes shut. She needed this to stop—needed Veronica to snap out of her drug-induced coma. But she just stood there with her arms crossed, looking down at the ground, doing absolutely nothing.

Brice leaned in and crushed his lips against Sloan's in a bruising kiss. He bit and nipped, trying to force her mouth open. She shook her head and pushed at him with her arms, but nothing could keep him away. In fact, the more she struggled, the more he seemed to enjoy himself. He grabbed her arms roughly and yanked hard, but thanks to her hip bones, she was locked securely in place and wouldn't be going anywhere anytime soon.

"What the fuck?" Detective Torren yelled from inside the house. Sloan felt his hands on her ankles, gripping hard, pulling her back through the window. Yet all the while, Brice maintained his hold on her arms. She'd become a rag doll in a vicious game of tug-of-war, but luckily the cop won out. He gripped her elbow with one hand and guided her back into the bedroom. Then he pushed her onto the mattress, causing her to bounce once before curling into a ball. He picked up her rubber-soled shoe and disappeared into the bathroom. Seconds later, she could hear the sound of nails being driven into the wall. It seemed the board was back in place, and so was she.

When he returned, the cop's face was full of anger. "I told you to eat your food and not go anywhere. *To fucking stay put!*"

Sloan winced as she watched him pitch her shoe against the wall. She feared his fist would come next.

"I've been nothing but nice to you!" he screamed. "Protected you from everyone! But you try to escape?" He threw his arms in the air in disbelief. "Do you want to be raped? If you do, then let's get on with it! I'll rape you right now if that's what you fucking want!" He climbed on top of her, grabbing her legs and spreading them wide before dropping his hip between them. Using one arm, he held her hands above her head. "Let's have some fun," he snarled.

"No! Stop!" She thrashed around trying to get free. Tears streamed down her face and into her hair. "Please, not again!"

Pierce sat up on his knees and looked down at her. He no longer held her wrists. His arms were held loosely at his sides. "You were raped, weren't you?" His voice was gentle, his anger gone.

Sloan couldn't talk. She couldn't stop crying. He climbed off of her and stood by the side of the bed.

"Sloan?"

She flinched at the sound of her name and curled back into a ball.

"Honey…talk to me."

More than anything, she wanted to be alone. She needed time to recoup—time to collect her thoughts and understand what had just happened.

Pierce sighed. She felt his hand next to the burn on her neck. "We should clean and disinfect this before it gets infected." The bed dipped and creaked as he got up from it. Soon after, he came back from the bathroom with cotton balls, cleaning alcohol, and Band-Aids. He sat back down on the bed and began to treat her wound.

"So are you going to tell me who it was?" he asked.

Sloan chose to ignore him. It wasn't any of his business if she was raped or not. The past was the past, and she intended to keep it that way.

Pierce continued to work on her neck and then spoke in a hushed tone. "I'm sorry about that. I wasn't really going to hurt you. I just thought I could scare some sense into you. It wasn't the best idea I've ever had, and not very professional either."

She closed her eyes, hoping he would believe she'd gone to sleep, but after a few minutes, she felt his hand smooth her hair. He continued the gesture—a calm, reassuring summons, willing her to lower her defenses. "You don't deserve all the bad things that have happened to you," he said softly. "No one does...especially someone as beautiful as you."

Beautiful? Sloan almost laughed out loud. She'd never felt the least bit attractive or worthy of love her whole life. And now even less so. *Where are my friends?* she wondered. Maybe they never existed outside of her imagination. They were as phony and wicked as the fairy tales she had once believed in—the fairy tales her language teacher had enjoyed reading in boarding school and had cruelly destroyed the night he snuck into her room. It suddenly dawned on her that, no matter where destiny took her, she would always be caged, always be trapped in her childhood nightmares. Begging for love, begging for power. Begging to wake up and be free.

✒

Sloan rolled over on her back and looked to her left, where Pierce had been sleeping. She sat up, realizing he was gone, and for a brief moment, she actually missed him. After climbing off the bed, she headed into the bathroom to relieve herself. Then she blocked the drain in the tub and turned on the hot water, hoping to wash away memories from the previous day—memories that made her feel dirty inside and out.

When it was filled, she climbed into the white porcelain tub and sloshed water as she soaped up and rinsed off. Since she had the only key to the inside door, she felt safe enough for the time being. But obviously, she couldn't live there. What about heat, exercise, and food? Pierce had supplied breakfast sandwiches, burritos, greasy fries, and burgers in four-hour increments in the warm bedroom. Her mindless activities throughout the day included reading movie magazines, pacing back and forth, and tuning stations on the blipping radio. Aside from clean clothes, her needs were being met, but the isolation was driving her nuts.

She grabbed a razor and was about to shave her legs when a strange thought occurred to her. Hairy legs might be the only thing protecting her from being raped by Julien, the unseen masochistic guy staying in the first room. More than once, she had heard the sound of the front door slamming and the voice of a female bitching after being manhandled, neglected, and screwed. How long would it take before he came looking for fresh blood and perverse entertainment?

Sloan pulled the razor back, took out the blade, and just looked at it, wondering if she could use it as a weapon against the bastard while Pierce was away. But then she'd have to strike out at Brice and Veronica as well. *Stupid assholes.* What was going on with Ronny, anyway? She had been in and out of rehab at least three times over the last eighteen months for drinking, drugs, and a botched suicide. Sure, she was messed up in a big way, more so than Sloan. However, that didn't excuse the sick game she was playing. The way she had zoned out and let Brice hurt Sloan. And for what? Cocaine, crack, and pain pills? A restocked supply turning them into the walking dead?

Sloan's eyes moved from the sharp, stainless blade to her wrist. Without even realizing it, she brought the blade down and sliced her skin. The sting brought her back to her senses. She pitched the blade to the other side of the tub. It bounced off the side and sank under the water. Blood slowly welled up on her wrist along with her tears.

What have I done? Was she really that depressed? As loony as the rest of them? She grabbed her arm and thrust it into the water to stem the bleeding. After climbing out of the tub, she opened the medicine cabinet above the sink and extracted a gauze bandage. She wrapped her wrist, still puzzled by her weird behavior. Undoubtedly, it had been brought on by her annoyance at being left in this place.

She covered herself with a fluffy blue towel and looked down at her clothes on the floor. They were dirty after being worn for three days, if the horrible flavor in her mouth was any indication of how long she'd been there. She needed a toothbrush, and she found a clean, packaged one next to the toothpaste and shaving cream. A thoughtful amenity for an unexpected houseguest.

She squeezed the tube and gave her teeth a thorough cleaning. Then she raked her fingers through her long damp hair and leaned into the mirror to study the slow-healing bruises on her face. Her stomach let out a growl, reminding her that the first meal of the day would be arriving soon. As a precautionary measure, she placed her ear against the door and listened. There was a rustling noise, a squeak from the springs in the mattress, and then a soft sound that could only be interpreted as light snoring.

Sloan cracked open the door and confirmed Pierce was sound asleep. He was stretched out on the right side of the bed with an arm draped over his chest. She opened the door the rest of the way and stepped quietly into the room. On top of the dresser, she spotted a packet of soda crackers. She popped one into her mouth and opened the top drawer on the dresser, hoping to find something to wear. After picking out an oversize white sweatshirt and pair of blue shorts that looked smaller than the rest, she turned around to make her way back into the bathroom.

"Shit!" Sloan yelped. Pierce was wide awake, propped up on his elbow, and his eyes were staring at the top of her towel.

With his clothes, she covered her cleavage, blocking his view.

"What happened to your wrist?" he asked, studying her warm face.

"Nothing." She took a side step toward the safety of the bathroom. *Please don't move,* she said over and over in her head.

Pierce sat upright. "That doesn't look like nothing to me."

"It's nothing, really," she assured him.

"You know you're a terrible liar."

"No, I'm not." Two more steps, and she'd be in the safety zone with a wood door between them.

Pierce stood. "Let me see it," he insisted.

"No way!" She hurried inside, closed the door, and put the borrowed clothes on as quickly as possible.

He waited a few seconds before pushing the door open. "Can I see your wrist now?"

"No. Go away and leave me alone!"

"Will you stop screaming? It's four in the morning," he hissed.

Four in the morning? Damn, that was crazy. Why did he sneak into the bedroom so late? She straightened the sweatshirt before asking, "How did you get in here? You told me that I had the only key to the bedroom."

"The door wasn't locked," he said with a shrug.

What was wrong with her? Did she really forget to check it? Forget to bar Julien access to the room? Somehow, it didn't seem likely...which meant the cop was lying. "Well...you should have knocked or something," she said.

Pierce rolled his eyes. He crossed his arms and leaned into the open doorway. "If you're done in here, I'd like to use the bathroom..."

"Oh yeah. Sorry." She relocated herself to the edge of the bed and filled her mouth with more crackers. He walked back into the room after finishing his business, and she immediately turned away.

"So I guess we're done talking then?"

"For now." She laid her head on the pillow and closed her eyes.

"You know it's really easy to tell when someone's pretending to sleep," he said. "They have soft, even breaths that get louder."

Sloan tried to breathe heavier. She even made a soft snore.

Pierce snorted a laugh.

"Damn it," she grumbled.

"So you talk in your sleep, huh? How's your neck, by the way?"

"It hurts."

"Maybe I should put a fresh bandage on it."

Sloan half shrugged in response.

"One more day to go. Do you think you can hold out a little longer?"

She snapped her head back to glare at him. "You said it would be over tonight. Why am I still here?"

There was a long pause before he answered. "It's safer for you to stay put. I can't keep an eye on you if you're running all over town."

"Safer? What's that supposed to mean?'

"It seems to me that someone's got a vendetta against your family. Possibly your grandfather. I need you to think, Sloan. Do you know if anyone has a reason to want to wreck him and bring you down in the process?"

Sloan rolled darts around in her brain, trying to zero in on a viable target. Two names immediately came to mind: Neville Murdock, the hack reporter Sloan had justifiably humiliated, and Veronica's horny blue-eyed brother. By shutting Damien down in the bus shelter and ignoring his rude remarks about Paul, she might have created a skillful enemy—a vengeful combatant capable of turning Brice and Veronica against her.

After sharing her suspicions, the cop nodded. "I'll see what I can find out. In the meantime, don't get any bright ideas about leaving. Julien comes and goes at all hours. I've been trying to keep tabs on him, and I even brought my partner on board to help out. If word gets back to him that you're on the loose, he might find you and rip you apart before I could stop him."

With every word, she drew further and further into herself. She looked at Pierce, confused and frightened by his intensity. "That's awful! Why would you say such a thing?"

"Because the truth isn't sugarcoated, Sloan. In my line of work, it comes with the reality of knowing you're alone in this world and everything about it sucks. Especially half the people living in it."

Sloan curled up into a ball and pulled the covers over her head. This was a dream…just a really bad dream. Tomorrow she would wake up, and Julien would be locked away where he belonged. Pierce Torren would disappear, and she would finally be free to get on with her life.

After a while, she lowered the comforter and stole a look at his sleeping profile. She should have been happy, thrilled at the prospect of separating herself from Pierce, but now the idea that she would never see him again ravaged her. It was wrong to have feelings for this jaded, self-absorbed man—allow herself to become another case of Stockholm syndrome. He was her protector and her pseudo kidnapper and nothing more. If she had any hope of maintaining her sanity, she needed to keep it that way as long as humanly possible.

She closed her eyes and thought about Sky—the man she truly loved, although he never knew it. The first time she'd felt the connection was the night they had joined friends for barbecue sandwiches at Pitt Cue. They had a great time reminiscing, laughing, and eating. Then, while leaving the restaurant, the

sole of her shoe caught, tossing her forward. She had reached
for Sky to keep from falling and took them both down. He kissed
her nose gently before rolling them on the wood floor so he was
on top. Sloan became flustered, averting her gaze. He seemed
to have realized the embarrassment and moved to get off of her.
After pulling her upright, he asked, "You OK?"

She nodded, and everyone laughed except Sky. He smiled
down at her, cupped her cheek, and sent her pulse racing. "Warn
me the next time you plan to attack me," he said before leaning
down and kissing her forehead.

Sloan looked at Pierce, sleeping soundly, and found herself
wondering how Sky would feel after discovering she'd been lying
in bed with a cop for days on end while he'd been doing everything in his power to find her.

13

FLIGHT TO FREEDOM

Sloan closed the last page of the *InStyle* magazine and shut off the radio. As with yesterday and the day before, she had no sense of time or place. She only knew the endless stretch of silence that came with Pierce's long, unexplained absences.

Click. The sound of a dead bolt disengaging came from the next room. She fully expected the door separating her from the maniac to be tested next. But the silence continued. Pierce didn't knock at the door or open it with his nonexistent key.

Who the hell was that? Her imagination went wild, conjuring up a tiptoeing intruder waiting for the right moment to strike. Seconds became minutes as she cowered in the corner, waiting for the unnerving creaks that accompanied the comings and goings on the floorboards in the next room.

Eventually, Sloan pulled herself upright and moved to her door. She placed an ear against the wood panel, straining to hear. Then she gathered her courage and released the lock. With bated breath, she cracked the door and slowly widened the opening. She surveyed the empty room before taking a step inside. To her amazement, she'd been left completely on her own. The only evidence to confirm anyone had been there were empty pizza boxes, trashy magazines, crushed beer cans, and filled ashtrays. She edged her way to the door leading to the outside world and couldn't help noticing the unlatched locks. With a trembling hand, she tested the doorknob, fully expecting it to catch, but when it turned easily, her breath caught in her throat.

Why did they leave it unlocked? Was it a mistake made by her unseen guard? By Pierce driving away in a hurry?

There was no time to question her good fortune. She needed to flee before her freedom was barred—before Julien and his gatekeepers returned. Pierce would undoubtedly be angry after discovering her gone, but it really didn't matter. She was going stir-crazy and had to get out of there. Headlights were rapidly approaching on the muddy, isolated road. Bouncing and coming closer and closer. If she didn't leave now, she might not ever. That was the only thought lifting her heels, directing her through the dense woods and driving cold rain—leading her to the only home she'd ever known at the end of her long, harrowing journey.

𐐒

Knock, knock, knock. "Mr. Cohen...Mr. Cohen. It's me, Margaret. I need to speak with you. There's something I haven't told you yet, and we only have a short time before everyone returns."

Chase had no interest in opening the door. The feeble-minded old woman on the other side of the wall had gotten him into enough trouble already. Thanks to her wacky stories and his overactive imagination, he was on the outs with Sara. After returning from the hospital and passing him on the staircase, she had remained obtuse, finally calling him an insidious

155

ingrate and a liar when he insisted his suspicions were innocently derived.

"Go away, Margaret," Chase told her. "I'm sure there's plenty of work for you to do in this house."

"Please, Mr. Cohen. Can you meet me outside in the garden next to the toolshed? It's at the end of the concrete path. I'll be there in five minutes. I wouldn't be bothering you, sir, if it didn't concern your fiancée."

Fiancée? Damn it! What was he getting sucked into this time? It seemed this woman would stop at nothing to discredit her employer. Gossip was certainly her bane. And yet, what if there was something she knew and he wasn't willing to listen? Could it turn out to be the biggest mistake he'd ever made?

"All right," he finally said. "Let me grab my jacket. I'll meet you outside. But if Heidi shows up again, you're on your own. Got it?"

Margaret nodded before walking away.

"How did I get myself into this mess?" Chase grumbled to himself. After buttoning up, he ventured downstairs and out into the garden. He followed the walkway and reached the toolshed where Margaret was waiting, just as she'd said. She appeared to be as eager as ever and determined to give him an earful.

"Remember what I was telling you about Sara's deceased daughter, Laura?" Before waiting for an answer, she continued, "Anyway, she came home from boarding school pregnant when she was only seventeen and told her mother that she had no idea who the father was. I overheard in the kitchen and was beside myself when they got into a terrible row over Sara demanding that she have an abortion. Laura wasn't having any part of it, and she drove off in the middle of the night during a heavy downpour. I knew something bad was going to happen, but no force on earth was going to stop it."

Chase clapped his hands together, rubbing them. "It's freezing out here, Margaret. Can't we go inside and talk about it there?"

She shook her head. "No, Mr. Cohen. I don't have much time. Heidi will be upset if she sees us together." She glanced around nervously before continuing. "Miss Lily told me that one of her nurses was at the hospital when Laura was brought in after a full-on collision. It wasn't long before Laura was declared brain-dead, and somehow, Sara got it into her head that she was being punished for demanding the death of that child. She paid a doctor a small fortune to keep her comatose daughter alive...just long enough to deliver her baby. But then something went terribly wrong, and that poor infant died. The doctor didn't have the heart or courage to tell Sara, not after all the money he'd been paid. He found out there was a woman by the name of Allison giving birth at Lily's house that same night, and he convinced one of the midwives to help him. They made the switch and told that poor mother that her baby had died. And what made it even worse was that Allison never believed that dead child was hers. The next morning, a doctor made special arrangements and had her committed, claiming she'd lost her bloody mind."

Chase jammed his hands in his pockets and looked down at the frost-covered grass. He rocked back and forth in place, trying to keep warm. "So what's any of this got to do with Rachel?"

Margaret dropped her eyes in shame. "The woman they committed was Rachel's mother...Allison Lyons." She wrapped her arms around her waist and rattled on. "Ten years after she got out, Allison showed up on Miss Lily's doorstep and threatened to ruin Sara, claiming she knew the truth about her baby. Then that poor woman came to the manor while Sara was away on her honeymoon and told me the same story. She said Paul Lyons was the baby's father, only he didn't know that the baby survived. I

KAYLIN MCFARREN

tried to tell Sara what had happened, but she had no interest…
She didn't want to believe any of it. Then the letters started coming. She issued a restraining order to keep Allison away from the
manor and from going anywhere near her granddaughter."

The shovel leaning against the toolshed fell, turning their
heads. A young, redheaded woman with tragic green eyes stood
before them, looking lost and dejected. The sound of their voices
must have drawn her there. She was in a pitiful, disheveled state.
Her hair was matted and hanging around her shoulders, and
her pretty round face was marred with scrapes and nasty bruises.

"Sloan!" Margaret rushed to embrace her. She hugged her
like she was never going to let her go. But Sloan's arms remained
firmly at her sides, and her grim expression remained fixed.

"I was so worried about you," Margaret told her. "Honey, are
you all right?"

"Don't do that!" Sloan screamed, causing Margaret to take a
step back. She narrowed her eyes at Chase. "Who are you?"

"I'm Chase Cohen…visiting from California," he said quickly.
"Your friend Sky stopped by a few days ago, looking for you. I'm
just glad to see you're OK."

Sloan returned her attention to Margaret. "How long were
you going to make me wait before telling me?"

"Telling you what?" Margaret looked to Chase for emotional
support, but he had none to offer.

Sloan expelled a heavy breath. "About my mother. The
woman who gave birth to me. The one that's still alive and looking for me?"

"Honey…"

"Don't call me that!" Sloan shouted.

Margaret glanced away, apparently feeling the heat from
her face radiating in the air around her. "Mrs. Lyons is a good
person. She would never intentionally harm anyone. But people

158

misrepresent themselves all the time. She had no way of knowing whether that poor woman was in her right mind or not."

"Of course you would say that," Sloan said, glaring at her. "You and Heidi have always defended Sara, even when she was wrong and you knew it. God, you only think about yourselves. Just like everyone else!"

Margaret leaned forward, as if she was trying to reach out to Sloan. "If you'd known the truth, what possible difference would it have made? You've had a good life here, haven't you?"

"Fuck you."

The housekeeper groaned and spun around, giving Chase the impression that the exchange was now officially over—that she wanted to get as far away as she possibly could from Sloan. But before taking two steps, an unfinished thought must have been triggered inside her brain, keeping her from leaving. She turned toward Sloan and shook her head. "What happened to the girl who shared breakfast with me each morning, the one who told me she wanted to be a better person?"

Sloan stared at her blankly. "I don't know who the fuck I am anymore, or why you would ever think I was better off because of that screwed-up...demented old woman. Don't you get it? I believed you; I loved you. And I never understood why she never loved me."

"C...Could you ever forgive me?" Margaret said pathetically.

A pensive, brooding look stole over Sloan's face. "Why did you...Why did everyone let me believe I belonged here? It was so wrong. Don't you understand?"

"I'm so sorry," Margaret offered. "But I think Sara loves you—I do. That's why she wouldn't give you up."

"And now she wants to disown me. What a lovely turn of events. Don't you think, Mr. Cohen? If that's not fucked up, I don't know what is. So how does Paul Lyons play into all of this?

Is he just an innocent, dim-witted bystander, or screwed up roy-ally like the rest of us?"

"Paul thinks his child died and doesn't know any different," Margaret said. "No one was allowed to tell him."

"His child?" Sloan's eyes narrowed. "What are you saying, Margaret? You're not telling me that cranky old man is my father? Paul Lyons...the right hand of God?"

She said nothing but simply nodded.

"Shit! It's worse than I thought." Sloan's eyes filled with angry tears. "That selfish, conniving old woman. As far as I'm concerned, she can go straight to hell."

"Umm, you might want to rephrase that," Chase said. Everyone turned to watch Sara rapidly approaching. By the frightened look on Margaret's face, it was clear the timing of her arrival couldn't have been worse.

"What's going on?" Sara demanded. Her eyes fell on Sloan, and for three full seconds, she actually seemed pleased to see her. Then Killian crossed the road to join them, and she turned icy. "I can't believe you had the nerve to come here. Your grand-father is in the hospital because of you."

Sloan said nothing. Hate was written all over her face, and her eyes were locked on only one person: Sara. The woman who had stolen her from her distraught mother and now had every intention of discarding her like yesterday's news.

"How did you get in?" Sara demanded to know. "You have no right to be here. Call the police, Killian. Get this...person out of my sight!" Sloan bolted from the shed, red hair flowing behind her. Chase followed after, but he lost her in the tall hedges. He scoured the rose garden for any sign of footprints in the spongy sod, but there were none to be found. Voices were trailing closely behind, forcing him to pick up his speed. In the distance, he saw Sloan cut through the orchard, and he ran for a while until he saw her again. She was heading for the barn at the far end of the property, losing everyone along the way. Chase followed a dirt road across rolling hills for ten minutes and then doubled back, believing he was lost. As he approached the back side of the stable, he heard pounding footsteps and bolted from his position, cutting Sloan off in front of the open doors. With a swooping arm, he caught her around the waist, throwing them both to the ground. She kicked and swung her arms wildly, trying to fend him off.

"Stop it! Let me go!" she screamed.

He held her in place until she calmed—until her voice dropped to a sorrowful plea.

"I beg you, please leave me alone."

He released his hold, sending her scampering into the corner of an empty horse stall. She stayed there, huddling close to the cold, hay-covered ground like a frightened, whipped puppy.

"I'm not going to hurt you," Chase said.

A stream of tears left her luminous green eyes. "How could she do this?" she mumbled. "How could she lie to me all these years? I thought she was my grandmother, my blood relative, the only family I've ever known. What kind of monster would do this to someone else's child?"

Chase let out a big, heavy sigh. "I'm only a houseguest," he admitted. "I don't know Sara Lyons from squat, and after five lousy minutes, you don't know a damn thing about me. So I'm not going to tell you to forget your instincts. In fact, I'm counting on them. Just know that I'm here for you, and I'll do whatever I can to get to the bottom of this."

She stood up, wiping her nose with the back of her hand. "Why would you do that? Why would you help me? Unless there's something in it for you."

Chase shook his head. "No strings. Honest. Under the circumstances, it might be hard for you to believe anything right now, but I assure you it's true. I was young once, didn't have parents, and ended up as lost and confused as you." He struggled to find the right words, fighting his own better judgment. Sloan was right, and he knew it. Most people weren't interested in getting involved. They had enough problems of their own to worry about. But this was Rachel's sister. A blood relative that she didn't even know existed.

He looked down at the ground and revisited his past, recalling the best reason for her to trust him. The only one that made any sense. "I hated everything and everybody who tried to help me. And then I met an incredible sea captain who was determined to turn my life around. I fell in love with his amazing, beautiful daughter who had faith in the impossible and saw something in me I didn't know was there. The truth is—if they hadn't been there for me when I needed them, I probably wouldn't be here today."

She listened quietly with her eyes downcast.

"You have to realize your value is far greater than you believe, Sloan. You've got a lot going for you, and you can't let anyone in this world dismiss that."

She gnawed at her bottom lip, just like Rachel—a family trait, no doubt. "I understand what you're saying," she said in a hoarse, halting voice. "But I've heard promises before. How... how do I know that you'll stand by me? That you won't leave... like everyone else?"

"I'm here, aren't I?" Chase said. "All I need to know is that you're as innocent as I believe, that you didn't have anything to do with the robbery at the Lyons gallery."

"The robbery? Oh, shit! They really did it, just like he said they would. You've got to believe me, Mr. Cohen. I had nothing to do with that. No way, no how."

Chase looked her up and down from head to toe, taking in all five feet and six inches of her. He had to believe she was telling the truth, and not only because she asked him to.

"There's also the money they found in your dresser at the gallery," he told her. "Paul said he gave it to you as a gift, and I know he's telling the truth, but the cops think he's covering for you."

"If I was going to rob the place, why would I leave money behind? That doesn't even make any sense."

"I guess they think you left in a hurry. Maybe forgot to take it with you after you broke in and set off the alarm."

Sloan dragged her hand over her forehead. "This is bad, isn't it? I saw Melina after I left the restaurant, after my lunch with Paul. I told her I'd leave the key on the reception desk before I skipped town. Now I can't find it. I might have dropped it at the club or somewhere in the parking lot." She glanced down at the ground and then angled a look at Chase. "The guy who grabbed me was named Julien. I never saw him, but I can identify three of the kidnappers, including Brice Stanton and my best friend, Veronica Hewes."

"Best friend?"

"Yeah. At least I thought she was."

"I'm sorry," Chase said. "I wish that was all you had to worry about, but I'm afraid there's another problem. When you were being held by those guys, there must have been a towel you used when you were cut and bleeding. It might have been left in a bathroom or laundry room. Anyway, the thieves dropped it at the gallery next to a broken window, turning you into a prime suspect in the robbery investigation. Right now, we need to stay as far away from the police as possible. At least until we can meet with Paul and get his attorney involved."

"Cops," Sloan hissed. "I knew that guy was dirty. That's why he didn't come back. That's why he left the place unlocked. So I could walk out the door and straight into jail." She ran her fingernails along the outer seam of her blue shorts. "Detective Pierce Torren. That was his name. What a joke. He had a gun and a badge and told me he needed my help to catch art thieves. It was all a setup, just like I thought. But I still don't understand why he took off the blindfold and let me see his face."

Chase's brow pinched. "Pierce Torren? Are you sure?"

"Yes, Mr. Cohen," she said with conviction. "I saw the name on his ID, and he admitted it was him."

"OK. That gives me a great place to start. Now, I need to know if there's anything else you remember. Anything that would help me locate Veronica and Brice."

"I'm not sure," she said. "I can show you where they held me and where Veronica lives. But something tells me she's not going to be there."

"That's a beginning. And what about Sky Nolan? Do you think we can trust him?"

She got very quiet, and then she smiled. "Yeah, I do. He's a really good guy. I know he'd help us."

"Great. As soon as I hear back from him, we'll put a battle plan together. And Sloan…I think you'd be surprised to hear that Paul Lyons is behind you. If you're OK with it, I'd like to take you to see him right now. Maybe he can even pull a few strings and get this mess cleared up before it gets out of hand."

"There she is!" Killian yelled. Four cops rushed toward them, appearing to come from nowhere. Chase stood back, helplessly watching as Sloan was handcuffed and read her rights. The whole time, Killian stood by, smiling and looking extremely pleased with himself.

"Damn it," Chase hissed. "You don't know anything about this, Killian. How could you give her up?"

He said nothing, only crossing his arms like an authority figure.

Chase watched the officers march Sloan toward their cars, which were parked a short distance away behind Killian's SUV. "This is wrong!" he called after them. "She's innocent!"

Sloan turned back to see Chase. Her eyes never left his as she ducked her head inside the second squad car and slid into the backseat. The door was slammed shut, and one car rolled after the other down the long driveway and through the open security gate, leaving Chase and his frustrations behind.

I've got to help her. There was no letting her down. He was going to be Paul's hero and Sloan's redeemer whether Sara Lyons liked it or not.

"So what were you planning to do, mate?" Killian asked him. "Harbor a criminal? Bring down the Lyons family and everyone connected to them?"

Chase snarled. "You seem to be doing that all by yourself, jackass."

Killian shook his head. "Come on, Chase, you're dealing with Sloan Rafferty. That girl's been in trouble with the law since she was twelve years old. No one's going to believe anything she says. Why should they?"

Chase wanted to beat the shit out of him then and there. But he had promised Rachel that he would rein in his temper and behave like the perfect gentleman she expected him to be. However, that didn't stop him from speaking his mind—from letting this asshole know his true feelings. "I don't know how or when it's going to happen, but one of these days, you're going to get more than you bargained for, and everything you love in your life will be gone."

"Yeah? Well, just keep hoping, Mr. Cohen."

Killian smiled and walked back to his car, leaving Chase feeling weak, depleted, and useless. Rachel would probably discourage his meddling when it came to rescuing Sloan, and she would undoubtedly oppose him digging up Sara's family secrets. But she was also well aware of his reputation for being tenacious, and she knew he would never walk away when someone was in trouble. Not when he had witnessed the injustice firsthand.

14

ULTIMATUM

C hase approached Paul Lyons's car in the driveway, his heart pounding at the prospect of seeing Rachel again. After the cool reception they had received at the gallery and his outburst at the dinner party, Chase was amazed that Paul had given his niece permission to drive his two-million-dollar car for the length of their stay. Perhaps her uncle's priorities had shifted after nearly losing his life. Or maybe her concerns over his health problems had increased her value in the household. Whatever the reason might be, Chase felt a slight twinge of jealousy as he passed by the volcano-red Aston Martin Vanquish— the same sports car he had seen featured in *Car Magazine* and could only dream about owning.

I have everything I need, he reminded himself. He entered the house and walked down the hallway toward the library. Rachel stood inside, eagerly motioning for him to join her. He closed the door behind them and stood listening while she informed him that a detective inspector and his sergeant had showed up at the hospital earlier that day demanding to speak to her uncle— but not about the missing art. They'd actually come to make a disturbing accusation regarding a drowning victim: a young woman her uncle had hired to work at the gallery and with whom he'd been romantically involved.

Rachel lowered her voice. "I don't understand it. Whether he had an affair or not, how could they honestly believe he had anything to do with that woman's death?"

"Did they actually say *murder*?" Chase asked.

"The sergeant inferred as much. He said that, before discussing any evidence pertaining to Miss Gallagher's death, my uncle would need to contact his attorney and come in for questioning. Chase, he said *evidence*. Doesn't that mean they found something incriminating?"

"It's possible, but it's even more likely that someone's setting him up."

Rachel was obviously distraught, and it wasn't healthy for her or the baby. He wrapped his arms around her shoulders and kissed the top of her head. All he cared about was marrying this girl and getting on with their lives. Proving once and for all they belonged together. Yet everywhere he turned there were complications popping up: kidnapping, swapping babies, robbery, and now another murder. Bodies were dropping everywhere, and the wrong people were being arrested. Life was getting more complicated by the second. But at that moment it didn't matter. Not as long as Rachel loved him, as long as he was the only one in her eyes.

"After this is done, let's run away to Scotland and get married," he said.

Rachel burrowed into his chest. He thought she might be crying, but when she pulled away, she was wearing a tremulous smile.

"So how's your uncle doing?" Chase asked, forcing himself back to his natural state of optimism.

Emotion choked Rachel's words. "As well as can be expected, I guess. But this...this will do him in for sure. I just know it."

Chase held her away from him and looked into her tear-filled eyes. "Sweetheart, I don't want to upset you any more than you already are, but there seem to be a lot of folks in this town dying from heart attacks. With four husbands all diagnosed with the same condition and her need for power, I'm still not convinced Sara isn't part of this. It's like she's turned into some kind of black widow and has been collecting on their insurance policies or something. For the life of me, I can't figure it out. There has to be a reason why she keeps them around for ten years. Maybe some kind of expiration date—who knows? Isn't that how long Paul's been married?"

Rachel seemed to be lost in thought. When she looked up, her hazel eyes were bright with clarity. "You're right. He mentioned that yesterday and said something about marrying people for the wrong reasons."

"Baby, I still think it might be a good idea to ask the doctors for a toxicology report. You know, just to be safe. If it comes back positive, there's every reason to believe Sara intended to kill him. Maybe even caused Gwen's death and made it look like a suicide. Especially if Paul was having an affair with her. What's troubling me, though, is why the police are so sure your uncle's involved."

"When I came out of his room, I heard them talking in the hallway. It seems an expensive silver knife turned up on the same beach as the victim's body. Even though they can't prove it was used in the crime, the engraved initials in the handle led them back here, and a member of the staff confirmed it was missing."

Chase shook his head and shrugged. "Maybe it was Killian. That guy has no loyalty or compassion for anyone. Do you know that while you were gone, Sloan showed up here, totally wrecked, and that jerk had the nerve to call the cops and have her arrested?"

Rachel rolled her eyes and huffed. "You're really determined to hate him, aren't you? Has it even occurred to you that Sloan might be guilty as charged?"

"No, it hasn't. You didn't hear the whole story, the part involving Sara Lyons and the doctor she paid." He needed to share the whole ugly truth, but the news that her mother had an affair with her uncle would be bad enough without also learning she had a half sister who'd been stolen at birth.

Chase looked down and blew out a breath. "Sweetheart, there's something else…something you need to know."

Her buzzing phone interrupted. "Hi, Devon," she said. Obviously aware of his curiosity, she turned away, shielding her phone, but he could still hear her side of the conversation.

"I've been thinking about it a lot," she said softly. "Yes, I know. What can I say? I've got mixed feelings right now. I'm not sure if it will ever happen. What? No, that's not necessary. I'll call you later. I can't talk right now." She waited a few seconds before turning around.

"So I guess we're not getting married," he said, his throat too tight to say more.

Rachel slipped her phone into her pocket and nervously looked away. "I don't think this is the right time, Chase. There are too many other things to worry about."

He tried to understand—tried to bury his feelings—but something told him the time would never be right. "Tell me, Rachel. Do you even love me anymore?"

"Of course I do," she said. "How could you think otherwise?"

"I don't know. I'm not sure about anything anymore."

"Including me?"

He shrugged, knowing it was only two days ago when he used the same words. "For some reason I was under the impression we were a team," he said. "That we could solve anything we put our minds to. I don't know what you and your uncle have been discussing, but if it concerns his thoughts on marriage, it really shouldn't matter to you. We came here for only one reason, Rachel. To show him we belong together."

Her eyes met his eyes. "I know you want to prove you're a great guy. And you are, Chase, believe me. But we're completely out of our league here. Our job is to look for sunken ships, lost gold, and missing jewels. What makes you think we're capable of solving crimes? We're not detectives or CSI crime stoppers. We're just ordinary treasure hunters."

"Nothing's ordinary about our job, Rachel, or us. We've been called heroes by the people we've worked for. By magazine writers, curators, and ticket holders who still visit the museums we've filled. This is our chance to be *real* heroes—to put the bad guys away. If there's a chance to clear your uncle's name, free Sloan, and get on with our lives, isn't that what we both want? To do the right thing for everyone?"

She nibbled on her bottom lip, glancing down and back up at him. "I've been trying to tell you for some time now, Chase. Everything in my life is upside down. I'm not sure how I feel about anything anymore."

"Especially me," he muttered. He looked away, feeling like he'd been punched in the gut. His mind told him that he was fighting a losing battle and it was time to let go. They were cordial roommates in every sense of the word. Since their arrival, they had barely kissed, barely touched, and hadn't made love at all.

"In four days, we're heading back to the States," she said in an even, emotionless voice. "In the meantime, I plan to do whatever

I can to help my uncle, and I would really appreciate any support you're willing to offer. After that, we're going to have to trust the police to do their jobs. We really have no choice in the matter."

"Really?" Chase sniffed. "Well, my gut tells me Veronica Hewes is connected to everything. If she weren't, she wouldn't be hiding out. Sky Nolan has offered to help me find her, and he has a good idea where she might be. If I'm right, and Sara's involved as well, it will only be a matter of days before the truth comes out. Oh, and one last thing. I promised I would help Sloan, so I'm not leaving here until she's free. If you want to stick around, that's great. If not, then any decision you're struggling with will be settled once and for all. When we get back to San Palo, we'll go our separate ways. I'll honor my obligations and do whatever I can to provide for our child."

She gasped and stared at him with her mouth sagging. "Are you really that self-centered? Oh my God, Chase. I can't believe you just said that."

Chase disregarded her words. His last grain of patience had dropped. "I'll be back in two days. Stay here and look after your uncle. I'll call you when I can. That is, if you're still here."

15

VISIONARIES

Rachel slammed on the brakes, avoiding a nosedive into the river. The rain was dumping hard, and the wipers were struggling to stay ahead.

"Are you sure you want to reroute?" the Aston Martin asked her.

Rachel glared at the GPS built into the dash of her uncle's expensive foreign automobile. "Of course I do! The stupid bridge is washed out!"

Pressing buttons angrily, she waited, casting a frustrated glance at the water rushing over what was left of the overpass.

"Calculating route," the pleasant female voice said after a few seconds of silence. Rachel tapped her nails on the steering wheel. She squinted her eyes to see through the blinding rain, pelting the sports car from all angles. "Make a legal U-turn. In fifty-five meters, turn left and proceed three kilometers to Route Ten," the woman's voice instructed, her annunciation haughty.

"Why can't you say *miles*? How far is a damn kilometer?" Rachel pulled back off the shoulder and tried her best to do as she was told. The car bounced along on the freshly paved road.

She looked around, trying to get her bearings while driving through the downpour. The entire trip, from the Cumberforge Manor to the B-and-B house outside Saxton, she'd faced the heaviest rainstorm she'd ever experienced. The closer she got to her destination and to reaching Chase, the worse it was getting. And now, she was lost in the middle of the map-charted roads that were washing out everywhere.

Chase was controlling her life again, ignoring her advice and opinions, and she didn't like it one bit. "Don't go anywhere," he had demanded on the phone. "It's not safe to drive. Not in this weather. Sky is meeting with Damien Hewes tonight. I'll let you know later what I find out."

Rachel had to be there. She needed Chase to have faith in her and realize she was smarter and stronger than he believed. It didn't help that her uncle had doubts about his marriage that left her questioning hers. When Sara had arrived at the hospital and bent down over his bed, he had reluctantly turned his face toward her and closed his eyes, as if hoping her kiss would be as simple and painless as possible.

Rachel snorted a laugh. Why on earth had they come here, anyway? It was all her fault, and she knew it. If she had listened to Chase months ago, they would have been married by now, enjoying a tropical vacation instead of freezing to death in this miserable place. From the day she'd become pregnant, her emotions were up and down like a damn roller coaster. But eventually, her hormones were going to stop running wild. If he didn't meet her halfway and back off on his control tactics, the only pathway to their happiness would be gone. As far as Rachel was concerned, she was a fully competent woman with determination and common sense, sufficiently tempered by tact and civility. She had come here strictly as a courtesy to her uncle—a way to make up for her rude behavior in California after accepting the keys to her father's yacht. Without her diving skills and intuition, two lives would have been lost two years ago, and the Wanli treasure ship would have never been found. She had to have some degree of intelligence to become Chase's full-fledged business partner. So why was he treating her like a child? And why had she allowed it to go on for so long? She needed to explain that to Chase. To get him to step back and trust her judgment, right after she figured out where the hell she was going.

The Aston Martin hummed along the narrow road for a few minutes before her confidence returned. She had to find her way out of this godforsaken countryside and head toward the shining lights of civilization. Damn it! Would this rain never stop?

"At this rate, the whole country is going to sink," she yelled at the windshield. "And I'm going to be floating around forever in this stupid car." A jolt indicated the pavement had ended and she was now on a muddy trail. The farther she drove, the worse the road got, until the car was completely hung up in mud. After becoming a partner in Trident Ventures, she'd grown accustomed to having Chase solve all their problems, and she wasn't prepared for the mess she'd gotten herself into.

"That's it!" Her patience for this ridiculousness was gone. Despite her high heels and dry-clean-only outfit, she stormed from her uncle's plush vehicle and into the blinding rain. She was an intuitive, resourceful woman, and after their successful exploits, she had more money in the bank than the vast majority of businesses in San Palo. So she could easily figure out how to get her car out of the mud, right?

Wrong. Rachel looked up from the mud-covered car and pushed the rain-soaked fringe of hair away from her face. A behemoth green farm vehicle charged up, spraying muddy water everywhere. It came to a stop right in front of the sports car, and the door swung open. Seconds passed, and then a man who looked like he was made out of all muscle and bronze skin jumped out of the monstrosity, staring down at her from the brim of his dripping, warped hat.

"Stuck?" he asked.

"How'd you guess?"

She watched his frown deepen and regretted her rude tone. It simply never made sense to her why people would ask silly questions, leaving her to restate the obvious.

She exhaled a breath and tried again. "My tires are grounded in mud, and I'm lost. I need to get to Saxton. Seriously, where the hell am I, anyway?"

The man was quiet for a few seconds, as if determining if he was going to help her or not. "No sense in going farther," he finally said. "I'll hook up your shitty car and pull you out. Then you'll need to follow me down the driveway."

Rachel glowered at the man. He could be an ax murderer or even a cannibal. There was no telling what kind of people lived this far out in the country.

He seemed to have picked up on her hesitation. "I'm not a murderer. You've got no reason to worry about me."

Rachel jumped and stared at him. Did she say that out loud?

"But I've been known to cannibalize, in a sense," he said with a grin and a tip of his waterlogged hat. He dropped down out of sight and hooked a chain to her car, leaving her wondering what exactly he meant by that. *A cannibal in a sense?*

Rachel climbed back inside of the Aston Martin and gripped the steering wheel tightly as the car fishtailed out of the mud. She followed his vehicle and parked. Feeling more than a bit uncomfortable, she walked behind him into his house.

"I'm just going to grab some dry clothes," he told her. "Make yourself comfortable."

While he changed, she looked around and was impressed. The living room was painted in a soft cream color, and fluffy plush furniture was scattered about on polished wood floors. The kitchen was a light-blue color with yellow accents. By all appearances, the place didn't look like a man had decorated it, which led her to believe he had a wife hiding somewhere.

"This used to be my grandparents' house," the man told her as he walked back into the main room, tossing a towel around his neck. Rachel spun around and stared at him, wondering if she'd accidentally spoken aloud again. His long-sleeved denim shirt was unbuttoned, exposing a massive tattoo covering his torso. It was a lavish black-ink landscape, as exquisite in detail as the tattooed, katana-wielding female samurai she'd encountered during her treasure hunting trip to Japan. But this wasn't beautiful orange koi, colorful geishas, or green scaly serpents. This was a journey through time into London's dark, wicked underworld. A place where carriages rolled, prostitutes ventured, and Jack the Ripper once played.

"Interesting tattoo," she said. "I don't think I've seen anything like it." She smiled quickly and looked for a distraction by surveying the room. "It's really nice here, by the way."

The man grinned at her and gave her a shrug, clearly skeptical that she meant it.

For some unknown reason, she felt the need to defend herself. "No, really, it is. It's not exactly my style, but it seems warm and comfortable all the same."

"Yeah, uh-huh," he said.

His eyes traveled over her wet shirt and soaked skirt. She suddenly felt very self-conscious and crossed her arms.

"You bring a change of clothes with you?" he asked her.

Rachel shook her head. "My suitcase is in the trunk of the car. I just need to run out and get it."

She reached for the doorknob, and the man's hand was immediately on her forearm. "It's pouring out there," he told her. "You're going to get sick. I've got clothes you can wear. Just hang tight."

He disappeared again and came back minutes later with a white T-shirt and pair of gray sweatpants. "These are from when I was skinnier, so hopefully they'll fit you OK."

She thanked him before looking around.

"Bathroom is the first door on the right."

Rachel nodded and disappeared inside the beige room, which was as comfortable and homey as the rest of the house. She removed her clothes and folded them neatly into a small pile before pulling his T-shirt over her head. It was rather large on her, but it was warm and dry, and she immediately felt better. She pulled the sweatpants on and cinched the waist as tight as possible, but the baggy garment still hung off her hips slightly. Noticing a mirror, she stepped closer and realized that her mascara was making a slow retreat down her face. She quietly pulled open the closet in the room and snagged a blue washcloth and bar of soap, providing her with the means to scrub her face. After draping the wet cloth over the edge of the tub, she ran her fingers through her long auburn hair and sighed at her spent reflection. For the time being, it would have to do.

When she returned, her rescuer was reclining on the couch, talking on his phone. "Hey, it's Wyatt. I'm sorry, baby. I wanted to see you tonight too. But all the bridges are out, and you know it's too fucking dangerous to come out there. So give me a rain check, and I'll hit that sweet ass up tomorrow, K?"

Rachel rolled her eyes. She slowly dropped into an overstuffed chair and turned her gaze toward the fireplace. After he damp, muddy escapade, she was chilled to the bone and appreciated the heat.

Wyatt put his phone down and smiled. "You feel better?"

"I do, thanks. My name is Rachel, by the way."

He peered at her. "You look as though you could use something to eat. If you don't mind my saying so."

She shook her head and instinctively touched her tummy. "Thanks, but I'm not hungry."

"You need to keep your strength up...for that baby."

"What? How did you know?" She sat up straighter and felt the hem of his T-shirt dragging across her stomach. She looked down and quickly fixed it.

"Your life is in your eyes. I see beyond them...who you are, what you've seen, and how it affects your future."

"I don't understand. Are you some kind of prophet? I mean, do you have a gift of insight or something?"

Wyatt chuckled. "Some people refer to me as a seeker, a gypsy fortune-teller. For twelve years, I traveled throughout Europe, performing like a freak at circuses, carnivals, and county fairs. But then the mental erosion caught up with me. The only way I could keep my sanity was to escape to a quieter place. Now I plant crops and try my best to eke out a living as a farmer in this godforsaken countryside."

A chill ran up Rachel's back. She needed to get out of here and fast. This guy was repeating words he couldn't have heard—words she'd spoken while driving alone in her car. The vision of choking sleep demons flashed in her brain, and it suddenly occurred to her that he could be one of them.

"I'm not a demon either, Rachel. I devour impressions and regurgitate the bones. It's my cannibal tendencies, you see. A Satan-given talent I've been damned with most of my life."

Rachel swallowed hard. "Damned with?"

"You'd feel the same way, if you were plagued with them day and night."

This guy was psychotic—he had to be. And yet there was something oddly compelling about him. She closed her eyes and allowed her mind to wander—to test her sensitivity, explored and developed during her trip to Japan. But there was nothing exceptional under the surface of this man. Nothing to see or feel. Only a wall of blackness blocking an intruder's inquisitive mind.

"How refreshing," Wyatt said, his deep voice opening her eyes. "It seems you have a hidden gift."

"It's not a gift," she told him. "If it were, I could end my nightmares. Wipe all the frightening memories away."

"It will happen in due time, Rachel. When your life is settled, happy, and complete. But your instincts will stay with you forever, and right now it's most important you use them." He stepped closer and looked into her eyes. "Someone is searching for you. A bald man with angry dark eyes who could cause you and your baby great harm. I want you to think back over the last few days. To recall a particular scene. You left a dinner party upset and walked toward the kitchen. Two men were standing alone in the hallway, looking at a photograph of your uncle at a party celebrating his Agatha Christie Award. You overheard one of them talking, saying something I can't quite make out..."

"He said no one remembers voices."

Wyatt nodded. "Then he turned and looked at you, and you saw the bag he was holding."

"He was there as a guest. One of the men from the Morris Graves fraternity. Why would it matter if I saw him? I have no idea who he is."

"But he knows you, Rachel. You mustn't forget." Wyatt looked away and tilted his head. "Do you hear that?"

"Hear what?"

"The rain stopped. You need to go home, back the way you came. When you reach the Cumberforge Manor, lock yourself in your room and stay there until tomorrow." He held her hand and looked into her eyes. "If he should find you, stay strong and keep your wits about you. The shining light that follows and protects you won't be able to save you this time."

Wyatt used his tractor to clear a path in the road, providing Rachel with a safe passage to the outside world. She waved a hand and continued onto the main road before considering driving in the opposite direction, where Chase would be waiting, hoping to get the answers they both needed. But then words from the fortune-teller came rushing back, turning her steering wheel to the right.

You need to go home. She had more than one soul to worry about. The child she was carrying was an innocent being, a life she needed to safeguard above her own. She looked down at her phone on the seat, in the same place where she had left it. She picked it up and turned it on. An urgent message appeared on the screen from Killian, who had been hanging around the manor for days and visiting Sara while Paul was away: *Chase's life is in terrible danger. Meet me at the stable at 6:00 p.m. It's the only safe place to talk.*

Rachel didn't understand. Was this a prank? A way to set her nerves on end? No, it couldn't be. For most of her life, Killian had been like a brother to her. She trusted him explicitly. When they were young, he could be huge prankster and an annoying tease. But there was no way he would joke about life-and-death matters. Especially with her uncle's health at risk. So what did his text message mean? Who was threatening Chase, and how was she supposed to save him?

Before she had a chance to gather her thoughts, her phone started to ping, and the same message was repeated again and again. But it didn't make any sense at all. If Chase was truly in danger, why wasn't Killian calling the police? Why was he warning her? The text messages continued to arrive on her phone, replacing her doubts with fear. She couldn't shrug this off, not if it meant losing Chase. Despite Wyatt's warning, she had to know what was happening and if there was any possibility of rescuing Chase. She glanced at her watch. It was 5:42 p.m. and getting dark outside. With a fifteen-minute drive ahead of her, there was no time to waste. She increased her speed and kept a watchful eye on the rearview mirror. With police officers encroaching on their lives, the last thing she needed was to be pulled over for speeding.

She reached the final bend on the long roadway leading to the manor's gated entry. But the railroad guardrail was descending quickly, blocking her. Empty passenger cars on the long train continued to go by, adding tension to her neck and minutes to her watch. There was no way to swerve around them; she could only sit tight and wait. When the caboose finally passed and the train guard lifted, Rachel jammed her foot on the gas pedal and drove through the automated gate, picking up gravel on the way. She parked the car and ran to the stables, where Killian would be waiting.

A quick look around inside confirmed he was nowhere in sight. She was only a few minutes late. Would he have left and returned to town so soon?

Damn it. Rachel stood in place counting to ten and was about to return to the house when the sound of crunching footsteps turned her around.

"I was hoping I'd find you here." It was Brandon, Killian's conniving cousin, approaching from the back side of the stable. He was only a few feet away when he halted and slowly smiled. From where he was standing, she could smell bourbon in the chilled air. She couldn't imagine why he was there or why he'd been drinking at that hour.

"What do you want?"

"Sweet, ravishing Rachel. The one that got away. And such a shame too. We could have been *so* good together. But somehow there never seems to be enough time for the two of us. Someone else is always in the picture, in the room…in your life. All these years, and I'm still fucked up over you. I can't stop thinking of that body, those lips…no matter how hard I try."

Rachel looked around. "Don't you have somewhere else you need to be?"

"Not at the moment. So what do you think, gorgeous? Wanna screw around? No one's here to stop us now." He took another step toward her and grinned.

She could feel her pulse racing. "I understand the police are looking for you, Brandon. They've been asking everyone who attended the gallery party questions about that night."

"I don't know why. I haven't done anything wrong, aside from getting Melina pregnant." He chuckled with unsuppressed mirth.

Rachel raised a disbelieving eyebrow. "You did what?"

"Well, unlike you, she spreads her legs like a friggin' peacock every chance she gets. And you know, I like dogs, but I've never been into kids. In fact, I actually detest the smelly things. So Killian's bride-to-be agreed to keep our little secret to herself." He chuckled before adding, "Although it's not so little anymore…"

Rachel spotted Killian, edging along the side of the stable, undoubtedly hearing everything Brandon was saying. She crossed her arms, stilling her shaking hands, and tried to find a way to delay the inevitable.

"Maybe you should go home," she told Brandon. "I'm sure you're just making it up. The same way you did when you told Killian about us. None of that was true either, was it?"

"Yeah, you got me there, at least when it comes to you. But Melina's a whole different animal," he said, swaying in place. "She can suck the chrome off of a muffler, fuck a man to death, and still want more. Never seen anything like it in my life…"

Killian sprang from his spot, slugging Brandon from behind and dropping him to his knees. Then he rolled him over and pounded his perfect face repeatedly until it was a bloody mess. Until he could no longer touch or take what didn't belong to him.

When Killian righted himself, Rachel recognized the real threat and ran straight for the house. She could hear him coming after her, calling out her name, and she wasn't about to stop. If she timed it right, she could reach the top landing and lock her bedroom door before he cleared the entry.

"Rachel, wait!" he yelled from outside. She was about to reach for the stair railing when she felt a man's large hand on her arm, jerking her around to face him. It was the bartender from the dinner party. The same Italian-looking guy with the tattoos who had brought Melina a glass of water at the art gallery. Only somehow he looked different…unshaven and unkempt.

"This way," he said, pushing her into an open closet. He slammed the door shut, leaving her in total darkness. Immediately, two hands came up, one wrapping around her waist, pinning her arms at her sides, and the other covering her nose and mouth with a damp cloth. She struggled to free herself, blasting muffled screams, and tried to hold her breath for as long as possible. But it was useless. Her lungs gave out, and the sweet, intoxicating scent filled her nostrils, fogging her brain and quickly draining her strength. She was being transported back to another time and place—to a dark, secluded parking lot in San Palo, where drug-dealing mobsters had been waiting to kidnap her for a money-grabbing scheme.

"What are you doing here, Julien?" Killian barked. "I thought Mrs. Lyons fired you three days ago."

"You're right, Mr. Reed. She did. I'm just helping out until she can find a replacement. Is there anything I can do for you, sir?"

Rachel couldn't talk or move. Her eyelids were fighting gravity, and she could barely stand. In the entry, Killian's voice was slowly fading, like a cloud drifting away.

"Rachel Lyons ran in here a few seconds ago. Do you have any idea where she might have gone?"

"Margaret and Heidi were loading up the last of their belongings in the car. You might want to stop by the garage and check with them...if they haven't already left."

"Left?" Killian asked. "Are you saying they were fired?"

"Along with two chambermaids and the stable master. Mrs. Lyons told everyone she's cleaning house today. Now that would be something to see, wouldn't it, Mr. Reed?"

Rachel couldn't open her eyes. Julien's voice echoed in the hollows of her ears as her mind descended into the dark abyss—back into the hellish place haunting her dreams. She was trapped in the arms of evil, just as the fortune-teller had predicted. No one was there to save her. No one would stop them from killing her. Not this time.

16

THE WITNESS

The foghorns were extra loud near the Sea Cliff Inn on the outskirts of Saxton. It was as if they were alone on a ship sailing through the thickest fog. Chase stood by, scanning the tiled rooftops and ancient church tower in the distance, while Sky stepped up to the door and rang the bell. The gray-eyed proprietor peered through a cracked window blind before slowly opening the door. For the umpteenth time, Sky told his story about searching for his innocent ebony-haired sister who had run off with an unscrupulous twenty-year-old playboy.

After scrutinizing them, the owner twisted his lips and spouted, "That'll be two hundred eighty dollars a night."

Chase was dumbfounded. "Are you talking US dollars?"

The old man stepped back inside and was preparing to close the door. "Pay or don't stay," he muttered.

"We just need to know if she's here," Sky told him.

"Might be in two-oh-one next door, but you'll need a paid entry key to find out." The old man scratched the stubble on his cheeks and added, "You want the room or not?"

"Looks like we have no choice," Chase said, pulling out his wallet.

In the adjacent building, they climbed a set of narrow winding stairs to the second floor; the lights flickered out. Sky pulled a lighter from his pocket and held it before him. He made sure the corridor was deserted before heading toward room 201. With one touch on the door, it creaked open, a noise that was amplified a million times in the room.

"Ronny, you in there?" Sky whispered.

Chase was straining his eyes to see through the darkness when the overhead light came on. A kid with spiky black hair was lying on his right side on the bed with his back to them, and for a moment, Chase thought the guy was sleeping. Then he rounded the bed and leaned closer. The large bloodstain was almost invisible on the blue bedsheets, but on the front of the guy's white T-shirt, it was stark and startling, like a splash of cold water to the face. Brice's expression was frozen in a grimace of pain. His hands and face had been sliced repeatedly before his throat was slit. It looked like a drug deal gone bad, judging from the trace of white residue under his nose.

Sky's eyes were enormous. He fled first, dropping the room key and trying several times before he finally unlocked the neighboring door. When they were both safely inside, Chase locked the door behind them. They sat on their beds, staring blankly into space, trying to determine what to do next. If someone was capable of killing Brice in this small, remote village, how safe were they?

"We need to call the police," Chase finally said.

Sky shook his head. "I've had too many run-ins. Never killed anyone, but came close a few times. Without having Veronica here to tell them what happened, who do you think they're going to haul in?"

An hour passed, and still she hadn't returned. Sky began pacing, and then he disappeared outside with a pack of cigarettes in his hand. Chase stared at the ceiling, thinking about the murdered kid in the next room and wondering how his parents were going to take the news. Sky returned, looking exhausted and blurry-eyed. They agreed to decide what to do in the morning, and then lay back on their beds and took turns sleeping. At six in the morning, the door slammed. Chase bolted upright and scrambled to his feet; Sky was gone. Yet outside the window, there was his car, parked right where they'd left it the night before.

Where the hell is he? Chase pulled on his shoes and jacket and was about to go searching when Sky returned with two cups of steaming hot chocolate.

He handed one to Chase. "It was the only thing working in the vending machine. As soon as you're wide awake, you might want to come with me."

"Why's that?"

"I found Veronica."

"Alive?"

"Mostly," Sky answered. "She's hiding downstairs."

Chase wasted no time. After reaching the first landing, he looked to his left. At the far end of the hallway, he spotted the young woman, hunched over, visibly shaken, in an oversize blue sweater and drippy black eye makeup, her dark hair a long, tangled mess.

He edged closer and sat, squaring an ankle over one of his knees. "Is there someone you need us to call?" he asked.

It seemed like Sloan's friend wanted to answer, wanted to speak so badly, but her mouth simply hung open. He wished Rachel was there; she'd have all the right questions to clear up this nasty mess.

Veronica's eyes stayed on Chase's face as he took a sip from his cup. She watched as he quickly licked his lips—his tongue darting out over his top lip and then slowly running over the bottom, ending with a soft smile.

She exhaled a deep breath and averted her eyes to her lap.

"I'm not sure what you want me to say..." her voice cracked.

He placed a finger on the side of her chin, forcing her to look at him. "Tell me what happened."

Her eyebrows knit in confusion and worry. "Who are you? Why are you here?"

Earn her trust, Chase reminded himself. *Just like Sloan.* He leaned back against the wall, relaxing as if he planned on being there awhile. "I'm Chase...a friend of Sloan's. She's been worried sick about you."

Veronica stared with cow eyes. "She is?"

"Of course. That's what good friends do. They worry about each other."

Chase glanced up at Sky, who was standing along the opposite wall with his arms crossed, quietly gauging their progress. Veronica traced his vision and began rocking in place. Then she looked back at Chase and stilled. "We've been friends since I was thirteen," she said. "We used to hang out on the weekends."

The conversation continued, slow and easy. Chase asked her every question he could think of and even shared parts of his life in return. She heard about Rachel and a few of their adventures, and her rocking eventually stopped. He learned how her passion for art was instilled by her mother, who worked at an advertising firm in Wales and snagged acting gigs in different shows all across Europe. While she talked, Chase brushed strands of her hair away from her face, touched the bracelet on her wrist that her father gave her, nodded his understanding, and stared into her eyes while she spoke, hanging onto her every word. He got the impression that Veronica had never had a conversation like this with anyone.

"If you have a nice home," he said, "then why are you staying here?"

She looked away, biting her lip again.

"It's OK, Veronica," he assured her. "You can tell me anything. Anything at all."

She took another deep breath and provided the explanation they needed to hear. "Brice and I met this guy at a party. He said he'd been seeing Sloan for a while. She was being harsh, screwing with him...cheating with other guys right under his nose. She'd stopped sharing personal stuff with me and was always putting guys down, so it sounded right. Anyway, this guy said he wanted to get even, and if we helped him, sort of scared her a little bit, he'd hook us up with some great shit, and she wouldn't even have to know about it."

"What happened next?"

"He grabbed her outside the club and took her to this old house his sister owned. We were supposed to keep an eye on her for a few days and let him know if she tried to leave."

"Was anyone else helping? Watching her and keeping her there?"

"Just this slick-looking guy, but I never got his name."

"Did you hear anything about a robbery or missing art?"

"What art?" Veronica's blank expression spoke volumes. Chase finished off the last of his cocoa, rolling the next question around in his mind.

"After Sloan left, did her ex-boyfriend come back and give Brice what he promised?"

"I don't want to talk about that..." Veronica rubbed her hand under her nose and sniffed.

"Sure. I understand."

Chase knew she didn't want him to push it, but he needed a name—a way to prove the coke dealer was responsible for killing Brice. "We want to make sure what happened to your friend doesn't happen to you. So what do you say, Veronica? Can you help us out? Can you tell me the name of the guy with the knife and if he was the same person who wanted to teach Sloan a lesson?"

Veronica shifted in place. She looked up at Sky for the longest time, as if needing his reassurance—a sign that he wouldn't hold her responsible for their friend's death and Sloan's physical abuse. "I'm not sure. He forced his way in and was wearing a yellow hooded raincoat. It might have been Julien," she said. "He's a dealer and part-time bartender at the Red Room, a place in Soho. He said he gets hired to work at private parties and for Sloan's grandmother. I guess that's how they met..."

"What's his last name?" Sky asked.

"I don't know."

"Tell me what he looks like, Ronny."

She gave a vague description that would match any muscle-bound, dark-haired guy on the planet. Then she started bouncing her leg in obvious agitation.

Chase leaned over and hugged her tightly. He pulled back, looking at her hopeful face. "You did a good thing."

She tilted her head. "I did?"

"You helped Sloan, and I know you're going to do it again because you care so much about her. That makes you a very special person, Veronica."

Chase looked down at his phone, noticed two missed calls from Rachel, and realized he had been sitting on the cold floor far too long. "It's getting late." He frowned, letting her believe he was reluctant to leave.

Sky sighed heavily and shook his head. "Get out of here," he said, tossing Chase his car keys. "I'll call you after the cops are finished with us."

"They're going to ask why you waited so long. What are you going to say?"

"That's my problem, not yours. Just tell Sloan I was here, OK?"

He punched in Rachel's number on his phone, and it rang twice before going to voice mail. "Hello," her voice said. "I'm available right now but misplaced the phone. Leave a message, and I'll call you as soon as I find it." The sound of her sweet voice reminded him of his parting words—the cruel remark about ending their relationship that he'd made to jolt her emotions and remind her of what was at stake.

What a jerk. Chase took a quick breath and began. "Baby, it's me. I'm heading back and just wanted to let you know that all that stupid stuff I said—"

It was at this point that all of the toxins Veronica had ingested, snorted, injected, and huffed over the past forty-eight hours decided to purge themselves from her body. She shoved open the exit door, which separated the hallway from the parking lot, and collapsed in front of a neatly trimmed hedge. While Sky hovered and Chase watched from the doorway, Veronica's neck muscles seized, and her spine contorted, pushing inward to her stomach, forcing her to heave over and over, leaving nothing behind except a trail of black tears rolling down her cheeks and, hopefully, regrets for her painful mistakes.

"I'll catch up with you later," Chase called out. Then he climbed into the car and pulled out of the driveway. He floored the gas pedal and headed toward Bellwood, wishing he had listened to Rachel and just let the cops do their job.

17

THE SCAPEGOAT

Rachel opened her eyes slowly and sat up on the green military cot where her kidnappers had deposited her. There were no windows cut into the brick walls, and the concrete floor was cracked and stained in places, making it easy to assume that this was a basement in an old building or deserted house. All she knew for certain was she needed to get out of there and back to where Chase would be waiting. If she had followed the fortune-teller's instructions instead of Killian's, she wouldn't be in this predicament. As much as she wanted to blame him for the deception, she couldn't. Not unless Killian turned out to be part of this plot.

She heard raised voices in the next room and moved next to the door to make out their words. "What are we supposed to do with her?" a woman asked.

"Keep her under wraps," the man replied, dragging out a folding chair. Rachel leaned closer to the crack and could see two people moving around in the room, but only glimpses of a shoulder or a leg. They both sat down at a table, picked up a beer, and sat back, allowing her a better view. She saw messy dark hair and a tattooed arm and knew it was the bartender immediately. But the blonde next to him was only vaguely familiar.

"This is so messed up," the woman said.

"What are you so worried about? She never saw you."

"She knows who you are, Julien."

"It doesn't matter. In two hours, we're out of here."

"Then what?'

"She'll wake up and go home. She won't even know what happened."

"All because of your father and his fucking paranoia. Why did he insist on being there anyway?"

"Hell, how should I know? He had his reasons. Sit back and shut up. It'll be over before you know it."

"I need a hit," she muttered.

While she rolled up a bill, he reached into his shirt pocket, pulled out a tiny white packet, and sprinkled it in front of her. She leaned down and snorted a line of cocaine, heroin, or whatever it was, up one nostril and then the other. When she was done, she sat back, wiping her nose.

"Feeling better, Britt?" he asked.

"Yeah...a lot better."

Julien followed her lead, snorting two lines, tipping his head back and closing his eyes. His chin dropped at the sound of heavy footsteps entering the room.

"What the fuck, Julien!" another man shouted. "I can't trust you to do anything right, even when I do all the work myself. Where are the vans?"

"They're coming. Just like I said they would. What's your problem, anyway?"

"Did you bring that woman here like I asked? The one I told you about?"

"Yeah. She's in back, lying down. Britt knocked her out good."

"You'd better hope so. She's the only one who can link us to the robbery."

"What about that other girl, Sloan? You said her grandmother would pay up. What the hell happened there? Tor told me she blew him off. I went to the house last night to check on her, and she was gone."

"I know. I left it unlocked."

"Why would you do that?" Julien asked.

The man with the herringbone cap drained the rest of Julien's beer. The same man Rachel had seen at the house without his disguise at the end of the dinner party. He crushed the can and tossed it aside. "I set her up to take the fall for us," he said, smiling. "She's in jail, cooling her heels."

"Huh. That's pretty cool, Dad."

Britt leaned forward on her elbows. "But what's going to keep her from telling the cops the truth?"

Julien's father practically growled in frustration. "Tell your girlfriend to keep her yap shut. I don't even know why you brought her here."

"She's been helping, Dad."

The old man looked into Britt's glossy eyes and then back at his son. "Yeah, right. Helping herself to your stash. I told you to keep clean tonight. You're both going to fuck everything up. Do you have any idea how long I've waited to get even with Paul Lyons and that rich bitch he married?"

There was complete silence in the room. Then Julien's father spoke again. "If those Chinese guys you've been dealing with don't deliver as promised, we're going to lose a million. Do the math, Julien. That's two hundred fifty thousand dollars apiece, including the drivers. I've got nothing if this doesn't work. You understand?"

"Don't worry. Tor's on top of it. He's not going to let anything go wrong. He's meeting us at the docks like I told you. That's where the deal's going down."

"What about Chase Cohen?" Britt said. "He's been asking all over…trying to find out who grabbed Rachel's sister."

Sister? Rachel's jaw slacked. They couldn't be talking about her. They just…couldn't.

Julien snickered. "We'll have to kill the fucker, I guess."

His father's face turned red.

Smack! The slap to Julien's face was the hardest Rachel had ever heard.

"Ow! Why did you hit me?"

"Because you're a complete idiot—that's why," he snapped. "Now go find something to inject that woman with before I break your neck. She needs to be out when we leave."

"Diazepam?"

"I don't care what you give her. Just put her down fast."

For the sake of her baby, Rachel had to find a way out of there. She stepped away from the door and walked around the room. Between the walls in one corner, there was a storage area that went back a long way. It was filled with assorted junk—everything from discarded bedding to a sad-looking Christmas tree. There were also four enormous water barrels next to an old washer and dryer. She tried to pull one of the barrels across the floor to block the door, but she wasn't strong enough. Approaching it from the rear, she pressed her back against the wall and shoved it with her feet. The barrel inched forward. She continued the slow progress, straining her back and legs until the door was partially blocked. It wasn't the best solution, but maybe it would slow them down, since there was no lock to hold them back.

Rachel returned to the crack in the door and leaned close to listen. It was quiet for several minutes. Then footsteps could be heard coming down the stairs. She turned and launched herself into the junk pile, penning herself behind the washer and dryer. She heard the door open in the next room followed by muffled voices, delaying Julien's approach.

With nowhere safe to hide, she looked up. *Whoa!* There was a hole directly above her. It wasn't very deep—maybe five feet at the most—but somehow she had completely missed it. Wood planks crossed along the edges, and it was filled with dusty spider webs. If she could just get up inside, she would have a better chance of protecting herself.

She scrounged around quickly and found a small camp shovel in the stack. After sticking it up into the hole, she heard someone at the door shoving against the barrel. It hardly moved, and it seemed the simple blockade was working, at least for the time being. She went back to work clearing the space while Julien became more determined. He rammed his body against the door, making the water barrel scrape across the floor a few inches.

Rachel pulled the shovel back down, coated in webs and hairy brown spiders. She tossed it aside and twisted her body around, pushing off the floor so that her feet could enter the hole above her head first. When she reached her chest, she felt the end of the cavern. She bent her knees, hooking her toes around the roof brace. Then she pulled herself up, using her feet and hands to stay inside.

It was a silly idea, leaving her as vulnerable as a coon in a trap. What if they found her crouched up like this? She'd be dead along with her child.

Rachel saw a shattered computer monitor almost directly below her. As the door slammed into the water barrel again, she reached down and grabbed it. Her arms took the weight easily. She lifted it up, just barely managing to fit it into the hole.

Although she could barely see past the monitor, when she shifted it slightly, she could view the entire room without being seen. There were no useful weapons as far as she could tell, but if Julien's father came for her, Rachel could drop it on him and do some serious damage.

Now she had to wait.

With a loud crash, the barrel scraped across the ground and came to a stop. Someone walked into the room. Rachel held her breath as her long hair swished in front of her eyes. She tried to shake it back so she could see more clearly.

The short-haired blonde was standing next to the cot. "I thought you said you left her in here."

"I did. There's no way she could have gotten out."

Rachel closed her eyes and tried to place the shapely blonde— the name that was unique when she heard it. *Britt Easton*. Wasn't this the woman she'd seen hugging Killian outside the gallery when they first arrived? The same person he claimed to have been friends with for years?

There was the soft click of a gun and then nothing. She felt the tension in the room rising. Her arms were burning with the effort of holding the monitor inside the ceiling. But she couldn't let go of it now. She had to keep hanging on to it, or she'd die anyway.

Footsteps could be heard leaving, and then came the sound of someone climbing into the tunnel. She felt her legs shaking with the effort of keeping them up. While the blonde moved clumsily through the junk pile, Rachel held her breath until she could feel her lungs burning. But she wouldn't let it out, not yet. The determined intruder peered behind boxes and tried to turn around, causing a stack of cans to topple over.

Rachel was about to explode.

"Is everything OK in there?" the older man called from the next room.

Britt struggled to pick herself back up, and she caught a glimpse of Rachel's face and let out a strangled cry. She raised a small gun, and Rachel dropped the monitor, hitting her on the back of the head.

Without a second to lose, Rachel dropped down, trying not to step on the woman before making a run for it. She dodged behind a large bucket full of hardened cement as Julien entered the room. He held a silver hypodermic needle in one hand and looked into the gap.

"Britt?" he asked hesitantly. Not getting an answer, he climbed into the tunnel, needle raised and ready. If he came much closer, Rachel would be discovered. She looked around for something to hit him with and spotted a baseball bat on the other side of the tunnel. If she reached over and grabbed it, he'd jab her with who-knew-what and send her to la-la land forever.

Rachel looked into the box behind her. It was filled with old dishes. She could throw a plate at him, right? But what if she missed? Then her eyes lit on something else.

Silver candlesticks! As quietly as she could, Rachel reached in and grabbed one. Julien crept even closer. She wanted to swing at him now, but she wouldn't have a good aim. With her heart racing, she gripped the candlestick hard, her knuckles turning white. She saw the end of the needle pass the edge of the bucket and huddled closer to the wall to avoid detection a little longer. She heard the sound of two pops, like a car engine backfiring. Then there was silence, and Julien was climbing again. For a moment, for one small moment, it looked like she might actually pull this off.

"*Tingzhi!*" The voice was low and deadly.

What was that? Rachel froze solid, her breath catching in her chest. Then she swung the candlestick as hard as she could. It collided with Julien's forehead, making a metallic thud. He dropped the needle, looking dazed. She swung a punch at his face, putting as much force as she could into it with the little space provided. Then, just to be sure, she hit him with the candlestick again.

Julien slumped to the floor, unmoving. Rachel hastily crawled over him and hopped down to the ground three feet below. She had just straightened when she heard a distinct click. When she looked up, she was staring straight into the muzzle of yet another gun. This time, a Browning 0.96.

"*Ladao!* Put hands up!" Rachel didn't have anything to drop, so she placed both of her hands on the back of her head.

The gun motioned for her to move forward. She did as she was told and walked through the door, wondering if they were going to kill her now or later…after the buyers left or before. Or could these be the men they'd been waiting for?

She felt the gun jab into her back and heard a man giving her directions. "Don't do anything."

Rachel wasn't about to. She wasn't some agent that had awesome karate moves or a detective with a hidden gun in her boot. She was terrified and pregnant. Despite her best efforts to escape, she was actually going to be killed. That was the only thought racing through her head. But as they left the house, her mind slowly started to accept it, letting other thoughts enter. Why were they going to kill her? She didn't have anything they wanted. She hadn't done anything to them, at least up until now. And as far as she knew, neither had Chase. So what did they want from her? What singled her out from everyone else?

Rachel saw a bald-headed man sprawled out and facedown on the ground with blood oozing from multiple bullet holes in his body. She prayed desperately that somebody would look out the window and call the police, but when a big white van pulled up in the street and two Chinese men joined the first, she knew there wasn't a chance she was going to get out of this one.

Rachel tried to take in everything at once: the men's close-cropped hairstyles, what they were wearing, the guns they were holding, the license plate of the van, how many people there were, and hopefully where they might be taking her. But she was running on overload. Even with her gift of insight—her fully developed sixth sense that allowed her to feel vibrations and detect magnetic fields most people were unaware they possessed, there was no way she could concentrate on everything at once. She memorized their Asian faces and repeated the license-plate number over and over again in her mind.

Someone jerked her hands behind her back harshly. She heard the sound of a zip tie, binding her wrists together tightly. There was no way she would be able to free her hands. She felt strong hands grab her arms just below her shoulders and pick her up off the ground. She tried to curl forward to protect her baby, before being thrown into the van. She struggled to roll over and managed to work herself into a sitting position. Two other men climbed into the van with her and slammed the door shut. The engine roared beneath her, and they rolled away, heading to who-knew-where.

18

THE ADVOCATE

For five hours, Sloan sat in the cold cell staring at the bars, listening to the hookers in the adjacent cage holler at the guards, waiting for the drama in her life to end. When she was finally released, one of the officers told her that she'd been cleared of all charges by Detective Torren and her ride was waiting outside.

"Tell him to let us out too!" One of the women screeched before the door slammed shut.

Sky was standing on the opposite side of the electronic door. As soon as Sloan reached him, he threw his arms around her and held her tight. After thanking one of the officers, he guided her to his car and helped her inside.

"Thank you," Sloan said in near whisper. She wanted to feel like Sky was her hero...that she trusted him more than anyone. And maybe she did, or maybe she just wanted to believe it was true.

He rolled his silver SUV into the parking lot next to McDonald's and turned to her, smiling. "Hungry?"

"Famished," she said, attempting a smile.

"Want to eat in or out?"

"Inside."

"Come on then, beautiful." They entered the restaurant and got a few funny looks when folks noticed the dirty sweatshirt and blue shorts she was wearing. But Sky didn't seem to care. Sloan got them seats while he got the food. He didn't ask what she wanted, but just ordered her favorite combo, and he took it to the table where she was waiting.

"Smells great," he said. He was about to sit down when Sloan grabbed his hand, urging him to sit next to her. He chuckled and kissed her cheek softly. Then he began eating his mega burger, and Sloan cuddled up to him, eating her fries.

"Remember when we first met?" she asked him.

"After that I was crazy about you." Sky laughed.

"I'm glad you were."

He finished eating and went to get another drink. When he came back, he watched Sloan devour the last bite of her chicken sandwich.

"You finished?" Sky asked, sitting down.

"I think so."

He smiled and touched her hand. "Can I ask you something?"

"Sure. Anything."

"Have you been hurting yourself?" he asked.

"No. Why would you ask that?"

His eyes were fixed on the white bandage covering her wrist. "When we get back to my place, can I look?"

"Sure." She cuddled closer to him.

Sky lifted her chin with his fingers to look in her eyes. "I love you," he said.

She smiled softly.

"I really do, Sloan." He kissed her lips gently.

"Stop being cheesy."

"Never." He kissed her passionately. Then he held her hand and walked her back to his car.

Fifteen minutes later, they were at Sky's loft. He pulled her down the hallway and into his bedroom. She teased him, saying she hoped it wasn't why he'd shown up to post bail. He laughed and denied it. She did what he wanted her to do, knowing it would make him happy. It was the first time in a long time that she cared about pleasing someone, and it actually felt good. Maybe her numbness was wearing off and genuine emotion was taking hold. There was no way to tell for sure. She only knew that as much as she wanted Sky to be happy, she needed the greatest fix of all.

Unconditional love.

She looked up at the ceiling and counted the lines in the air vent's grill. Her voice came out in a hoarse whisper. "I don't know why all this shit keeps happening to me. There has to be a reason. Maybe God is punishing me for all my screw-ups."

"That's silly," Sky told her. "You didn't deserve any of it... especially going to jail."

"What about Ronny? What are they going to do to her?"

He explained that it was best for Veronica to stay in jail...at least for the time being. It could be detrimental—life threatening, even—if their friend returned to the streets, especially after not doing drugs for two days.

Sloan smiled sarcastically and shook her head. "She's not going to last. As soon as they let her out, she'll be using again."

"Then we'll stand by her and get her the help she needs."

"It seems you've turned into the custodian for misfits."

He smiled. "Probably because I am one." He brought her injured wrist to his lips and kissed it, his eyes never leaving hers. She could feel her cheeks warm. "You're not alone, you know.

Lots of people care about you. Especially me. I'll support you, no matter what."

Sloan closed her eyes and swallowed hard, desperately wanting to believe it. In some strange way, the time she'd spent with Pierce Torren, locked up with her thoughts, had forced her to reexamine her beliefs and relive the fears she'd kept hidden. She knew that in order to have any chance of surviving, she had to overcome her despondency, learn to stand up for herself, and have faith in the people who loved her.

Even if Sky was the only one.

The locked entry door opened and closed in the next room, and suddenly there were footsteps crossing the wood floor, heading into the kitchen. Sky's arms wrapped around Sloan, holding her tight, as if waiting for the threat to become real.

"Who is it?" he called out. The white sheet and down comforter were tucked all around them, and their clothes were strewn all over the floor. Sky's switchblade was still in the pocket of his jeans, but could be accessed quickly if needed.

"Oh, there you are," Damien called from the hallway. "Hope you don't mind that I used your extra key." He stepped into the bedroom, and his eyes instantly dropped. A blush spread across his pale cheeks, changing him from a twenty-year-old to an embarrassed preteen. "I didn't know you were both here." He lifted his eyes a fraction and smiled.

"What is it?" Sky demanded. "It had better be damn important for you to come here without calling first."

"I tried, but I kept getting a busy signal." He motioned his head toward the nightstand. "I guess we can understand why."

Sky's eyes lit on his black Panasonic phone with its handset dangling from its coiled retractable cord. He stretched down to retrieve it, leaving Sloan clutching the bed sheet against her bare chest. "So why are you here?" Sky said, dropping back against the headboard. He drew Sloan against him in a protective embrace.

"I came here on account of Chase Cohen. You know, that treasure-hunting guy from California."

"What about him?" Sky asked.

"He stopped by my house, looking for you. He said something about needing your help with finding his girlfriend. We were on our way here when this cop named Tor pulled us over. He said everything was under control and we needed to stay out of it."

Sky's eyes narrowed. "What does that mean?"

"It means you don't get involved," Sloan said.

Damien jerked a shoulder. "Yeah, I guess. All I can tell you is this guy was packing some heavy artillery. He had twenty...no, thirty guys with him heading south toward the harbor in black armored vans. I'm telling you, it was like a scene straight out of a Stallone movie. You would have loved it."

"So where's Chase?" Sky asked.

"He followed after them, of course." Damien tilted a smile. "What do you think? Wanna check it out?"

Sloan shook her head. "What don't you understand about staying put?" Now where had she heard that before? Oh yeah. Pierce Torren. The cop she was still trying to figure out.

Sky lifted her chin and smiled. "Since when did any of us follow directions?"

19

THE TREASURE TROVE

Determined to stay strong, Rachel reined in her fears and tried to concentrate on the turns they were making. Down the hill, right, and then an instant left. After a few moments, another right. They slowed, turned left, and came to an almost-complete stop. Then another left and speedy acceleration. If Rachel was correct, they were on the highway now. Not a good thing, since they could easily pass exits without her knowing. She closed her eyes, estimating that ten minutes had passed, and wished with all her might that she could see where they were going. A quick look around confirmed the van was empty. Stripped of anything useful. She half wanted to say something but was afraid of being shot. But she was keenly aware that they hadn't taken precautions with her. They hadn't tied up her feet or taped her mouth.

More time passed, and then they began to slow down. Had they reached an exit? They slowed to a stop. She heard the unmistakable sound of a clicking blinker. They turned right and then went straight for a while. All the sound of traffic faded away. The road grew bumpy and then smoothed back out again. She hadn't the faintest idea where they were. After all, she was in a foreign country, completely out of her element.

Suddenly, there was a loud shriek, and the car veered dangerously to the left. It seemed the driver had tried to turn too fast and too hard. The van tipped on two wheels. Rachel threw her weight across the van to keep it from toppling, but her weight wasn't enough. It crashed onto its side, leaving the sliding door as a ceiling. She smacked her head painfully on the wall, and sparks popped before her eyes. With her arms still behind her, she shook her head hard, trying to rid it of the blackness. Then she looked down at her stomach and thought of her baby, struggling to survive inside of her.

Both of the guys in the car pounced on top of her and pressed her against the wall, squeezing air out of her chest. She heard the unique sound of tape being ripped apart. Before she could react in any way, a thick piece of duct tape was slapped over her mouth. One of the men grabbed a fistful of her hair and yanked her head back painfully. He jabbed the muzzle of his gun under her jaw and held it there, watching the door of the van. The other crouched on the opposite side, his gun pointed up toward the sliding door.

Rachel could hear the engine of at least two other cars outside, slightly muffled by the metal. Two gunshots fired, and then she felt the gun pressing steadily harder into her skin, almost cutting off her air.

Rachel was practically panting; she couldn't help it. She had been thrown into a surreal movie; only real bullets were flying around. She listened hard as everything went quiet outside. She heard footsteps crunch over loose gravel. Suddenly, the metal above them dented in with a loud slam. Her body jumped, her breathing sped up, and she closed her eyes, knowing she was going to die.

There were muffled voices outside. Then the door slid open, revealing at least four guns directed at them.

"Point at me, and I shoot her!" her captor screamed, jabbing the gun against her neck. Rachel convinced herself not to struggle against him and concentrate only on the people standing above them. Three men were standing in the opening. Their eyes darted from Rachel to her captor to the other man in the corner, visibly shaking. They didn't look old—maybe in their late twenties or early thirties. They all had on thick green bulletproof vests and green cargo pants with pockets running down the lengths of their legs.

Cops? Secret forces? With their Aircutt 0.86 machine guns, they made it look like they were on a mission to destroy.

"I kill her!" her captor yelled.

The men lowered their guns. Rachel couldn't think straight. She couldn't tear her gaze away from the men standing above her. Were they going to shoot through her just to kill him?

Rachel heard a slight squeak as the man's finger tightened on the trigger. He was going to shoot her anyway. It looked like her rescuers weren't going to be able to save her in time. That left it up to her. A spike of adrenaline shot up her spine. Rachel jerked her head away and tried her best to elbow her captor in the gut. She came in contact with something as a shot went off and hesitated only a moment before falling over sideways. She kicked savagely at the other man whose gun was directed at her and caught him on the side of the jaw. He slammed his head against the wall and lost his gun. She glanced behind her to see her other captor shooting up at the machine-gun owners. Carefully, she worked her tied hands under her butt and pulled her legs through the opening. Now Rachel's hands were in front of her, making everything easier.

Pushing herself upright into a sitting position, she saw out of the corner of her eye the man crumple to the ground. She looked around, and as she did, the hard metal of a gun whacked the side of her face. Pain erupted down from her right temple, blocking her vision. She felt warm liquid dripping down her cheek as she shook the hair out of her eyes. The man's foot came in contact with her shoulder hard. Rachel fell over sideways, feeling like her skin was on fire. She heard a click of a gun and looked up to see the man pointing his weapon straight at her.

My baby!

There was a loud hammering sound, and the man dropped the gun and crumpled to the floor. She looked up at the hole. One agent was already inside the van, and two more were waiting above. The one inside walked toward her in a crouch, lowering his gun. From her view, he was upside down, and he was surprisingly handsome. He had long brown hair, beautiful brown eyes, and a slightly rugged look about him.

"You OK?" he asked in a gentle voice, placing one hand on the ground as he bent closer to her. Rachel scooted away from him and got to her knees. "I wouldn't hurt you," he said, holding up a hand. "I'm Pierce Torren. I've been working undercover on this case. I'm sorry, Miss Lyons. This wouldn't have happened if I hadn't been recognized by one of the drivers."

Her heart was still pounding, her breathing was unsteady, and adrenaline was still pumping through her bloodstream.

"Are you hurt anywhere besides your head? Did they break anything? Did they inject you with anything?"

Rachel began to wind down. Her breathing slowed, and she began to feel more like herself. She hadn't died. She was still breathing...still shaking, but she would hardly call this safe. She gingerly touched her stomach to make sure everything was all right before slowly shaking her head. Then she reached up with both tied hands and peeled off the duct tape covering her mouth.

Ouch! It hurt more than she thought it would.

"You've got yourself a great guy," he said, taking a few steps closer. She drew back instinctively but then sat down with her feet in front of her and let him approach. He cocked a half smile. "He followed us here and told me to tell you that he was letting the pros do their job for a change."

Rachel was too shaken to respond.

Pierce looked up and called out. "Giles, throw down the nippers." He reached up and caught a wicked-looking metal clipping thing. They were like garden shears but shorter and thinner. The tie snapped apart, and she rubbed one wrist and then the other.

When she looked up again, Chase's pale face came into view. It was slackened; his brow was furrowed, and his eyes were dark. Never in her life had she seen so much fear in a man's face before. When their eyes met, his face instantly brightened. He held out his hand to help Rachel stand, and she took it.

"Are you OK?" he asked urgently.

Her only answer was to throw her arms round his neck and burst into tears. She clung to him for dear life, afraid to move— afraid to speak.

"I drove up just as Julien and Britt were driving away," he told her. "I saw your head in the back window of their car and tried to keep up, but they got away. Detective Pierce tracked me down and said they had everything under control. They knew the situation and would get you out safe." He looked into her eyes. "Everyone was ordered to stay back, but when I heard the guns firing, I swear I wanted to jump in front of them. If it weren't for Pierce, I probably would have."

Rachel didn't know how to react. Her eyes lit on the detective. He smiled and nodded before resuming his debriefing.

"Anyway, from what I hear," Chase said, "you were incredible. Almost took two of them out by yourself. I just thank God you're all right." He leaned down and kissed her forehead.

The sound of police officers barking orders drew their attention. They both stood and watched from the sidelines as the team of detectives and investigating officers went to work, opening the doors on the second and third van. They were filled with stacks of paintings in all sizes and shapes. One of the men pulled a steel briefcase from a passenger seat and pried it open. Inside were neatly bound hundred-dollar bills.

"Wow...can you believe it?" Chase said. "All those paintings were heading to China. I don't know how those guys thought they'd get away with it. The MI5, detectives, and enforcement officers they have in this country are...incredible. It was just a matter of time before they were caught." He sighed and draped an arm over her shoulder.

She glanced around them and noticed three faces in the crowd. One of them was distinctly familiar, at least from the framed photos she'd seen decorating the manor. It was the red-headed young woman Chase had been looking for...only now she was linked arm in arm with Sky Nolan. The same young man who had charged into Cumberforge Manor searching for her after she had disappeared.

"I heard the strangest thing while I was in that house," Rachel said, staring straight at her. "Britt Easton said Sloan Rafferty was my sister." She looked up at Chase and quirked a brow. "Isn't that crazy? Now why would she say that?"

A look of surprise shaded his face. "Oh, she did? Well, I'm sure it can all be explained away. Let's get back to the manor and put you in a warm bath. I'm sure you need to unwind after that experience."

Rachel felt like she'd been caught in a bear trap a second time that day. All that song and dance about telling the truth, about sharing her deepest secrets. And now he was holding back. Why would he think she wasn't strong enough? She'd already survived a mountain of emotional disaster and almost died at the hands of Chinese hoodlums.

Chase grabbed her hand. She felt the current run up and down her arm. The attraction felt so inappropriate in this setting. He looked into her face, his eyes at once cool and pleading. Rachel took a step back, breaking his hold. No matter how thorny this moment, she would stand firm because she wanted him—no, needed him to tell the truth.

"Is Sloan my sister?" she asked.

"Yes. I wanted to tell you. There's so much involved here that you don't understand. I just need a few minutes to explain."

"I don't want to hear it. Not now. Not until we get back..." Her voice trailed off. Her hands started to shake despite herself.

A look of concern contracted Chase's face. "I'll get you out of here as quick as I can."

20

ABSOLUTION

As Rachel sat across from Chase in the manor's vast living room, staring at the flickering flames in the fireplace, she realized she had never felt so bewildered and exasperated in her whole life. While playing the hero, Chase managed to solve any problem that arose with the people around her that she couldn't fix. He prevented major disasters that threatened their lives in Japan and California, leaving things running smoothly again. She kept asking herself why she would allow this. But she knew. She had a craving, a weakness as all-consuming as the needs of a junkie. For the last two months, if someone asked for Chase's help, her wants and frustrations were put aside. Forgotten, discarded…as insignificant as she had allowed herself to become. And now, after taking matters into her own hands, resuming the role of a dismissive partner had become even less appealing.

The silence between Chase and Rachel stretched until he finally spoke. "I thought you'd like to know that Julien Lancaster and Britt Easton were arrested. They'll probably spend the rest of their lives in jail. Even though Julien swore he had nothing to do with it, his fingerprints were all over the knife that killed

Brice Stanton. The one that turned up at the B-and-B where we found Veronica Hewes." Chase surveyed Rachel's profile, evaluating it with a critical eye. "His dad and two of his drivers died from their wounds. When your uncle heard the news, he was completely floored. Turns out Max Lancaster was his book agent. Unbelievable, huh?"

Rachel barely nodded.

"You can rest easy now, knowing everything's been handled."

She turned, locking her eyes on his. "What about my mother? The letters I received years ago, right after she left? How am I supposed to react after discovering you knew the real reason she disappeared and still said nothing?"

"Baby, I only found out two days ago, and then everything went crazy..."

"It doesn't matter. You promised not to keep secrets from me, and you did. You stood in the library knowing the truth and kept it to yourself. I don't understand why you would do that when honesty is so important to you. It goes both ways, Chase. You want to know everything about me and my deepest feelings, but you share nothing."

He looked down, avoiding her gaze. "It almost literally killed me when I heard you'd been taken, tied up by those gang members and held at gunpoint. I know you're angry at me because I wasn't there to keep you safe. I should have been, but I can't promise that will always be the case. You're strong, resourceful, and resilient. You proved that today, Rachel. You're the center of my world; you always have been. You'll always be my life." When his eyes came back to her again, he made a near smile and puffed a breath—not a laugh, but a bleak sound of amusement. "I need you to get it through your head that I want to know everything about you because I care so much...because you're worthy of love and respect. That's it, sweetheart. Plain and simple."

Tears of vexation showed themselves in her eyes. "Then why is it necessary to share my mistakes with you? Why do I need another person to judge me?"

"That's not what this is about, Rachel. No one's trying to judge you. Least of all me. My blunders far outweigh anything you've ever done or will ever do. And today, that was amazing. Beyond heroic. I honestly don't know if I could have pulled off what you did and still lived to talk about it."

She angled her head to look at his face. There was no point in sharing the root of her problem—the fear of abandonment that plagued her at night. It was too close to her, and she was afraid he'd brush it off as silliness. Just like her counselors had done years ago. They assumed her surface complaints were the real issues and wasted all their efforts by striking at shadows. "If I am worthy of love and respect, why are you trying to control me? Don't you trust me, Chase?"

Chase's stoic expression didn't change, but a flicker of fear darkened his eyes. "Maybe I'm afraid of losing you."

"If that's true, then you need to trust me. You have to believe that I love you and I'll never go away. But if you suffocate me, I'll die, and so will my love."

"But how can I trust you if you won't tell me everything?"

"That's what trust is, Chase. Opening your heart and believing in the other person."

He looked away and seemed to be contemplating her words. When his eyes returned to hers, he asked, "Do you trust me?"

She searched her heart for the right answer. Although it had been her greatest fear, she honestly believed he would never leave her again. He could be arrogant at times and unintentionally self-absorbed. He occasionally ignored her feelings in favor of doing what he thought was right for her. But, undoubtedly, he did so out of love. In spite of everything they'd been through, she still cared deeply for him.

Rachel's lips curved into a soft smile. "Yes. I believe I do."

"I've never been great at sharing my feelings. I don't know if most men are capable of stripping down and baring their souls. I can only tell you that the time we spent apart was excruciating." He twisted his lips and blew out a sigh. "I thought about you constantly…even dreamed about being together. When you came back into my life, all the darkness fell away. I didn't mean for it to happen, but I became obsessed with the fear of losing you again. I was so afraid of disappointing you by saying the wrong thing that I kept my opinions to myself. I guess that's why I didn't tell you about your mother and uncle. I didn't want to be the bearer of bad news and witness your pain from hearing it. All I've ever wanted to do was protect you, Rachel. If you can help me understand that it's not necessary…that you have faith in my ability to learn, then I'll try to be better. I'll back off and give you the space you need. Because I love you more than life itself."

Rachel closed her eyes and thought about the sincerity of his words. She realized that the fix she was looking for came from deep within herself. Without even realizing it, she held the key to her destiny and was stronger than she knew. With Chase at her side, encouraging her to test her wings, she could soar higher than she dreamed possible.

Paul was standing just inside the doorway, eavesdropping on their conversation. "I learned a valuable lesson from all of this," he said. "Your strength not only comes from yourself but from the people you allow yourself to love." He offered a weak smile. "I'm sorry about your mother, Rachel. For being the reason she left you behind. But nothing I can say or do will change the past, or make up for the mistakes we made. The only way to move forward in your life is to think about the future."

Rachel looked at Chase. She could see the worry in his eyes—the fear of losing her completely. How could she have been so blind? Self-doubt drove him the same way it drove her. Only in her case, she tried to pull away rather than be hurt. And he tried to control her so she couldn't leave.

"I want you to be happy," Paul told her. "Your father didn't live to see this day, but I'll be damned if I don't. Marry the man you love, with my blessing, and build a beautiful life for your children. That's my gift to you. The happiness you both deserve."

Rachel's bottom lip trembled, and tears began to fall. Her love for Chase had been buried under a mountain of fears and doubts. From the first day of their trip, she had been stretching her insecurities to the limit, like a slingshot—pulling them tight until they snapped back with stinging pain. The only thing she knew for certain was that she needed him in her life. She didn't want to lose him; she only wanted him to understand the depth of her feelings and not have to be reminded on a daily basis. They would never be the idyllic couple that never argued, never walked away, never reached the end of their rope. Their emotions were intense—a crazy mix of love and hate that no one would ever understand. They shared an unforgettable history… years filled with adventure, thrills, and romance. They met, separated, and came back together stronger than ever. And now it was up to her to permanently bind those paths and allow their passions to grow into something special—something more powerful than the two of them could ever imagine.

She looked into his eyes. "I don't know how to live without you. I don't think I ever will…"

Chase dropped to his knees. He wrapped his arms around her waist and laid his head on her lap. She smoothed his hair with her hand over and over until his eyes closed and the silent spectator in the room quietly walked away, leaving them to a world of their own.

⚜

Rachel heard a soft rap on the bedroom door and was surprised to see the reflection of Sara looking back at her in the vanity mirror. In spite of her perfectly coifed auburn hair, glimmering diamond earrings, and elegant, high-neck crème dress, her downcast eyes gave her the appearance of a woman in mourning.

"I hope you don't mind my intrusion," she said in a soft, wavering voice. "I simply wanted to let you know that all the arrangements have been made to your specifications. The minister from the local church has agreed to perform the service in our chapel this evening at eight. The seamstress should be up with your dress any moment, and the flowers just arrived. Our cook is preparing a simple dinner in the kitchen, just as you asked. If there's anything else you need, please let me know." She offered a quick smile before adding, "With the fairy lights shining through from the garden and the snow falling, it's going to be a lovely ceremony."

Rachel turned in her seat to face Sara. For the last hour, she had considered various ways to broach the subject on her mother's whereabouts and finally settled on a straightforward approach. "When was the last time you saw Allison Lyons?"

"I'm sorry. What did you say?"

"I asked about my mother...the last time you spoke to her." Rachel could see the disquiet in Sara's face; her eyes nervously brushed the carpet before venturing an upward glance.

"Perhaps this isn't the best time," Sara said. "If you would like to sit and talk when we're alone and no one is waiting..."

"The only one waiting is me." Rachel wasn't interested in another postponement. Sloan had been given twenty years' worth. It seemed that if this woman had her druthers, Rachel would never know the truth.

The room was silent. Sara looked at the curtains, pursed her lips, and smoothed her collar. "I believe it was four years ago," she finally said. "She showed up at a country-club luncheon and asked me about Sloan. Of course, I couldn't speak to her in front of my friends, so I excused myself to another room and listened to what she had to say. It turned out she was leaving for parts unknown and wanted to know if Sloan was happy. When I told her she was, she said that was all she needed to know. And then she said she wished things had been different and that she hadn't lost two children in order to keep one. I wasn't sure what she meant by that until I asked my husband last night." Sara exhaled another shaky breath. "He said that when your father found out Allison was pregnant with his child, he forced her to leave in the middle of the night and told her that she would never be welcomed back. That she would never be allowed to see her children again."

Rachel watched Sara's face, trying to determine the validity of her story. "When did you find out the truth?"

"The truth?"

"About Sloan not being your granddaughter."

A small frown creased Sara's forehead. She appeared to be genuinely confused. "But she is, my dear. She always has been... and always will be."

It was Rachel's turn to be perplexed. She watched Sara's unchanging expression and realized this woman was completely serious. After a brief moment, she tried again. "You do understand that your daughter died as a result of a car accident? That there were complications and your granddaughter died three months later?"

Sara smiled and shook her head. "Oh no, dear. That's... entirely untrue. My granddaughter might be a hellion and sometimes drive me to drink, but she's very much alive and doing very well for herself. In fact, she's leaving to start her new career in the theater first thing in the morning."

"Sara, I think you might be a bit confused. There was a death certificate from the hospital in my grandmother Lily's belongings. She told you what happened just before her heart gave out. Don't you remember?"

"Oh yes. We were sharing recipes that day. She was particularly fond of my chocolate-truffle tea. After two cups, she said she was suffering from mild indigestion and needed to lie down for a while. No one would have believed it was something worse. Especially me."

"Hmm...you don't say." Rachel realized it was useless to go on. Any wrongdoing had been ruled out years ago, and from the sounds of it, this woman had mental issues reaching far beyond her husband's comprehension.

"You know, my dear," she said, "sometimes it takes years to find the right person. And when you do, you never want to let him go...even when his time's up." Her kind, motherly eyes were back, light brown and gentle. "I've always felt that way with husbands, but even more so with Paul. He's my rock, you see," she said, smiling reassuringly. "After ten years together, I'm hoping to keep him around as long as possible."

21

PARLEY

Sloan stood outside on the manor's doorstep, nervously waiting. Her long red hair and black wool coat were dusted with snow. After her eye-opening experience and dismissal of charges at Detective Torren's insistence, she had promised herself that she would never set foot in Cumberforge Manor again. Not as long as Sara Lyons was living there.

Paul opened the door. "Thank you for coming, Sloan," he said with stiff formality. "I'm so glad you could find the time." From the deep worry lines on his face and the frantic phone call she had received an hour earlier, there was no doubt in her mind that he was as upset and confused as she had been for the past four days.

Sloan shook her head, unable to move forward. Then Sky stepped up and reached back for her hand. The door opened wider, exposing Margaret's simple brown dress and downturned eyes. Seeing her there, standing behind Paul, was just another reminder of the deception she'd endured.

Paul anxiously beckoned with his hand. "It's cold outside. Please come in." The man looked haggard, his face drawn, his eyes mirroring his concern. It wasn't difficult to believe that the conspiracy by everyone involved had rocked his perfect world. How disappointing it must have been to discover he had dismissed, ridiculed, and banished a resentful, ill-mannered child who was surprisingly his own.

Sky stepped into the entry with Sloan following. The four of them moved in a quiet procession through the hallway and into the library. After closing the door softly, Paul waited for his three guests to be seated before taking his place behind his large desk.

He cleared his voice. "I'm not exactly sure how to begin. This is a very difficult time for everyone."

Sloan stole a quick look at Margaret, sitting alone in the corner, her face tightened and her eyes reflecting her despair.

Paul rested his hands on the desk. He gazed at Sloan and spoke concisely, as if presenting his case to a jury. "I was informed this morning that twenty years ago, a child was delivered at Saint Vincent's Hospital by Dr. Samuel Watson. She died two days later and was buried in Buckingham Road Cemetery. Without my knowledge or my wife's, a second child was born at my mother's house in Creighton to a woman I loved but had no right to be with at the time. This baby girl was brought to Cumberforge Manor."

Sloan wrinkled her brow, attempting to grasp the meaning of his words.

"Ginny Elizabeth Myers's death certificate was found in my mother's personal effects, but I had no frame of reference as to its meaning or significance. My attorney researched the matter and discovered that Allison Lyons's maiden name was Myers and that Ginny was the name she had chosen for her daughter. In addition, a woman who acted as the midwife for my mother was tracked down in Hastings and confessed her part in switching the babies. As for Dr. Watson, he committed suicide several years ago after it was discovered that he had done something similar in Clovelly."

Surprisingly, Paul had confirmed and filled in the blanks of Margaret's story. For all intents and purposes, Sloan had been a pawn in Sara's life. But the end of her opponent's board was now in plain sight. With an anonymous call to a hack reporter, she could bring down the queen of Cumberforge Manor and destroy her precious reputation. Maybe even bring her to justice for her part in the cruel deception. The thought was empowering, legitimately valid in every possible way. She could be the one holding all the strings, controlling the lives of so many. But what would be gained by it? How would she be any better than Sara Rafferty Lyons?

Sloan smiled. "I'm Ginny?"

Paul nodded. "Ginny Elizabeth Myers."

Sloan looked down, astonished by the sound of her name.

"I can only tell you that I'm sincerely sorry for any wrongdoing in this matter, and I want to assure you that I intend to honor my responsibilities and acknowledge who you are to the letter of the law. There's nothing I can say to make up for the past, but I promise I will do whatever I can to better your future."

Sloan scoffed. "Is that the answer to all of this? I told you before, Paul, I have no interest in your money. I just want to understand why it's taken so long for the truth to come out." She looked to her left, where her dearest friend was seated. He squeezed her hand reassuringly and smiled.

"Sloan and I talked it over," he said. "We agreed that leaving Bellwood is the best thing for us. I have a job waiting, and Sloan has a position in the theater. The change will give us a leg up, a fresh start in our lives. A chance to figure out who we really are... together."

Sloan closed her eyes. The time had come to open the cage doors and test her wings, but one reoccurring thought was holding her back. Preventing her from moving on. She turned to Paul. "No matter how long I live, I'll never understand how your wife didn't know."

Paul was silent...perhaps rehearsing a strong defense on Sara's behalf. "Your grandmother has suffered a great deal over the last thirty years," he explained. "After losing everyone in her life, she wanted to believe more than anything that you belonged to her. I know you're angry right now, and you have every right to be. But given time, I hope you'll find it in your heart to forgive her." He glanced at the photograph of Sara on his bookshelf. "Ten years ago, I promised to stick by her through thick or thin. She's become more confused over this situation and has agreed to undergo intense therapy with a doctor of my choosing." Paul's lips curled into a sad smile. "I believe everyone in this world deserves a second chance and an opportunity to find happiness in her life. Don't you agree?"

Sloan nodded. "Yeah, I sort of wish you'd done that years ago, Gramps." She released a humorless laugh. "I know you would like it to be different, but that's the best I can do for now." She remembered Margaret and found herself wondering why the housekeeper had been called to join them following her dismissal. Perhaps she was needed to validate Paul's story—to lend him emotional support. Or maybe she was there to supply the missing piece to the puzzle.

Sloan turned in her seat. "Where's my mother, Margaret?"

The housekeeper lifted her head. Her dull-brown eyes remained fixed, staring into space. "Allison was sent to a mental institution right after you were born. Miss Lily told me, but Sara refused to believe the truth, so I kept the secret to myself."

Her eyes tried to reach out to Sloan, but they failed miserably. Her nose was running along with her tears. "The only thing I haven't shared is that Dr. Bradshaw was involved. He told me

that she hung herself five years ago...after seeing you at a restaurant in town. She came up to you but didn't know what to
say. She just stood there...watching you leave. But I don't believe
it's true. I really don't. I never trusted anything that man said.
I'm convinced she's still out there, wandering around, lost and
confused." Margaret sniffed. Her eyes met Sloan's. "I'm so sorry,
honey. I truly am."

Paul stood up and approached Margaret. He laid his hand
on her shoulder and leaned down to whisper in her ear. She nodded and unbent her knees. She walked out of the room and out
of Sloan's life...at least for the time being.

Paul came back to his desk, and Sloan reached for his left
hand. She held it tight and looked up, staring into his hazel eyes
with hope welling in her chest.

"Please help me find her." It was a plea without dignity or
care. "I know it's been years, and she might be different. She
might not even realize who you are. I just have to know she's all
right. Can you do that for me, Gramps? Please?"

He nodded. "I'll see what I can do."

Sloan released his hand and rose to her feet. She slipped her
arms around his waist and hugged him for the first time. After a
few seconds, she stepped back and shook off her emotions.

"I've got to get going," she said with new vitality. She looked
at Sky and smiled. "We have to pack tonight."

"Yeah," he said. "And she's got a shitload, believe me."

Paul smiled and patted him on the back. "Take good care of
my girl, will you?"

"Oh, I will, sir. She's going to make sure I do."

Paul opened the door just as Rachel was about to knock. The
look on her face appeared to be one of surprise that Sloan hadn't
yelled or screamed or stomped out of the room but only sat
across from her father while they conducted a civil conversation.

"I'm sorry if I'm interrupting," Rachel said. "I just wanted a chance to officially meet my half sister and to let her know that I would be honored if she and her boyfriend could stay a bit longer to attend my wedding in the chapel. I realize we don't know each other," she said, softly smiling, "but something tells me that will be rectified before long. Please say yes, Sloan. It would make Chase and me extremely happy to have you there."

Sloan looked at Sky expectantly.

"I think we could manage it," he said. "If you help me pack first thing in the morning."

"Done deal." She smiled at Rachel, intrigued by her beautiful eyes—mostly green like hers. "I've never seen a real wedding except for Princess Diana's on telly reruns."

"Oh, it won't be anything like that," Rachel said. "Just a small gathering—nothing fancy. And my brother Devon will be there. I haven't got a clue what you'll think of him, but I'm sure he'll love the idea of having a little sister. Which reminds me—don't you have a birthday tomorrow?"

"Yeah, I almost forgot about that."

Sky leaned down and kissed her cheek. "Well, I haven't. I've got some great friends in Scotland. They're planning a blowout in your honor. But we're sticking with brats and suds this time. Got it?"

Sloan threw her arms around his neck and kissed him hard. She looked over his shoulder at Rachel. "He's amazing, isn't he?"

A smile spread across her lips. "Actually, I think we're both pretty damn lucky."

22

SHARED VOWS

A silent witness stood in the garden admiring the bride's ivory satin gown through the chapel's leaded-glass window as candelabras flickered and cast their glowing light on the freshly laid snow. It had been a long time coming, bringing together these two sovereign, adventurous souls, and now it was possible to sit back on the iron patio chair and simply enjoy the moment. Chase's shimmering eyes looked into Rachel's with an expectancy surpassing any dream in a lover's mind. She represented the epitome of perfection with her long waves of auburn hair, green-hazel eyes, blushed cheeks, daring neckline, and single red rose. The minister mouthed words, and they repeated them line by line, revealing heartwarming emotions capable of cutting the chill on the coldest night in October.

The witness ached to come out of the darkness and reveal her presence, but doing so would reveal her deep-seated shame, allowing everyone to see her ugly truth. After being diagnosed with akinesia, she no longer had a voice and existed silently in a world that had become twisted, waking every morning after viewing split, fractured images—horrible glimpses of death and depravity that would transform her conscious hours into a living nightmare. But tonight, the witness was clearheaded for the first time in many long years, and she stared down at the melting snowflake in her hand, instantly reminded of David Harkins's words from her cherished book of poems, memorized after four repeated readings: "You can shed tears that she is gone / or you can smile because she has lived. You can close your eyes and pray that she'll come back / or you can open your eyes and see all she's left. Your heart can be empty because you can't see her/ or you can be full of the love you shared."

Chase and Rachel's wedding ceremony came to an end with a powerful kiss lasting for endless seconds. This was it… the moment she'd been waiting for. The view of perfect love with the depth of emotion one could long for and never experience in one's lifetime, no matter how hard one might have searched.

Rachel happened to glance in the right direction, meeting the witness's stare—eyes so like her own. She walked closer to the window and peered through the partially fogged glass. The witness quickly slipped back into the shadows behind the tall hedges. Rachel remained motionless, as if questioning what she'd actually seen. A few minutes later, the witness stole a glance, only to be taken aback by a shocking sight. The beautiful bride had escaped her cocoon and was now tracking footprints in the snow. Within seconds, the witness's self-imposed exile would be over.

Panic rose to the highest level. The witness's head was throbbing. It was impossible to think, impossible to focus. Impossible to stop Rachel from knowing. A sudden sound stopped the determined bride in her tracks. She turned to investigate, allowing the witness the precious time she needed to cloak herself in obscurity.

"Baby!" Chase called from the doorway. He followed Rachel out into the snow. "What are you doing? Come inside before you catch your death." He wrapped his arm around her shoulder and drew her close.

"It was the strangest thing," Rachel said, glancing back. "I saw a woman standing out here, but now she's gone."

Chase looked around. "Are you sure? I don't see anything."

"She was right there."

He squeezed her tighter. "Come on, sweetheart. You've had a long day, and I think we've got some catching up to do." He released his hold and reached for her left hand. After appraising her wedding band, he turned her hand over and kissed her palm like a prince from a wonderful fairy tale. "Thank you for accepting me and my flaws. I promise you won't regret it."

Rachel touched his face. "I'll never regret marrying you. Not as long as I live." She walked with him back inside the house, glancing over her shoulder one last time.

※

Sara wandered into the living room where Paul was stretched out in his favorite lounge chair, enjoying the warmth from the glowing fireplace. From the direction of her inquiry, she seemed to be confused as to where everyone had disappeared. "I couldn't help noticing that Sloan's car is gone. Was she planning to come back tonight?"

Paul looked up from his newspaper. "No, dear. She's staying with Sky tonight."

"Do you think it's appropriate for a young unmarried woman to move in with her boyfriend? I know it's a different time and she's not a child anymore, but we're responsible for her all the same."

Paul quirked his brow. "We are?"

"Yes, of course," she said.

"But I thought you disowned her last week."

"That was just a lesson, darling. A way to teach her to be more responsible. It seems to have worked, wouldn't you say?"

"I suppose. It seems to me that you've been concerned about the responsibilities of everyone lately, including the new members of your housekeeping staff. But then I would consider it warranted with Julien Lancaster being a drug dealer and murdering one of his customers." Paul scratched his forehead. "Come to think of it, he did more than that, didn't he? If the cops hadn't found that missing steak knife from the kitchen in Holderness Cove and the second one Julien used to kill Brice Stanton, they never would have linked your former bartender to Gwen Gallagher's death. That's rather miraculous when you think about it, isn't it?" Paul returned to his paper, but his mind remained on Sara's strange lapses of memory and her frequent, unexplained disappearances. There was actually a period when he found himself suspecting his own wife for his mistress's death. But then he realized the foolishness of believing something so outrageous.

"You're absolutely right, darling. It's important to know more about the people who work for you. Which reminds me— is Killian Reed still an employee? After he damaged his cousin's face so severely and put him in the hospital, I would hate to think what he might do to one of your disgruntled artists or disappointed customers."

"Oh, I don't think you need to worry about Killian," Paul said. "He moved his family to Yorkshire while his wife is being treated for some type of addiction."

"I do hope it's not alcohol with that new baby of theirs."

"Haven't got a clue, dear. But I'm sure it will be handled appropriately."

"That's good. That's very good."

Paul folded up his paper and laid it on his lap. "So I've been wondering if you might have seen my missing rain jacket. You know, my special yellow one that you bought me for my birthday a few years ago. It seems to have up and walked away."

Sara pursed her lips, pushing out an unenthusiastic hum of acknowledgment. "Oh, I'm so sorry, dear. I borrowed your jacket for one of my outings and somehow got it stained beyond repair. I had no choice but to discard it. If it's all right with you, I'd like to go shopping first thing tomorrow and pick you up a new one."

"Hmm...I suppose that would be all right."

As she sat down on the edge of Paul's chair, the smile on her lips bloomed. "Oh, by the way...happy tenth wedding anniversary, darling. This is the longest I've ever been married."

Paul wasn't sure how to feel. With all the craziness that had been going on, the terms of their marriage contract had been the least of his concerns. Although he could end this farce with one phone call and move on with his life, he feared the unknown more than the role he had assumed. "Happy anniversary, Sara," he mumbled.

"Shall we head off to bed now?" she asked. "I know the newlyweds are still here, but that doesn't mean we have to be good tonight." She stood up and tugged at his arm with more strength than he thought her capable of possessing.

"All right, all right. Run upstairs and get ready," he told her. "I'll be up shortly."

Paul watched her cross the room before he noticed her oversize Gucci bag sitting on the floor next to his chair. "You forgot your purse, Sara," he called after her. Apparently, she didn't hear him. She was already halfway up the stairs, and there was no point in bringing her back. He picked up the heavy black bag and weighed it in his hand, wondering why she would overlook the expensive accessory, when she had always been obsessed with her personal effects.

Against his better judgment, Paul separated the handles on the purse and noticed the top of a canning jar—an item he had never seen before. Curious, he pulled out the filled container to examine it more closely and discovered a strange mix of odds and ends—earrings, watches, pens, and necklaces that had apparently accumulated over time. One particular item caught his eye and left him gasping for air. It was an all-too-familiar gold hoop earring, one of a set he had given to his beloved Gwen. His mind was racing. Could it be? Could Sara have had something to do with her death? She obviously loved him, but was she capable of killing the woman he cherished in his heart to keep him from leaving?

Oh my God. Was Sara his just reward for his years of adulterous acts?

"Are you coming?" his wife called from the top railing, wearing her white lacy slip.

Paul walked toward her, clutching the jar of disturbing mementos. He stared at her in astonishment, his lips moving in one or two tries at speech before his mouth at last made it into motion. "What d...does this mean?"

Her nose wrinkled with childish amusement. "I'm not sure how you found those," she said, "but you need to put them back, darling. I'm telling you right now if you don't come up here and join me for a nice romp, then I'll have no choice but to go searching for a new husband." Her smile grew into a devious little grin. "And I would hate training a new one."

EPILOGUE

When the house was quiet, Rachel and Chase sat side by side on the couch in their bedroom, still dressed in their wedding attire. She talked to him about her fear of drowning, her anxieties over having a baby, her doomed engagement with Killian, and her embarrassment at lusting for Brandon. "And like the idiot I was," she said, "I took full responsibility for what happened. But what can I say? I was eighteen years old, a stupid girl, and insanity ran in my family."

"Guess I must be crazy too," Chase said, "because I'm nuts for you."

"Oh, that's terrible! Did you find that on a greeting card or something?"

Chase grinned. "It was attached to the gift from Devon and Ian...the one you refused to open."

"And for good reason. Devon is the absolute worst at keeping secrets. He told me that Ian gave us a silver engraved frame with a photo of them mooning us inside of it. Now why the hell would I want that?"

"Maybe they think I'm going to keep you away from them. Which sounds like a great idea to me."

The gravity of her features fell away as she tilted her head and smiled. "So that's the plan, is it?" She rose to her feet, bare after kicking off her stilettos. "Care to help me out of my dress, sir?" she asked, glancing seductively over her shoulder.

"Yes, please," he replied as he put down his whiskey glass, stood, and quickly went to work on the silky buttons that lined her back.

"After dinner, I passed Sky and Sloan in the entry on their way out and heard the sweetest thing."

"What was that?" Chase asked.

"She said, 'For what's it worth, Sky, I've always loved you.' He held her and kissed her in the most romantic way. Then she saw me and smiled and said she would write as soon as they were settled."

"Ah, that's great, honey." Once Chase had undone the majority of her buttons, he lowered Rachel's dress off her shoulders and kissed the back of her neck. Then he continued lowering the dress until she was able to step out of it. He took her hand, lacing his fingers through hers, and led her to the suite's massive bed. She loosened the tie from his neck and began unbuttoning his shirt. Before long, they had shed every single item of clothing. She didn't move away or object when he allowed his palms to skim her curves, trailing them down her sides to her hips and then around to her tight bottom. Rachel ran her fingers through his hair as he kissed his way toward her shoulder and then down to the little hollow between her collarbones. He placed two kisses there before working his way down to her abdomen, where he lingered a bit longer than usual, thinking of the lucky baby inside of her.

The anticipation of where he was headed was palpable throughout Rachel's entire body, and she began to spread her legs, encouraging him further.

Chase gave her a crooked smile and then moved to her inner thighs. He kissed each one slowly, teasing her at first before zeroing in on what she'd been eagerly waiting for. With a few broad licks, he separated her silky folds to discover that she was wet and ready. He slid two fingers deep inside her and began pumping in and out, focusing on pressing just where he knew she liked it.

Rachel arched her back and let out a small groan, signaling he had found the right spot. While keeping his finger action constant, he put his mouth to good use, expertly working her over until he felt her legs quiver. He quickened the pace of his fingers and tongue until she was panting and rocking her pelvis in tune to his movements. Then he stopped and closed his eyes, remembering Sara's sexual therapy and the way she had pleaded with Dr. Bradshaw not to stop—not to allow her pleasure to end.

Chase studied his beautiful wife spread out on the bed in a daring display of tantalizing flesh. He would begin with small, gentle kisses and, given time, eventually make sure she was taken care of one way or another. The times she was able to climax with him inside of her would be extra special. He would press a little harder, rub against her a little longer as he continued thrusting in and out. She would groan her approval as he held back his release until he was sure she was about to have a second or third one. Then he would quicken his pace as Rachel reached for his ass with both hands pressing him further inside of her, leaving him grinding faster and faster until she screamed out his name.

That was all he needed to hear as he came inside her. That was all he wanted to see as he opened his eyes and witnessed her smiling, lowering her head to kiss him. When they were completely spent, he would slowly roll to her side of the bed and enjoy watching her bask in the afterglow of their lovemaking. But until the time was right, he would taunt and tease her, leave her begging for her release. Then he would kiss her hard, hold her tight, and gladly provide it. And if his new bride was determined to test his strength and endurance in their cozy bedroom back in San Palo, there was no doubt in his mind that he could beat her four out of five times, hands down.

"Good night, Wife," he murmured against her skin. Chase listened to her soft, even breathing—serene, blissful, and content for the first time in months. He spooned up behind her and lowered his hand to trace a slow circle over the top of her tummy. "Sleep tight, Baby Cohen," he whispered. "Great adventures await you."

ABOUT THE AUTHOR

 Since launching her writing career, Kaylin McFarren has earned more than a dozen literary awards in addition to a finalist spot in the 2008 RWA Golden Heart Contest. A member of RWA, Rose City Romance Writers, and Willamette Writers, she also lends her participation and support to various charitable organizations, as well her own foundation benefiting cancer research in the Pacific Northwest. McFarren currently lives with her husband in Oregon. They have three daughters and two grandsons and enjoy traveling the globe and making monthly visits to their second home in California. For more information about McFarren, her writing process, and her books, be sure to visit her website at www.kaylinmcfarren.com.

KAYLIN MCFARREN

Inspiration behind the Story

For most of her life, Kaylin McFarren has been fascinated by the arts—visual, literary, and performance. At the age of eight, she penned her first poem and won her first award, in a short-story-writing contest sponsored by the Seattle Rotary. Throughout high school and college, she continued to write in journals, and she attributes her interest in a literary major to Lonny Kaneko, a highly respected English professor at Highline Community College in Des Moines, Washington.

Her dream of opening and operating an art gallery became a reality on June 5, 1999, and the gallery joined the list of twenty-seven diverse companies under her husband's Yoshida Group umbrella. In her eight years of running the gallery, she became a committed champion of more than four hundred artists in the Northwest, exposing their talents at monthly shows and through national marketing efforts. Her love of this visual medium, combined with her enjoyment of writing and entertaining readers, equipped her to weave this remarkable, action-packed tale.

30637813R00145

Made in the USA
Middletown, DE
01 April 2016